LAST RIDE

A HULL GANGLAND STORY OF REVENGE

CHRIS SPECK

Flat City Press 2025

Cover photo by Specky

'If you want to win, you're going to have to learn to lose.'

Howlin' Mad Murdock
The A-Team

ISBN–13: 978-1-0687183-3-5

CHAPTER ONE
Above The North Sea
Present Day

She's nineteen years old and called Jerusalem. It's not a common name even back home but her father used to say it was beautiful, like she is. On her forehead and chin are dark, thick homemade cross tattoos that are already blurred – they are the Niksat, and for those who know, they mark her as a Tigray woman from the north of Ethiopia. She is a long way from home – but not at all lost.

They are high in the night sky and the plane she pilots is a 1992 six seater Cessna. The control column is a little sticky, but other than that, the plane handles well. In the back are the family she collected from the airfield to the north of Amsterdam this afternoon, and the seat next to her is empty. Jerusalem checks the dials and controls on the plane's dashboard, and then scans the dark horizon below for the lights she expects to see from the towns along the coast. Her phone is plugged into one of the sockets and she looks down at it to check the time.

Europeans don't expect to see an African girl in a purple hijab flying a plane, and if she is ever caught, Uncle George seems to think she will not be charged as heavily as if she was a huge, middle aged Albanian or a Russian. Jerusalem helps him to smuggle people. She has been doing it for just over a year in these regular night flights from Amsterdam across to a remote airfield in East Yorkshire just north of a little town called Pocklington.

The people she carries are different from the poor souls who sail the English Channel to seek asylum. Her clients are those of significant means and can afford to be smuggled in more comfort. Of course, they are not so rich that they can do it legally, or perhaps they have something they need to hide. When Jerusalem lands there'll be a van waiting to take them somewhere into the UK – she doesn't know where and doesn't care either. Her job is to fly. Most of the compassion has already been knocked out of her. Uncle George is good at that sort of thing.

The family behind her are Iranians, possibly. She doesn't know their language, and the two little, dark-haired boys look frightened. They take turns cuddling the mother, if that's who she is, while the man in a pale suit with a moustache looks out the window at the black nothing of the North Sea. She has twice told the man not to look at his phone, any light could give their position away even this far up. Jerusalem pushes the stick forward slightly to drop their height. The lower she comes in, the less chance they will have of being spotted.

She hasn't spoken to her passengers so far, the less she has to do with them the better because this is just a business transaction. It's not like getting a cup of coffee in a café where there's a smile and a warm chat – this is illegal and dangerous for all of them. Jerusalem is no good at the small talk anyway, she doesn't care about their story either. She has one of her own.

Ethiopian girls don't usually learn to fly or get a pilot's licence, nor do they end up living a street life in Amsterdam at nineteen, but Jerusalem is far from a normal woman. Once upon a time, her father was rich. He owned a little house in the grounds of the Kokholo Yohannes Orthodox Church west of the city of Mekele on a hill; they kept a donkey, there was an old woman who cooked for them, they had an internet connection, the priest taught her English and classics, her father had a flatbed truck that you could sit on the back of. It wasn't rich by western standards, but back in Ethiopia, she was a lucky girl. That's all gone now, but Jerusalem has been left with riches yet. She has the confidence and guile of the rich. Her father taught her never to apologise for her actions, and that the world was hers to take. She'd never have survived if she didn't believe that.

Jerusalem picks up the phone from the seat next to her and examines the coordinates, she can hardly make out the numbers in night mode. She checks the instruments on the dashboard too. Like always, she has flown low to avoid detection. It would be much easier for them to fly to somewhere closer in the UK like Norwich or the Suffolk coast, but the land is populated with people and police. Up north here in East Yorkshire, it's deserted, flat, and just far enough away for nobody to notice. The journey still only takes an hour and a half.

The phone bleeps for her to change the course slightly and to start the descent. She adjusts the bearing with the yoke and feels the engine slow as she begins to lower the throttle. It will be ten to fifteen minutes from here. As they come out of the night sky, Jerusalem's ears pop and there's pressure on her nose. One of the Iranian kids behind begins to cry and this sets the other one off. The man bellows angry, foreign sounding words that have no effect on the boys.

"Be quiet, please," she whispers to him, but not to the children. The little plane shakes as it gets lower to the ground. They can see streetlights on the roads becoming more lifelike as they descend. She checks the coordinates and the map on the phone, it all looks good. It would be much easier if there were more lights on the strip of this little airfield, but then everyone and their dog would know they were coming in, and they would not need such a good pilot. Uncle George would not have to pay her quite as many Euros for her trouble either.

The wheels connect with the tarmac and the whole plane shudders and rumbles as the brakes take the strain. For a moment, the Cessna thunders across the runway slowing down with every yard it moves. This is just a strip of road north of a sleepy East Yorkshire town, a few miles off the main highway. There's no control tower, just a shed where the local gliding club keeps their planes. Jerusalem taxis up to a dark van waiting at the end of the strip and comes to a halt.

She looks over her shoulder. "Here you are," she says. "You will get out now." The man nods. She is not going to turn the engine off because once this family has left, she is going to turn round and take off again. She will be back in Amsterdam before twelve o'clock and Uncle George will transfer her the money tomorrow morning. The man opens his door and steps out onto the runway. The woman hands him one of the boys to carry before she gets out with the second one in her arms. Jerusalem watches them walk to the dark van and a figure slides open the door for them to climb in. It has gone well. Like the last few times, Jerusalem will get going without any fuss. That's what she's paid for.

A big man with dark hair and a black jacket walks from the van to the aeroplane. He puts his head through the open back door. Jerusalem turns to him:

"What?" she yells over the sound of the engine.

"You have return passengers," he shouts. This man is not English. He could be southern European with his dark hair and clean shaven face; he could be Albanian or Spanish. She shakes her head.

"No. This is not part of the deal. I return alone."

"You will carry these two men back to Amsterdam, Uncle George says so." She shakes her head. This has not been agreed.

"No," she repeats. It's not that she doesn't want to carry people over borders illegally; it's just that she does not know who they are and has no orders to take them, meaning they could be unpredictable, and dangerous.

"You will carry them," says the man.

"I will not fly them." Jerusalem speaks with authority; she will not be swayed by someone she does not know. It is for her safety. The man steps back as if he expected this answer and produces a handgun from inside his jacket. He shows it to her rather than pointing it. She sighs.

"I will not fly," she repeats.

"Then get out."

"This is Uncle George's plane."

"You can get out, or I'll drag you by your hair." Jerusalem narrows her eyes.

"Have another pilot, do you? What will Uncle George say?"

"Get out," says the man.

She opens the door and steps onto the tarmac. There's a light wind and the propellor in front whirrs in the darkness. A small figure in glasses steps past her and climbs into the cockpit while the man with the gun moves aside for another two big lads to climb into the back seats one after another. She can't see their faces but from the light of the dashboard she can see that the smaller man knows what he's doing with the Cessna. He closes the door with a clunk.

Jerusalem steps back away from the aircraft as the man with glasses begins to taxi forward so that he can turn it around. She hears the door to the van slam and its engine start. Then, without ceremony or communication, the van lights come on as it drives away and the engine of the Cessna roars into action after it has turned around. Jerusalem watches it thunder down the tarmac and somewhere in the darkness, it takes off into the autumn night sky.

She rubs her face with her right hand. She's been dumped here. Ten minutes ago, she was high in the sky and now the silence of the countryside at night rings in her ears. Her phone is in the aircraft like her wallet, and she doesn't have a passport. She's wearing a pair of white trainers, jeans and a t-shirt under a purple headscarf. She takes this off. Uncle George suggested she wear it anyway. How will he be when he finds out she's missing? She's not sure. As her eyes get used to the darkness, Jerusalem considers the man who she works for back in Amsterdam, she is not his slave anymore but she's bound to him by what he has done to her.

To the right she can see the lights of the main road a mile

or so away, to the left nothing but dark fields and beyond that, houses shrouded in darkness. In all honesty, Jerusalem has been in far worse situations than this.

She begins towards the lights of the main road. This could be a test from Uncle George, or maybe he's letting her go, either way, she's not at all afraid as she steps into the stubble of a corn field. She has everything she needs to get by already with her, like always, she has her two clever hands, her two strong legs and her two keen eyes. Jerusalem takes what she wants and she is sure of herself.

That's how she's got this far.

It takes a little under half an hour to get to the main road, and she guesses it's nine o'clock. From the signs at a big roundabout, Jerusalem decides to hitch south to the little town of Pocklington. She'll sleep under a bush if she can't get a ride soon. From there, she'll find a way to get online and contact Uncle George. Then he'll transfer money to her somehow, and she'll go back to Amsterdam, maybe.

The traffic is almost non-existent at this time of night. She stands on the other side of the roundabout and holds out her thumb to show that she wants a ride. A little car whizzes past with one lady driver but doesn't stop. Jerusalem has seen people hitchhike in the Netherlands before but she's never had occasion to do it. She's not particularly worried; apart from Uncle George, Europeans have never really given her any trouble before and they mostly follow the rules. If anything, whoever picks her up has got more to fear from Jerusalem herself.

Out of the darkness, and moving at a steady speed towards the roundabout, is a big truck with tacky neon lights across the cab and along the side. When the driver sees her, it starts to slow down. There's no traffic and Jerusalem steps back from the edge of the road as she watches it pull up. It's a fairground truck and carrying some sort of ride stored in two parts across the back. Against the bright lights along the rim, she can see the faces of badly airbrushed celebrities and hear the hiss of the airbrakes. The truck has a double cab and as it slows down, the back door opens up to a woman with an ugly face, big bulbous nose, and curly short hair:

"Where are you going, love?" she calls down.

"The city," says Jerusalem.

"We can take you as far as Hull. We're off to the fair." Jerusalem has heard of Hull but not the fair. It's a city on the banks of the River Humber south of here. This is the best offer she's going to get at this time of night.

"That would be good," she calls up. The fat woman climbs down from the back seat and stands in front of Jerusalem. She smells of fags and has what looks like a big wart on her neck as she points up to the darkness of the van. She doesn't look friendly, but she's a woman, so Jerusalem is going to trust the spirit of sisterhood. In a few steps, she climbs up and into the dark, smoky back of the cab and the woman follows then closes the door. Jerusalem sits in the middle of the back seat and the cab is full of people.

There's a big man with a flat cap next to her. He's wearing a denim jacket with the arms cut off to show tattoos on his muscular arms. He's smoking a rolled up cigarette. In the front, a fat bloke is driving and there's a tall, thin young man in the passenger seat.

"What's your name, love?" calls the fat driver over his shoulder as he starts the engine and pulls back onto the road.

"Carla," she answers. It's habit to lie to people you don't know. Jerusalem has a bad feeling about the way the tall, lanky looking man in the passenger seat in front leers back at her in the dim light from the cab.

"We're off down to Hull for the fair," says the driver. He's bald and his hands are stubby as they hold the big wheel of the truck. The headlights cut a path through the lonely darkness of the road in front. The lanky man in the passenger seat continues to look at Jerusalem with a kind of grin, he has a thin goatee beard and one of his front teeth is blackened.

"Where did you say you were going, love?" asks the fat driver.

"I'm going to the city. I need to get in touch with my employer." Jerusalem's accent is clear and bright. She rolls the r sounds slightly; it's the Dutch influence on her English even though her mother tongue is Tigrinya.

"You stick with us, love and we'll see you alright. Won't we lads?" The fat man at the wheel glances over his shoulder to get a brief look at the woman they have picked up. "Time was," continues the driver, "that we always collected a little something on the way to fair. We used to stop in Middlesbrough and pick up a lass to take to Hull with us. That was before I met you, Mother," he calls out. The ugly woman next to Jerusalem huffs with her arms folded as she looks out of the window. "How much do you charge, love?" asks the man.

Jerusalem feels fear beginning in her legs. When Uncle George brought her to Holland, after he'd spent a bit of time on her, she lived in and out of the whorehouses. The authorities would like the tourists to think that it's all regulated, but there are things that go on there. She knows what this man means. She must answer with force and conviction.

"I'm not a whore. The next chance you get you'll stop and I'll be on my way." There's no need to be afraid. They will read it on her voice if she is.

"What else are you, thumbing a lift on the main road at this time?" asks the fat driver into the windscreen. "There's no need to be ashamed about it, lass. We're happy to pay."

"You will let me out," she says as clear as day. The driver doesn't answer, and the man in the passenger seat looks at her with that half grin. There's the noise of the big wheels on the tarmac below and the whoosh of the air as they speed through the darkness of the East Riding countryside. Jerusalem waits a minute, in silence, before she reaches over the woman next to her and pulls the door handle – hard. She expects that it will fly open but there's just a click.

"Get your hands off me," says the ugly woman she has reached across.

"We've got locks in the back, love," calls the driver. "If you fall out from this high up, your head'll pop like a watermelon on the concrete." Jerusalem returns to sitting in the middle of the back seat and the cab is silent.

"My employer will be very upset if anything happens to me. He is not a man to be messed with," says Jerusalem as she leans forward. "I'm of value to him. Now, you will pull this vehicle over and let me out."

The driver gives a half chuckle over the wheel. Jerusalem takes a deep breath and she feels a hand go around the back of her neck – it's the man she is sitting next to with the cut off sleeveless denim jacket, the muscles and the tattoos. She feels her whole body go rigid. The hand is soft at first but when she turns to look at him, the big fingers grip her like a vice.

The truck begins to slow down, and the indicators make a tick tock sound as they move right to pull into the layby in the darkness. The man with the flat cap and the tattoos leans close to Jerusalem. She looks into his pock marked face with wide and frightened eyes and smells the smoke on his breath from the rollie. She's been through worse than this.

"You'll live," he whispers in a thick Geordie accent.

It's just after ten on a Saturday night. Bev is driving home in her big white BMW in the darkness of the country road. She hasn't got the radio on as she speeds over the deserted Wolds towards Bishop Burton, and there's the rush of the air as the tyres grip the road below her. Her eyes feel like they're full of grit.

It's been another disaster of a date out at Pocklington with a man in his mid-fifties. Bev thought she was good at sussing out weirdos and drunks on the dating apps. She met him for a coffee a week back in Beverley and he seemed nice enough to see again with his swept back grey hair, and smart shoes. He invited her to a pub out in Pocklington near where he lives; he was sleazy and three pints drunk. He went in for a snog as they parted ways in the car park and she had to push him off her. As Bev drives the deserted night road, she reprimands herself – there's to be no more online dating. She already knows what she will find there.

Just after the layby outside Bishop Burton, she hits the brakes as she spots movement to the right of her in the headlights. It's a figure stumbling on the side of the road. Bev acts on gut instinct alone and stops a couple of hundred yards ahead. She looks in the rear view mirror but it's too dark to see whoever was behind. Bev blinks and sees the shape of the figure in her immediate memory. It was a woman. She had black frizzy hair and a ripped t-shirt. Any other person would just drive off and call the police later. They might write a post on social media as to how worried they were about the woman, but ultimately, they would be more afraid for themselves. Bev is not that sort. She fumbles for her phone, activates the torch, and opens the door into the darkness outside. She calls out into the black night behind her:

"You alright, love?"

It took her a few minutes to get the woman into the back seat of the car where she sits now. She's hurt. She has no trousers or shoes, and all she will say is 'no police and no hospital' in her foreign sounding voice. It was only by promising this that Bev managed to get her in. Her face is bruised as if she's been belted and she holds her stomach while she sits there in the back seat. Bev picks up speed out of Bishop Burton and onto the main road into Hull.

"You need to see a doctor," she calls over her shoulder.

"You promised, no police and no hospital." Her accent is

not English. "I need only somewhere to rest." Bev glances back at her through the rear view mirror and sees her nostrils flared and her eyes wide and white under a frown.

"Who did it?"

"I do not know." She pronounces all her words clearly without the run on that British English affords. "If you get me somewhere safe for now, I can pay. I will see money is provided for you later when I contact my employer."

"I don't want paying, lass," says Bev. Her eyes are moist as she grips the wheel of the white BMW. "The doctors won't ask any questions; all they'll do is help." Bev swallows. Her blood is up for this young woman in the back seat, and she can feel rage flowing through her chest and stomach. It makes her angrier to see the lass trying to cope.

"I do not need any help."

Bev grits her teeth. "I'll look after you, lass," she says.

She says her name is Jerusalem and that she has a Dutch passport but it is not with her. She is in too much pain to be able to explain much. Bev gets her back to Hull at half ten and parks up on her drive on Lynton Ave just off Chants. She helps the girl into the house and puts her straight upstairs into Chloe's bedroom – this is Bev's daughter and she is away at university. She gets the girl under the covers and turns on the soft light of the bed stand so she can look at her. She's African with smooth skin and two faded, amateur looking cross tattoos on her face. She looks pale.

"I'll get you a drink," she whispers but by the time she gets back from the bathroom with a glass of water, the girl is already asleep.

It's Saturday morning and these days Bev's body will never let her stay in bed past seven o'clock regardless of if she's been drinking. She looks at her eyes in the mirror of the bathroom and wipes off the thick eyeliner that she couldn't be bothered to remove last night. She will soon be fifty years old but she is still pretty, the curves are still in the right places too, and she knows how to wear make-up. Bev gets hot flushes all the time, second guesses her judgements, feels the roar of emotion for no reason and unleashes her anger on any that deserve it. The doctor has given her cream to rub into her upper legs before she sleeps to replace the hormones that are falling away from her body as she gets older. It's the perimenopause, as if nature couldn't take the piss enough, it had to invent something before the menopause itself. Back when Bev was a teenager the family consensus was that their mum was just 'off her head,' and that was the end of it. That's who Bev is these days. Unlike her mum, she knows why she feels like this.

Last night, while Jerusalem was asleep, she sat at the table with a glass of neat gin and googled all the immediate effects of rape on a woman. Her rage made the tumbler shake in her hand, she felt sick, and in the deserted kitchen, with the work tops scrubbed and smelling of bleach where she only ever cooks for one, she drank another neat glass of gin to knock all the blazing anger out of her and so she could sleep till the morning.

On Chants Ave, it's autumn. She walks out of Lynton Ave and turns right past the estate agent towards the chemist next to the Italian Bistro. Much earlier, she ordered the morning after pill and said it was for herself. It takes an hour or so for the pharmacist to approve, and at the counter she waits in line and gives her name to the blonde lady before collecting her paper package. Bev is not working today. She's a taxi driver at Avenue Cars just five minutes' walk from here, and she has no council runs on Saturday. It's a steady job. It's been good for her.

She crosses the road to the cheap supermarket. It's early and so it's not so busy. She buys lemons, honey, posh butter, eggs, bacon, crumpets, and coffee. At the counter, the check-out girl is dressed in a blue and yellow tabard, she has long black hair and big eyelashes. Bev knows this woman, she is one of the girls that Our Dave, her boss at Avenue Cars, helps out. They don't like each other. Her name is Lilly. She looks Bev straight in the eyes as she bleeps the items through the checkout.

"Making someone a breakfast, are you? Did you pull last night?" It is no secret that Bev has been with men in the past, just as it is well known to certain people that Lilly here was once a working girl off Beverley Road. Bev's age and the fact that she does not have a regular partner make her feel insecure against the youth and make-up on Lilly's pretty face.

"I've got a friend staying over," she whispers back, "and I get to choose who I pull, love, and they don't leave me twenty quid for the privilege neither." It is overly nasty for Bev to say this. Lilly did not mean any harm by her comment; it's her nature to expect the best from people. She should know better from Bev, they have had run ins before. Six months ago, Our Dave tried to get Lilly a job at the taxi office, but she couldn't drive, answer the phone or use a computer properly so he helped her get a job here at the supermarket where she can chat to people. Lilly gives Bev a wide smile to show her bright white veneers. She knows that Bev is a more dangerous beast than she is, but she can't help herself.

"I bet he feels really lucky this morning," she says. "Hit the jackpot, hasn't he?" Lilly says this in the lightest, most pleasant voice she can, but the sarcasm runs deep through the comment. Bev swipes her bank card and then loads the items into her handbag.

"Have a lovely day," says Bev. She holds Lilly's eyes for a moment, just so she knows that's not at all what she means.

In the house and sitting at the kitchen table is the girl who says her name is Jerusalem. She has wrapped a towel around her middle to form a tight dress and is in the same t-shirt from the night before.

When Bev comes down the hall from the front door, the girl stands up and her hand goes to the towel to stop it falling. Her nostrils are flared and her brown eyes look down on Bev. She is well built at five foot eight with smooth slender shoulders and a proud neck. Her hair is a frizzy, loose afro and she has high cheekbones between the two cross tattoos on her forehead and chin.

"You should be in bed," says Bev.

The African girl stares down at her. "I must go. I have no money to give you now, but I will see you are paid for your help." Bev reads her straight away, she sees strength, pride and also, that Jerusalem's leg is juddering slightly as she stands there – like lots of women who are afraid, she is presenting a front to the world.

"You'll need to eat before you can go anywhere, and you haven't got any clothes." Bev sets her handbag down on the counter and begins to unpack it. She knows how this woman feels, wherever she's from, and she will help and not with questions or judgement but with support. In all this, Bev has to suppress the urge to be her mother and she must not let the emotion spill out of her. Bev walks over to the kettle, fills it up and sets it down to boil. Jerusalem stands looking at her.

"You'll have to sit down, lass," says Bev.

Jerusalem eats fried bacon and eggs, she drinks coffee and orange juice, and there's a refined way to her even though she is hungry. Bev has kept the chatter to a minimum and so has the girl. They both like this. Most people will natter on because they are afraid of the silence, not this girl, and not so Bev either. They like the space. Bev sits opposite at the round table and watches Jerusalem eat. She has long fingers and good teeth.

"I got you something," says Bev. She goes to her handbag and pulls out the package she got from the chemist. Inside, there's a little box. She opens it and pulls out a blister strip of plastic with a single pill on one side. She sets it down on the table in front of Jerusalem.

"What's this?" she asks.

"It will stop you getting pregnant," says Bev.

Jerusalem looks up to her. "How can I trust you?" she asks.

Bev frowns. This girl is more direct than she is used to. She licks her thin lips before she speaks. "You'll have to trust someone, lass."

Jerusalem's eyes examine Bev's blonde hair and the dark mascara around her light blue eyes. "Why?"

If this girl is going to be direct, then so is Bev. "I know how you feel."

"You do?"

"Yes," answers Bev.

Jerusalem wants to ask this blonde woman how she could possibly know how she feels. She can still hear the grunts of the men in the truck, and feel their strong hands around her throat. It makes her catch her breath and sends a wave of fear down her legs. Anger gets the better of Jerusalem, as it often does. "How would you know?" she asks.

"It happened to me."

"What did?"

"The same."

Jerusalem fixes Bev with level and cool brown eyes, behind the mascara she can see her honesty. It's not the kind of thing you would make up. Jerusalem is now sorry that she did not accept the help quicker. "When?"

Bev swallows as she looks back into the past. She's about to reveal a part of herself that she does not want to, and the memory sticks in her throat before it comes out:

"I was a bit younger than you," she says. "I don't know how many men." Her mouth is dry, she can feel her lungs taking in the smell of the bacon that has just fried, the blue tits natter on the bird feeder hanging on the side of the garage. Bev does not want to think about that night ever again. She's hidden the memory of it, even from herself.

"What's your name?" asks the girl.

"Bev."

"I will return this kindness," she says. Jerusalem's eyes have begun to water. She wipes them with the palm of her hand, then takes the blister strip, pops out the pill, and washes it down with the rest of the orange juice. "When this happened to you, who helped?" she asks.

Bev breathes in as she gets flashes of the nightmare hidden far away in the late eighties. "Who helped me?" she repeats, but in a whisper. "Nobody did."

HULL FAIR ONE

Rattling along at sixty miles an hour on the M62, two bits of a kid's drop tower are strapped to the flat bed of a truck with smiling frogs painted at the top. On another lorry, there's the garish airbrushing of celebrities along the side of a fair ground ride, and the top dome of a helter-skelter squashed tight between two crates. It will be the first night of Hull Fair next week. Everything is being set up. For the last few days, big wagons have rolled in off the M62 motorway from Leeds towards Hull. They've brought their fair rides in pieces ready to be put together when they get there.

The fair appears once a year in the second week of October and lasts just a week. The rides come from all over the UK and Europe sometimes. It's the final big meet of the season before winter. Last week the big wheel was in Nottingham, the Authentic Burger Van was up in Newcastle, and Mystic Lynn the tarot card reader had her caravan in Lincoln.

The people of Hull loathe and love the Fair in the same measure. Little kids like the bright lights and the spinny rides, gangs of teenagers roam in packs, new mums and dads struggle through the crowds pushing prams, older lasses go to pick up brandy snaps that they can't seem to get anywhere else.

The lights and the noise are magical, and the air takes on a sweet, oily cinnamon smell from the food vans. By the same token, motorists are pissed off that Walton Street is closed so the traffic backs up. Residents get upset by the noise and the mess, struggling dads begrudge the hundred quid they'll spend on their kids when it could go on food, and those down Chants Ave grumble that there won't be anywhere to park their car for the full week.

It brings rumours too. The showmen who work the rides have reputations for being thugs and thieves. People say burglaries get worse when the fair is in town. They claim that pickpockets come along with the rides to pinch money from punters. They say the attractions are built in a few days only and without any regard to safety, and then they cite past accidents.

The truth is much more pedestrian. Turns out those that run the fair are called showmen. They have a guild and are bound by traditions as well as by history. Families have worked Hull Fair for generations. They bring their kids with them on the road, and they work the rides too when they're teenagers. There may be thieves at the fair, but they are nothing to do with the showmen who work it. Indeed, if they get wind of a pickpocket, they'll be quick to rough them up or turn them over to the coppers because they want the money the punters spend, and they don't want them frightened. Like the farmer needs his animals, these showmen need their punters. It's the same for the rides; the council has a group of fifteen inspectors who check the site for safety before it goes live. The owners don't want them to break and they don't want to have an insurance claim if anyone gets hurt. There may be flashing lights at the fair, the thrill of the slingshot, the screams of excited lasses and the mystery of the fortune teller, but make no mistake – this is hard and cold business.

Mally Kemp stands at the bottom of the big wheel in the bright afternoon and looks up to the white crisscrossed wires and steel tubing that make up the ride. The fair is very nearly finished and most of the equipment has been checked already. It's changed a lot since he was a young man and first came with his auntie and uncle in the early eighties. It's not only the rides that have changed. Mally is just over five foot five, and he wears a thick black jumper with red braces over the shoulders – just so you can recognise him from a distance. He's kind of important. He puts his flat cap back over his bald head and turns to walk to the council official with a wax jacket and a clipboard. Mally takes a big pull on the chunky vape he has in his left hand. He switched from cigars five years ago, and billows of the artificial smoke issue from his nose like he's a steam train.

"It's all checked and done," says the official.

"Then we'll open her up next Friday night, as always." The man smiles and these two shake on it. Mally has been overseeing the fair for the last ten years, and though he doesn't run any of the rides, it's he who controls the lot in one way or another. Once the whole thing kicks off, he'll look after the families, the machines; he'll liaise with the police and the council and the local residents too. It will be as busy as a nightmare – just the way he likes it.

CHAPTER TWO
It's Face

It's Wednesday at twelve o'clock, and Bev has done all her morning drop offs. She's parked her white BMW in the tiny car park. This is Avenue Cars, a taxi office on Chanterlands Avenue, Hull, that is somehow still here when all the biggest taxi companies have merged together or been bought up, and mobile technology has done away with the need for a central office. Bev walks in the back door and goes to the kitchen where she flicks on the kettle. It's more social than anything else. She pops her head around the door to the main office, and there's Our Dave sitting at the round table with the newspaper in front of him.

"Do you want a coffee?" she asks.

"Aye, go on then," he answers with a smile. He's in his sixties, maybe, but looks younger with an allotment tan across his face, a thin white beard and an open necked shirt. His sleeves are rolled up to his elbows and his forearms are powerful in a wiry sort of way. Our Dave has changed over the summer just past. He spends more time on the allotment than in the office, and Bev no longer senses the uneasiness on him that he used to keep covered with smiles. He'd still rather talk about you than himself, but Bev feels that the worries he had are blown away. The business has changed too. Our Dave has someone who handles the running of day-to-day affairs. His name is Tom, but everyone calls him Face on account of the burn scars all over his cheeks, nose and down his neck. He started off as a kind of loser, but as the summer went on, he ballooned to be a successful arsehole, and Bev has had to cut him down to size more than a few times. It's not just that she wanted to do it, Our Dave asked her to.

She brings in two mugs of coffee and sets them down on the round table in the back office of Avenue Cars. Our Dave likes his black. The only reason this place survives at all is because of all the council jobs the two drivers do. There's a Kurdish girl called Dilva who makes a lot of the school drop offs, but it's Bev who drives the wayward, dangerous kids who have been thrown out of normal schools – she's a bit like they are. There was a hippy type of lass called Liz who used to drive the disabled folk, but she's set up her own charity for families on Westbourne Ave.

"How's tricks?" asks Bev. The older man gives her a wink.

"I need you to have another word with Face."

Bev sips her coffee: "What's he done now?"

"Womanizing," says Our Dave.

"I did that last time."

"Well, you didn't do a good enough job."

"Can't you talk to him?"

"I have."

"What's it got to do with you anyway, or me?"

"It's not good for him or any of the lasses neither. He's only doing it because his wife left him." Our Dave said this before. Bev rubs her face. Six months ago, Face was a drunk and a loser; after his missus walked out on him, he lost his lecturing position up at the University, and Our Dave gave him a job sorting out his business affairs. Fast forward to today, and the man has changed a lot, he's lost weight, stopped drinking and started dressing like he cares. He's saved the business in more ways than Bev could realise, but he carries himself with an air of confidence. The biggest arseholes are usually the ones who don't start like that, they learn and grow into it. Bev blames herself partly. It was she who trained him how to use the dating apps and explained to him what some women might want to hear. He's taken it up a couple of levels since then.

"Is he upstairs?"

"Aye, he will be. His pushbike is round the back." Bev didn't see it when she came in, but Face has one of those sleek, trendy fixies that he rides up Westbourne Ave. "There's something else, lass," says Our Dave.

Bev cocks her head. "Go on," she says.

"I'm selling up."

Bev squints at him as if she doesn't quite understand what he's saying. There are laughter lines from his blue eyes and his grey hair is cut short to the side of his head. It was Our Dave here who gave Bev a job even with her criminal record. He took a chance on her when nobody else would.

"You can't," she says. It comes out without her thinking. "Where would you go, what would you do?"

"I dunno," he says. "I could go travelling or something. I just wouldn't be here."

"Who'd look after your allotment? What about the people along this street?" Over the past ten years or so, Our Dave has become the de facto support for many of the businesses and people up and down Chants Ave. He's got a basic knowledge of plumbing and electrics, he can change a car tyre, he's alright to borrow money from, he will buy you a pint in the Avenues pub across the road, he's good at listening. Bev is ashamed sometimes, that she is one of these people.

When his wife died, Our Dave kept it secret, even from her and it hurt to think that he didn't have anyone to go to. Bev has kept close to him since this, even if he tries to shoo her away. It was Bev who bin-bagged all his wife's clothes from the house; she emptied the cupboards of memories and cleaned the dusty rooms so they were fresh and alive again. Our Dave has become Bev's concern and, like the women of this city, once she has decided to love someone, there is nothing and nobody that can keep her from it. Hearing that Our Dave is selling up means that she has failed in some way.

"It has to happen sooner or later, lass," he says. "I won't be here forever. You'll do okay out of it."

"It's that tosspot who calls himself Face, isn't it? It's him who's put you up to this."

"No. He likes things the way they are, he's told me so."

"Well, he would do, wouldn't he? He'll be trying to get this place for himself."

"Face doesn't need my money, and Avenue Cars isn't worth anything. You can trust him with the business, of that, I'm certain. I wouldn't leave him near my girlfriend if I was a younger man, but other than that, he's put me steady."

"You'd sell it to him?"

"I would."

Bev takes a deep breath into her chest but only so she can do a big, huffing sigh. "He's got you where he wants you, then. Have you already done the deal?"

"Nearly. I'll have my hands off completely by Christmas." It's early October. Hull Fair is just setting up a five minute walk around the corner.

"What's going to happen to me and Dilva?"

"Nothing. You'll keep your jobs. It will all be the same."

"No, it won't, Our Dave. You watch, this taxi office will get changed into a bloody vape shop or a café the first chance he gets, and we'll get slung out. That's how it'll go."

Our Dave shakes his head as he looks at the blonde woman. "We can't stop the future, Bev. If that's what happens then we'll deal with it."

"I'll have to deal with it, you mean." Bev feels her chest swelling with fire, and she is about to launch into a full scale rant before she catches herself. She thinks to the poor lass she picked up the night before last who's still in bed in her terraced house on Lynton Ave. She can deal with change – that's not what she is angry about. As she is getting older, Bev is beginning to know herself and despite the wrinkles on her face, she did not realise that age would bring her wisdom. "I'm only here for you, Our Dave," she says. "I'm only here to help you." The older man frowns at her in confusion. She's not usually nice.

"I'd never have thought that," he says.

Ever since Chloe went away to university, Bev has felt the

grip of loneliness around her throat. "If you're not here," she says calmly, "then I won't be either."

"I knew you'd understand," says Our Dave and there's a twinkle in his eye. Bev hasn't really understood at all. She puts her mug down and moves off to the bottom of the stairs. She'll have that word with Face after all. It might make her feel better.

It's still Wednesday morning. Jerusalem waited till Bev left at half eight, then got out of bed. Her bruises still hurt even though she slept for the best part of two days. She looks over the room that she's been left in. It smells of air freshener and the light grey duvet on the bed is clean. She drinks the glass of water left on the bedside table and then stands up to look into the little, well-ordered garden. She'll have to get up and out.

In the wardrobe, she finds a pair of jeans that are a bit too tight, a black t-shirt and a denim jacket. There's a cap with 'Marx HU9' printed on the front and Jerusalem scrapes her curly hair back and fits this over her head. Downstairs, she tries on some of the trainers on the shoe rack. They are too small. In the cupboard under the stairs there's a pair of khaki boots that fit just fine with a thick pair of socks on. Jerusalem isn't stealing this stuff. She's borrowing it. She'll be back to repay this woman who calls herself Bev.

Now she just needs a bit of time to get herself together and find her bearings. She eats a handful of nuts from a packet in the cupboard, drinks a pint of water and peels a banana as she looks out the window. It would be better if she could get out of this house before the woman comes back.

She opens the Yale lock, slams the door behind her and is off down Lynton Ave towards Chants. Jerusalem is an Ethiopian woman but she has lived in Amsterdam for the best part of two years, so she is familiar with these European streets. She glances down the alley at the end of a row of terraces and sees piled up junk and an old mattress – the UK is a little less organized than Holland. She turns left at the chemist and walks along Chants Ave even though she does not know where's she is going. She goes past Maya Spice, the wedding dress shop, the cheap supermarket, and the library. She walks next to a lass pushing a pram and then in front of an old man with a walking stick. There's a fella with a curly haired dog, a kid on an e-scooter and a blonde lass carrying a guitar. Jerusalem fits right in here and she feels it. Like Amsterdam, you can be almost anyone you want.

Opposite Avenue Cars she sees a black lad on an electric mountain bike with chunky wheels riding towards her. He's carrying a brightly coloured square backpack and has a facemask – Amsterdam is full of these delivery kids. Jerusalem holds out her arm to stop him and he comes to a halt on the footpath in front of her then pulls down his mask. She thinks he might be from Eritrea, Jerusalem knows his language, Tigrinya. It's her language too even though their countries have an uneasy peace.

"You can help me, brother?" she asks.

He narrows his eyes. He doesn't understand.

"Arabic," he says to her.

"Do you speak English?"

"A little." She got it wrong. This kid doesn't speak Tigrinya.

"How far away am I from the centre of this town, brother?" She should not really be calling him this, but it makes her seem more confident. She examines the lad more closely. He is young with thick curly hair spilling out from under his hood and earnest brown eyes. You learn to read people. He's no threat at all.

"Turn left at the cemetery and follow the road straight on. It's twenty minutes." She smiles in thanks.

"Where is your home, brother?"

"Sudan." He sees the cross tattoos on her forehead and chin, the bright white teeth and calm stare. He can guess where she's from. He looks at the phone strapped to the crossbar of his bike and sets his foot on the pedal, before he speeds off down the footpath into Chants Ave proper. Jerusalem knows these men; their stories are different but all the same. They were brave enough to run away from poverty and war somewhere and now they work hard, even if they are at the bottom of the ladder today. Jerusalem is not like this at all. She has the confidence and bravery of the rich inside her guts, so you can knock her over, but she will get back up again, and then belt you across the face rather than go back to work. She will start at the top, not like these delivery boys.

She walks until she gets to Spring Bank. There, she passes Kurdish and Polish supermarkets, men standing outside barber shops smoking cigs, white blokes drinking cans in the bus stop and a beggar with a ratty sleeping bag sitting on the floor outside of the supermarket. It doesn't take her long to get into town proper and at the big railway station, she sits outside on one of the benches watching the people going in and out. She is used to the busy hustle and bustle of Amsterdam Central Station, especially inside where the people are more crowded together. This might be a new city, but she doesn't have any choice about what she's going to do. It's all she knows. Jerusalem watches a beggar asking for change, sees a woman pushing her pram with her handbag hanging off her elbow, and examines two students with their backpacks over their shoulders.

Inside, in the bus station, she leans against the glass front of a shop and looks up at the information screen with place names she has never heard of before. Jerusalem doesn't have a lot of time, but she won't do a sloppy job. She makes her move through a big crowd and bumps into the lady pushing the pram, says sorry, then brushes past a big man wearing tracksuit bottoms. As she leaves the station, she fishes coins out the purse she just took from the woman's bag and drops them on the floor in front of the beggar with a clink.

This is how it's done.

Jerusalem walks a little further into the city centre, finds a newsagent and buys a packet of cigarettes and a lighter to see if the stolen debit card from the wallet will work contactless. When it does, she buys two more packets and some chocolate. You have to start small.

There's a beggar on Monument Bridge outside the glass shopping centre that sticks out over the water. Jerusalem gives him a packet of cigarettes and asks where she can buy things in this city – he's selling some sort of magazine, and she can see that he's a street person but that he's trying to get out of it. He's reticent with his answers. This is not the kind of person she's looking for at all.

In one of the charity shops, she buys the biggest handbag she can find with a ten pound note from the purse she just pinched, then wanders back to the shopping centre. In the sports shop, she nicks a pair of size ten trainers and two official Hull City football shirts, socks, and cheap perfume. Ten minutes later she sells all of it for fifty quid to a rough looking druggie in the old town. His teeth are yellow rotten from heroin, and after they agree fifty, he gives her forty. It crosses her mind to kick him in and steal what he has, including the drugs, but she doesn't know this city, and the difference between forty and fifty quid is nothing to her.

In a café she buys an iced coffee and takes out the phone she nicked from the man wearing tracksuit bottoms. It's not unlocked and she quickly accesses the settings, gives it a new pin number and resets it. She waits for it to start up again while she looks out of the window. This is a provincial town for sure, there's way less crime than Amsterdam and fewer police as well. When the phone starts up again, she makes a new pin but stops just before she adds her email address. She hasn't been in contact with Uncle George for days now, and in some ways it feels good. If she fires up her email account, he will be able to find her. Maybe he doesn't know where she is, maybe he doesn't care even. A thought crosses her mind. Perhaps she could go this alone. She's learned so much from him, and now, she's free. This little trip may be worth something after all. Jerusalem has a backup email account that she uses, one that Uncle George won't know about. She'll use that.

It's two o'clock when she walks back down to the train station. With the phone, she accesses a map and finds the way back to Bev's house. Now she has money, she stops at the big supermarket next to the station and buys water, tuna sandwiches and the largest bottle of gin she can find. The big bag from the charity shop is good to carry this.

On the walk back up to Chants Ave, her stomach hurts from what the men did to her a few days before. She stops on a bench for a smoke at the bottom of Spring Bank and gets hit on by a drunk man who sits down next to her. He's cross-eyed and she gives him a cigarette then listens to him prattle on for five minutes. He says she can come back to his place and she thinks about what he might have to steal, he smells of weed and sweat and hopelessness. She gives him the rest of a pack of cigarettes, pick pockets his phone and then walks up Spring Bank West past the cemetery, leaving him feeling like he's got the better of her. She's good at that.

Jerusalem stops to rest again next to the 'Welcome to Chant's Ave' sign painted on the side of an end terrace house. The pains in her groin and between her legs are worse. She should really get back to Bev's house. She will ask if it's okay to stay another night and then be off in the morning. With the phone she can contact Uncle George, he'll send her money and she can return to Amsterdam. Maybe.

When she gets back to Lynton Ave, Jerusalem knocks on the door even though the car is not in the drive. Bev is not home, so Jerusalem sits on the step and lights up a cigarette. She'll wait. It's sweet not to be rushed and for nobody to know where she is either.

Bev returns in half an hour. She sees Jerusalem sitting on the step as she pulls up, sees the Marx cap that belongs to her daughter, Chloe, and the boots that are hers. Bev's face doesn't give anything away as she gets out of the car, but she is relieved. She came back earlier to check on the girl to find her gone. Bev knows how to deal with these tough and broken kids. You treat them like adults.

"Help me with this shopping," she says. Jerusalem stands up and moves to the back of the white BMW. She grabs a heavy yellow shopping bag and then follows Bev to the door where she opens up. Jerusalem won't show how much this hurts. They set the bags on the kitchen table and Bev begins to unpack the contents after putting the kettle on. She has questions for the girl, but she won't ask them right away – it's much better for the answers to come out themselves.

"Are you hungry?" asks Bev as she opens a cupboard and stacks two tins of tomatoes on top of each other.

"I would like to stay one more night," says Jerusalem as she stands in the kitchen.

"I see you borrowed my daughter's cap."

"Yes. I have something for you." Jerusalem steps forward and pulls the big bottle of gin from the charity shop handbag. She sets it on the counter. "I saw that you drink this, there's an empty bottle in the cabinet next to the TV." Bev cocks her head and Jerusalem pulls a small wad of notes from her pocket and puts this down next to the gin. "It's twenty pounds. There will be more."

"I didn't ask for this," says Bev.

"I am not charity." The way she speaks is clear and bright, her brown eyes are focused.

"Where did you get it?"

"It was earned," she says. Bev goes back to putting the shopping away – she might have got this one wrong. This girl is a long way from the mixed-up kids she drives to the special school. She is capable and self-aware. Bev doesn't like to think how she got the money. Perhaps this outward show of strength and independence is how Jerusalem deals with what happened the other night on the road outside Bishop Burton. It's how Bev dealt with it as well.

"You can stay as long as you need to," says Bev. "How do you feel?"

"Good. When you've put this food away, I'll cook us something." Bev turns back to her with a grin as if she is taking the piss. Nobody cooks for Bev. The lass is serious.

"Alright," she replies. There's no need to show her surprise.

HULL FAIR TWO

There's a big, black rook perched on the top of a streetlight overlooking Walton Street Car Park in the Thursday morning sun. Ordinarily, this big patch of gravel serves the stadium behind when Hull City play at home. It's where you come for the big market on Sunday, and the little one on Wednesday. It's where generations born in Hull learned to drive a car for the first time over the huge puddles and uneven ground.

The big rook adjusts its wings as it peers down. Where once there was nothing but empty space, Walton Street Car Park is rammed with stalls. Hull Fair kicks off tomorrow and though it is all closed and boarded up now, every inch of this big car park is full. There are fairground rides of all sizes and a big wheel motionless in the autumn sunshine. Power cables are tarmacked to the floor, there are food stalls, a coconut shy, the helter-skelter and nearer to the train tracks, there are mobile homes and caravans where the showmen stay. There's the silent carousel near the entrance and the little Gypsy caravan where for a tenner, or twenty quid these days, the old woman will read your palm and look at your future in a crystal ball. It's all silent now, ready for tomorrow night when there will be lights, the boom of music and the screams of the punters riding the waltzers.

Primary school teachers give out worksheets that say the fair is seven hundred years old, that it moved to Walton Street in 1888 and that it isn't open on Sunday because of religious reasons. It was more of a spectacle back in the days before mass communications and colour photographs. Freak shows brought skinny tigers in cages and pale-faced underfed monkeys; there were halls of mirrors, coconut shys, boxing rings, pick pockets, the smell of magic and the foreign and the unusual. Today the magic has lifted, it's given way to spinning rides, overpriced chips and huge stuffed toys that hang as prizes above the electronic bingo. Everyone knows what a tiger looks like these days and showing off a fat man or a woman with a beard is cruel, just like watching two men belt hell out of each other in a boxing ring. You can get weirder pictures of yourself on your phone than in a house of mirrors.

The rook takes off and flies low across the white caravans and boarded up fairground rides. It will be rich pickings for the next week or more, there'll be chip wrappers, discarded toffee apples, half eaten pizza slices and the rest, all blown up and down Walton Street and life will be good. She flies north over the caravans and the railway line, over the trees of the western cemetery and past Dundee Street with Avenue Cars on the corner. She flies over these tight packed terraces on the way to her rookery in the big trees over at St Ninian's Church at the end of Chanterlands Ave. Below her, and leaning against the wall in the back garden of a house on Lynton Ave, smoking a cigarette, is Jerusalem.

CHAPTER THREE
Jerusalem

In the evening, Jerusalem makes Bev tomato pasta as if she lived there. She finds the herbs from the spice rack, looks through the tins in the cupboard, and adds pasta water to the sauce. She opens the gin while she cooks, and they drink thin measures mixed with lemonade and ice in tall glasses. Nobody looks after Bev with this day to day stuff and so she feels oddly uneasy but warm as she watches the girl cook. There is a no nonsense way to Jerusalem, and Bev can see that she is self-sufficient in a manner that other broken young people are not.

The chatting between them is light. Jerusalem has not given too much away. She explains that she was hitchhiking down from Newcastle to get the ferry from Hull to Rotterdam after visiting a friend, and that she lives in Amsterdam but is from Ethiopia. She tells Bev she works in an immigration centre in the middle of Amsterdam, which is sort of true. It's all very believable. Jerusalem doesn't mention Uncle George at all. It's best to leave him out of any conversation, but she alluded to leaving her home country when she was seventeen, and that it was not pleasant – this is real.

Uncharacteristically, and because Jerusalem does not really care, Bev spills her guts. She lives alone and drives a taxi. She is forty nine but says she's forty five on the dating apps because the algorithm will show her to younger men. Her daughter is away at university studying forensic science. She only drinks at the weekend and got divorced from a thug many years ago. Bev likes the Sunday night police dramas with a glass of wine and doesn't tolerate dickheads. Jerusalem's calm silence reminds Bev of herself.

In the garden the next morning, Jerusalem puts out her cigarette on the wall. Her body is healing up, and now that she is rested, she thinks about what she might do with regard to

Uncle George. She only needs to fire up the phone she stole, and she can contact him on social media. Probably within the hour he will have some way of getting her back to Amsterdam. He has told her before that pilots are hard to come by, and those he can trust even more so.

She looks down Bev's little garden in the October morning light and sees a big rook flying overhead. She thinks of the men in the truck who picked her up, and what they did to her. It makes her stomach bubble in anger, but Uncle George would be angrier than she is even, because she is his property after all. Every day she leaves it without getting in touch will make it worse.

Jerusalem knows what Uncle George is like behind the smiles. He sees details. He will not let this rest. Two years ago, in Saudi, he paid a hefty price to smugglers so he could take her. Uncle George explained that Europe would be the place for her to make her fortune. She did not realise what would be expected, for Uncle George has done much worse to her than those men in the truck the other night. She was hard to train at first, but he managed it. If Jerusalem did not comply, Uncle George told her that he could contact her father back in Ethiopia, and that he would tell him all the monstrous acts she has done already. She was strong willed but Uncle George won out in the end. He always does. That's why she knows he won't let her go.

Face stands at the window of the office looking down on the mid-morning traffic of Chants Ave. Opposite, Dundee Street Fisheries is just opening for lunch, the man from the orthopaedic bed shop is having a cig outside and cars flash by with the odd push bike. It's turning colder after a hot summer. Our Dave stands leaning on the door frame of Face's upstairs office that once upon a time would have been a front bedroom.

"The fair starts tomorrow," says Our Dave, "you going?"

"Not me," answers Face. "I must have been every year for the last forty years. What about you?"

"I always go," says Our Dave. "Just for a look around. I like the noise and the lights. Did Bev have a word with you?" he asks.

Face turns to him. There are burn scars all over his nose and cheeks and down his neck, but he doesn't seem ugly for it, especially when he smiles. "She did talk to me."

"There's no point in all these lasses you're meeting, Face. It won't make you happy. I don't know what you're trying to prove." Face has heard this kind of thing before.

"Why did you get Bev to tell me when you're happy to do it yourself?"

"She used to do the same thing, kid, and she's lonely. If you're going to be with someone you'll have to learn to compromise."

"I was married for sixteen years."

Our Dave knows this but he is conscious that Face is missing out. They have become friends over this last summer, and Our Dave has shared his business with this man as well as, on very rare moments, how he feels. Our Dave is from a generation of men that do not speak about their feelings. Face is from another generation that pretends they will but definitely won't. They understand each other.

"You can't just go from one to another, I can promise it won't make you happy."

Face has explained to Our Dave about many of the women he has seen; there's the artist from round the corner with the dark hair, the primary school teacher, the holistic therapist, the nurse, the truant officer up at the secondary school, and there was something wrong with all of them. One has cats and smokes, one drinks and likes to row, one wants to control him, another is mean, another wants him to perform sex acts that he can't bring himself to do.

"You're turning into an arsehole," says Our Dave.

Face nods as if this is a given. "That's what Bev said. It's not as if I lie to anyone."

"You don't just lie by not saying stuff." Face really is straight up with the girls he meets, but he leads them on.

"You'll have to let me get on with it, Our Dave."

"Just admit the reason you don't like them is that you really want your wife back. Nothing'll work until you do that." Our Dave is good at getting to the truth, but he hasn't come out with this one before. Once upon a time, Face had a pretty, petite half-Spanish wife with a pixie haircut and a bright white smile, but she left him for a handsome chiropractor from down the road.

Face sits down at his desk and looks into his laptop screen. He is not in the mood to discuss his personal life. Right now, he is in a happier place than he's been for a long time with his son living at home and peace in the big house on Westbourne Ave. He called Our Dave up to his office to discuss business after all and not the girls he's been seeing. There is something that is bothering him. Face clears his throat and he puts himself into lawyer mode:

"Last week I was doing some chatting to our contact in Holland, the guy who runs the furniture factory you use."

Our Dave frowns. "You mean Lars?"

"Actually, his son, Henrik."

"Go on." Apart from the flagging taxi office, Our Dave has a string of properties throughout this city. He also runs an import business that is not quite legitimate. For a long time, he has smuggled booze. It's mainly spirits and it comes direct from distilleries in Germany and Holland straight into St Andrews dock hidden in furniture trucks. Our Dave is not greedy, and so the operation has been small and profitable. He handles the distribution at this end and everyone makes enough money to be quiet about it.

"I've crunched some figures, Our Dave. You know that Henrik and his father's factory actually make good furniture.

They sell it up to Sweden and even some to the States."

"They're a reputable business, Face. They sell to the UK too." They don't. The furniture that comes in the trucks to Hull is junk and is only there to hide the booze.

"They've moved into renewable furniture as well, you know. They make tables and chairs out of old plastic bottles and plastic bags, but it's not your normal rubbish. They've got a team of Swedish designers on board."

"So what?"

Face licks his lips before he says what he's about to. "If we sold that stock over here, legitimately, we'd make more money on it than we do with the alcohol from Germany." Our Dave narrows his eyes.

"There'd be tariffs and taxes, all sorts of forms and admin, and who do we know to sell furniture to?"

"I've got the contacts for that, Our Dave. We wouldn't have to pay any of the bribes, the customs people wouldn't have to look the other way. We'd save a fortune. It'd be legit."

Our Dave blinks down at this man with his scarred face and smooth black shirt with an open collar. "Are you suggesting we go straight?"

"Yes."

Our Dave shakes his head. "It'd be more trouble than it's worth. The customs and the police rely on that money. If we didn't pay then they'd come down on us, besides, what about all the nightclubs that buy our cheap booze, where would they get it all from?"

"Be honest, that side of the business is falling off, Our Dave. You've said yourself that in the nineties you were doing ten times the amount of trade as you're doing now. People don't drink as much as they used to. Half of the clubs have closed down. The world's changing. The kids who used to get hammered in nightclubs would rather sit on trendy Swedish furniture these days and smoke weed while they doomscroll."

"And you've looked it all over, have you?"

"It'll bring in more. Henrik isn't like his old man; he's a modern lad with his eyes on the future. He doesn't like running our stuff across on the ferries. He wants to be bigger than all that. He wants to be legitimate as well."

"What if I don't need any more money, Face?" Our Dave is scared of sudden change, like everyone.

"It's safer. I'm not you. I don't know how to talk to people the way you can. I don't have the same kinds of relationships. I don't have your contacts either."

"It'd be the end of an era."

"It would be change. The only thing that isn't normal is that things stay the same."

"That your university education, is it?"

"Maybe. If I'm gonna buy Avenue Cars off you, Our Dave, it will have to be legitimate. I don't do loopholes and backhanders – I'm a lawyer. I need it all laid out clear with no grey areas."

Our Dave runs his big joiner's hands across his greying beard. "It'll take time for me to close it down. I'll upset a few people in the process. I'll have to think about it."

"Be quick, then," says Face. "It was six months ago that you asked me to shut up shop for you because you thought someone was going to put a bullet in your head."

"Things have changed since then; a lot has gone on." It really has. Our Dave no longer worries that he'll be bumped off and he has opened up about his wife's death as much as a man can from round here. He's moved all her stuff and tried to make a new life. There is also something else that he now guards from Face, and especially from Bev, not because it's illegal or dangerous, but because he's not sure if it's right. Her name is Wendy, she's sixty-two, and he's been seeing her for nearly five months.

"So, what do you say, Our Dave? Are we going straight?"

"It won't be easy, Face. I'll have to think about it. I'll sound my contacts out in Leeds and on the docks. They're in this just as much as we are. There might be a ton of shite too, from the people we pay off as much as the people we buy and sell from."

"I'll be ready." Our Dave is about to comment that Face will not be ready because he's spent most of his life teaching law up at the university. Then he remembers that the man sitting in front of him shot Hull's biggest gangland player through the neck in March this year – without hesitation. "I'll need to know soon, Our Dave." Face has a way of getting things sorted.

"I'll have a think about it," answers Our Dave. Face might be an arsehole at times, but he likes to run a clean shop. The tenants of the properties that Our Dave has bought over the years now pay up on time. Face has sorted the tax affairs and it is all clean and above board. Where Our Dave used to get cash in hand for the rent on some places, the tenants now have a contract and a direct debit; they don't pay as much as they should, but it is very near the going rate. Our Dave can feel the menace of spreadsheets creeping into a place that he built quite by accident. "You know it's not just about the money, Face."

"Yes, it is. Money pays to keep the heating on, it puts food on the table for my lad, it pays Bev and Dilva's wages. Money keeps us safe, Our Dave. You told me that."

The kid is right. "I'll make some calls, Face."

"I just want it to be watertight, Our Dave. I want no confusion and nobody coming knocking when we don't expect it. I want us to be secure."

"So do I," says Our Dave. He stands up from leaning on the doorframe and turns to go back through the door and down the stairs. Face calls after him:

"There was a woman came round this morning; she dropped something off for you. I left it in the kitchen." Our Dave turns to look back at the man sitting in front of his laptop. He's wearing a slight grin.

"Oh aye?" asks Our Dave. This is what you say round here when you are not too sure about what you've been told.

"It's a biscuit tin. She said she'd baked them fresh and I wasn't to look inside neither."

"Did she say her name?"

Face grins wider. "Wendy." Our Dave turns away and begins down the stairs. As soon as he knows Face is not looking, he breaks into a wide and beaming smile.

Face locks up the office these days because he's usually the last one to go home. It has been a busy afternoon of sorting out tenancy agreements. In between, he's been messaging a thirty-nine year-old social worker who lives up in Swanland, she has older teenage daughters and a cockerpoo called Gary. Face is not a monster. He doesn't like that Bev thinks he's an arsehole either. He locks the back door and is about to go to collect his bicycle that he fastens to the drainpipe in the corner, when he notices something. There's a figure standing in the little, rundown car park behind him.

She's five-foot-six and has grown out her pixie cut so that her black hair is a little longer and just over her ears. He hasn't seen her for a while. She's wearing a dark t-shirt and trendy denim dungarees over the top. This is his ex-wife. Face feels his skin run cold. His first instinct is to defend himself.

"How can I help?" he asks. Her name is Inma, and she left him for a square jawed chiropractor who she began seeing when she and Face were together. She hurt him.

"I just thought I'd say hello, Tom. It's been a while."

"My name is Face these days," he answers. She gives him a kind of wince, as if his new nickname is beneath her. She was always good at belittling him, but that's not really why she's here. "You've grown out your hair?" he says.

"Yeah. It's nice to have a bit of a change. It's good to see Alex is doing well at college." This is their son. He has grown a lot since they split up.

Face gives her an honest grin. "It's probably better if we just communicate by email or your lawyer, then we can be clear in everything we want to say. I'd really prefer it that way, just so there's no misunderstanding."

"It costs me a fortune to send letters like that, Tom." She can't bring herself to say the name.

"What is it that you want, then?" Inma looks anxious as she stands there in her flowery, Doc Marten type boots.

"I heard from Bev that you've been seeing women."

"What about it?"

"It's not like you."

"It is now. I'm another person these days."

"I'm worried how it will affect Alex. I'm worried that he'll think sleeping around is acceptable."

Face wrinkles his already deeply scarred features at this. "You shouldn't listen to all the shit you hear."

"It's not like you to swear, Tom."

"It is now," he repeats. "I work in a taxi office. I'll tell you what happens with the girls I meet, shall I? We go for a drink or a walk in the park, we might go for a coffee. Maybe they'll make it to date three if they're sweet or interesting…"

"I don't have to hear this," says Inma. She takes a deep breath in and folds her arms.

Face carries on. "Maybe we'll have a day trip to York or I'll take them to a restaurant or to Parkrun, or we'll walk across to Cottingham for a pint in the Billy, and if we get any further than a month in – I dump them. I'm getting good at it."

He's learned a lot in these months about himself and the world as well, especially from Bev. Sometimes you have to speak your mind even if it will hurt someone; even if the person it will hurt the most is you:

"I don't sleep with them, Inma, and I dump them because I want them to be you and they're not. That's the truth of it." He watches her swallow and her nostrils flare as she hears this. She takes a step back and disappears around the corner.

Now she's gone, Face puts his hand to his forehead. He did not know he would say this. He isn't an arsehole, whatever Bev says and he isn't over his wife however much he wants to pretend that he is. Face hadn't even admitted it to himself, until now.

HULL FAIR THREE

It all starts today – Friday afternoon. Little kids and teenagers have been excited all week. Mums who have promised they will go on the opening night; have now said they'll go on Wednesday when it will be quieter. Extra buses have been timetabled. Metal fences have been put up on the grass verges on Spring Bank West to stop people parking on them. Traffic wardens are going to work late nights. Mrs Turner from two streets across is going to have to keep her cat in for a whole week. Mr and Mrs Parkinson who live on Walton Street itself have moved to her sister's in East Hull because of the crowds, the noise and the mess. On the corner of Pulman Street, Amir who runs the Kingfisher Chippie has spent nearly a grand on extra potatoes, fish, cans of pop, and sausages for the punters at the fair. It is his best time of year, and he must capitalize on the opportunity.

At five o'clock, at the Spring Bank side of the fair, the Lord Mayor of Hull, dressed in his red gown and tricorn hat, gives a speech to three journalists and a handful of other local dignitaries. He says the same old sort of thing about enjoyment and community and historical tradition, and Mally Kemp is pleased that he does not go on too long. Then, he rings a big brass hand bell to signal that the fair is open, and the noise sounds out over the rows of caravans and tents to the larger rides and the big wheel in the centre. The music starts straight away. The carousel beside them creaks as it begins a slow spin, and the lights of the rides flicker on.

So, it starts.

Mally does the required hand shaking and smiling with the Lord Mayor and some of the councillors. He takes off his flat cap and grins for the cameras. It's just a formality.

In half an hour, Mally is back at his caravan fighting issues; the power is out on the funhouse at the rear of the ground, there are two food van workers rowing, and the coppers have already caught and ejected someone smoking weed from the Anlaby Road side. It will be like this, on and off, for a week or so. Mally knows how to handle it all. He'll deal with the food van workers himself, then be off to sort out the electricity for the funhouse. He'll let the police do what they want with the weed smoker.

At the back of the fair, metal railings fence off the train tracks, and behind them, crouched in the darkness of the undergrowth is a young dog fox with his eyes wide and frightened. The sweet autumn evening is ripening into night, and the orange sunlight is bleeding out across the horizon of the city. He can smell the vinegar from the chips already and the sweet perfume from the fatty burgers in the food vans. His orange fur is soft and new, his ears have white tips, and his whiskers are keen and straight. He knows how to wait. Once the darkness sets in fully and the people disappear, the lights will all go out and he'll have his fill from the stacked up bins. The only real problem will be who he has to fight to get at it.

CHAPTER FOUR
Wendy

It's Saturday morning again. Bev leaves early for one of those runs with West Hull Fitmums. They sometimes do Parkrun together at 9 o'clock but, more often than not, they go out to the fields just north of Cottingham. If you'd have told Bev twenty years ago that she would get up on Saturday morning without a hangover, she would have thought you were taking the piss. It's funny how age changes you. There's half a dozen of them and they go out to Risby to run around the lake and through the fields. Bev and the girls chat about men and she tells them about her last disaster of a date at Pocklington. She feels better when her school teacher friend explains about her husband's porn addiction, and Bev is fleetingly happy she isn't married, even if she is lonely sometimes. She doesn't say anything about the Ethiopian girl she picked up on the road the other night.

Jerusalem has swept and mopped the downstairs floors, done a basket load of washing, and hung the clothes on the line. She found frozen croissants in the freezer so she is baking these up. When Bev walks through the door at half eleven after a coffee with the Fitmums ladies, she is surprised. Her house smells lightly of bleach and sweet baking.

In the kitchen, Jerusalem is wearing the same jeans and shirt that she took from Chloe's wardrobe a couple of days before. Bev is not used to having guests, and not at all having guests who cook. The girl opens the oven to look at the croissants inside.

"They'll be a few minutes," she says. Bev puts her keys down on the table. She likes the girl, but she needs some answers before she is going to settle. This is how Bev works.

"You said you only needed another night here? You've been here a week."

Jerusalem closes the oven. There is no malice in Bev's tone.

"I thought I would be gone already," she says.

"You're welcome to stay here, but I need to know what's going on. When I picked you up, you were a mess, and you won't let me go to the police and you won't see a doctor. You didn't have a penny to your name, and then yesterday, you disappear and come back with money and gin and you say you earned it." Bev notices the smartphone on the table next to her bag. "And is this yours?" Jerusalem nods. "When did you get that?"

"I earned it as well." she says.

"How? I need to know." Even though Bev wants to help, she isn't about to take any shite. Jerusalem stands up straight.

"I stole it, the phone and the money too."

"That's not earning it then, is it?"

"If they are stupid enough to let me take it, then I've earned it, haven't I?" She says this like it's true.

"That's not how it works," says Bev. "I need to know who you are and what has happened, really." Jerusalem likes this no nonsense way of being, it shows strength, she will respond in kind.

"I told you my name and I told you I'm Ethiopian and living in Amsterdam. That much was true. I work for a man there, and I belong to him also. I came to England to do a job for him, and I was attacked before you picked me up. There were three of them. I found myself here and I wanted to pay you back, so I did what I know how to do, I found where there are people and I stole from them. Now, I wonder whether I should go back to that man in Amsterdam, or if I should run from him." This is the truth.

Bev stares back at her from eyes ringed with mascara and foundation that is mixed with sweat from her run. It sounds a bit far-fetched and Bev is only usually gullible when men are telling her things that she wants to believe are true. "How did you steal these things?" she asks.

"I live in Amsterdam. I can pickpocket."

"How can you belong to someone?"

"I was sold."

Bev cocks her head and fixes the girl with her blue eyes. Jerusalem is a commanding woman, but so is Bev, especially in her own house. "You'll have to go to the police," says Bev.

Jerusalem shakes her head. She bends down to open the oven and uses a tea towel to pull out the tray from within.

"You Europeans don't really understand," she says as she sets the tray on top of the cooker. "It's not as bad as you think. His name is Uncle George. I work for him." She goes to the cupboard to find two plates.

"What does he make you do?"

"I have done many things, but these days, I'm a pilot." Bev wrinkles her nose as if this is nonsense. "I fly people into the airfield north of Pocklington. I've been doing it for months. Someone stole my plane the other night." Bev narrows her eyes. She is not stupid. This sounds like shite. Jerusalem continues:

"My employer is paid good money to traffic these people. He says they're refugees but I don't think they are." She looks back to Bev. "These croissants are ready," she says.

Bev takes a seat at the table and the girl puts a plate down in front of her. She goes back to the drawer to fetch two knives and butter from the fridge then sits down. Bev does not pick up her cutlery, she is not finished with the straight talking.

"What are the tattoos?" she asks. She means the homemade crosses on Jerusalem's forehead and her chin.

"They are a sign of beauty where I come from. They are the Niksat."

"You say this man bought you."

"Uncle George, yes. I am his property, but I am not a slave. I am paid but I cannot leave his service." The croissants steam in front of them. "This is information you do not need to know," says Jerusalem. "It is best you forget about it, and me. You'll keep the money, and I will be on my way tomorrow.

Your kindness should not affect you."

"I wasn't born yesterday, love," says Bev. "I know how it is. You work for a man and you think you're free, but you won't leave. It sounds like being married." Jerusalem does not quite realise where she has ended up. This is Hull. It doesn't have the heavy, organised crime of a city like Amsterdam, but the people are not saints. Bev here is as tough as they come. "He says he loves you, does he?" Bev cuts her to the quick. Jerusalem's face reddens suddenly, her throat is tight. He did say this, yes, and part of her believed it too. She did not realise she was so easy to unpick.

"Who do you think you're talking to?" asks Bev. It's rhetorical. "You've been raped. Sounds like your being used. You said yourself a minute ago you didn't know if you'd go back to him, whoever he is. I don't know anything about you, love, but I know fellas. That's how they control you. Some things happen for a reason. Maybe I was driving down that road the other night because I was meant to. Do you think anyone else would have stopped for you, at that time? All they would have done is call the police when they got home. Not me." Jerusalem can see steel in this blonde woman.

"If I do not go back to him there will be trouble."

"There's going to be bloody trouble anyway," says Bev as she waves her hand. She is getting into her stride. "What do you think happens every day? There's always trouble. You just have to make sure you're on the right side of it."

"He's not a man to be played with," says Jerusalem.

"Played with you for long enough, hasn't he? You'll have to start standing up for yourself and stop doing things for other people. Like this money you've stolen to give to me. I don't want it. You only got it to make yourself feel better. Maybe that's why you work for him."

"What are you helping me for, then?" Jerusalem will fight back if she has to.

The truth spills out of Bev. Her defences are down but

there's no self-pity. "I'm lonely. I live alone. I meet fellas off the internet so I've got someone to go out with. I'm divorced. I'm nearly fifty. Doing something for a lass like you is the best thing that's happened to me for weeks."

Jerusalem peers back at Bev over the anaemic looking croissant that is underdone. The clock ticks on the wall. There's beeping from a car horn a few streets away. Bev's chin wobbles as if she is going to cry. This is too much honesty.

"You'll have to stay here," says Bev.

Jerusalem looks down at the croissant. She is suddenly not hungry.

Our Dave enters the back office of Avenue Cars and smiles a hello to Dilva who is getting something out of the printer. She gives him a big grin and points to the open biscuit tin on the counter.

"They're really nice," she says. Our Dave stops to look inside and sees the square rows of lemon drizzle cake within. These are from Wendy. He forgot to take the tin home yesterday, and whoever was here would have opened it up and helped themselves. He grabs one – it's moist with not too much drizzle, but enough to make it sweet. It makes him like Wendy even more than he already does.

"What you doing here on Saturday morning?" he asks in his friendly tone.

"I'm printing off something for Ryan." Dilva is a Kurdish woman who started working here a year or so ago. She has grown in confidence in that time, her English has improved, and her partner is a man named Ryan who has matured as well. Our Dave didn't expect anyone to be in the office. He's only here to pick up this tin of lemon drizzle slices and the white transit van. He says goodbye to Dilva as she's printing something else off from her phone and goes outside.

Once he's in the little car park, and alone, Our Dave pulls out his phone. He looks at the blur of icons and colours then fiddles to get his glasses from his top pocket so he can see what it all says. Six months ago, the weakness of age was telling him that he was about to die. These days, getting old just pisses him off. Wendy has sent him a message. There it is, under a round green icon, and he reads it with his glasses on his nose:

Wendy Police: *I dropped off some cakes at your office yesterday. The man with the scars is very charming…he didn't seem like an arse at all.*

Our Dave types with two thumbs for speed – Bev showed him how to do this. He replies: *He isn't all the time. Thanks for dropping them off.*

At his white transit van, Our Dave opens up, gets in and closes the door. He looks at his watch then takes off his glasses. He said he'd drop the van with Gaz before twelve. The man borrows it to do airport runs for holiday makers or professionals, and once he's saved enough, Gaz says he's going to get his own vehicle. Our Dave likes him. He's the opposite of Face up in the office in many ways, he's quiet, unsure of himself and loyal. Gaz used to be a doorman and he did personal protection for individuals as well. He's helped out more than a few times in the past and these days, he lives with a lass called Kate down Belvoir Street. They are made for each other even though they did not realise it before. Our Dave knows they are in love because of the way Gaz looks at her. It makes the old man happy to know they are together. Our Dave starts the engine and pulls out of the little car park into the busy traffic of Chants Ave.

His brain whirs as he thinks about the woman who left the lemon drizzle cake. Wendy is in her early sixties but looks younger. She has a twinkle in her eyes, and straight white teeth with blonde hair to her shoulders. She says she doesn't live in Hull, but in Willerby. It's a leafier part of town which residents say is a village, however, there is no discernible disconnection with the city of Hull apart from a sign on the busy main road that reads 'Welcome to Willerby' as you drive in, and

'Welcome to Hull' as you drive out.

Our Dave has been seeing her since May and it is a secret, but she seems to be testing this by coming to the office and dropping off cakes. He likes her, and it is changing the way he thinks about himself and the world around him.

Our Dave met her at the Hull University Student Hub in May when he took Dilva's kid's bikes to get them security marked by the transport police. That's why she's still in his phone as 'Wendy Police'. She works for the coppers as admin and did all the computer registration while the officers marked the bikes. Wendy has a big, bright smile and a dirty laugh. She has the air of a movie star to her, and when she'd finished taking his details, and he'd made her laugh and she him, he noticed that there was no wedding ring on her finger. So, as the actual copper talked to the next customer, he asked for her number and if he could take her for a cup of coffee. Our Dave is a born chancer, and you can't take it out of him just because he's old.

They went out for a coffee in the garden centre at Swanland. She was funny and self-deprecating but not defeatist at all. Wendy drives a little sport-injection Fiat, she has her own money and her own house. Her late husband worked for Humberside Transport Police and got fairly high up till he got cancer in his late fifties and struggled on to die at sixty one. Wendy kept on working in the admin of the transport police depot because she enjoyed it but just part-time. The coppers are like a family, even when you leave you don't, you still get invited to their get-togethers and weddings and you still get phone calls making sure you are okay and a lift to the Christmas party.

Our Dave didn't think anything of it when he learned who her husband had been and the friends she has. He assumed it would just be a cup of coffee between them and nothing more.

It developed.

They met for meals at the café under Skidby Mill on hot

summer days. They walked the sides of fields and round the big lake out at Welton Waters. Our Dave knows lots of her stories and she knows some of his. Wendy struggled when her husband died, and she could not have got through it without her friends and her only son, Brian. He's a plainclothes police sergeant with the CID department at Clough Road Station. Like many of the people Our Dave knows and gets on with, he is willing to let Wendy do most of the talking. Our Dave is naturally a listener, partly because there are many things he has to keep secret and also, since Hazel died, he is not sure anyone would be interested in what he has to say. Wendy is cleverer than Our Dave by a country mile, and on their long walks he finds himself giving away how he has come to terms with his wife's death, about his allotment on Raglan Street, and even about Face and how he has drifted into womanizing. When Our Dave catches himself talking like this, and too much in his opinion, he looks up to see Wendy looking at him with that bright smile as if she is listening. It is a new sensation since Hazel left. She is cracking him open, slowly, even though she cannot know any of the details about Our Dave's smuggling business, especially with a son who works for the CID. It's not ideal by any means. It's like playing with fire when you live in a house made of paper.

Our Dave drives down Chants Ave and stops at the traffic lights. He taps his fingers on the wheel in mild worry. There is no way he can tell Wendy what his business is, and no way he can tell his employees that he is seeing a copper, even if she is retired. Like a fifteen-year-old boy who has fallen for a girl from the wrong family, Our Dave has got himself into a pickle and like always, there is nobody to talk to about it. Face would caution against seeing her in the interests of safety, Bev would say it is too soon after Hazel's death, so would Gaz, and these walls that Our Dave built up to protect himself before are rebuilding themselves.

As he follows the one way system off Princess Avenue

onto Belvoir Street, he thinks about her. He likes the dirty laugh, the way she squeezes his arm. He likes the way she smells and likes too that she knows more about him already than some of the people along the Avenues who have known him for fifty years. She makes him feel young.

Our Dave parks the van up in a spot on Belvoir Street, puts on the handbrake and gets out. He's a bit early, as always, so he walks the little way back down to Kate's house, taps on the door and stands back. Gaz opens up with a smile. Kate has changed him for the better. He's dressed in a tight dark suit like a non-descript chauffeur and has sunglasses in his hand.

"I've come to drop the van off with you, Gaz." He likes to see that this young man is happy. He holds out the keys for him to take and Gaz collects them as he stands on the step in his socks. Kate comes down the hall behind him with a lunchbox. He has changed her as well; she is less gaunt and more organised. They are a good couple.

"I'll have the van back with you this evening, Our Dave," says Gaz.

"No rush," he answers. He doesn't want to take up either of their time. They're young people with young things to do. Kate steps in front of Gaz towards Our Dave, she's dressed in a grey jacket with a smart pale blouse. These days, she works at the counselling office on Princes Ave and like Gaz, she is there to provide a service without being noticed.

"I need a favour, Our Dave," she says. It is unlike her or Gaz to ask. She produces an envelope that she passes to him.

"What's this?"

"My friend's got a play on at the Truck Theatre, nothing big, but she needs people to go to make up the numbers in the audience. I'd go, but me and Gaz will be working. Will you see if you can get there? It's in a few weeks, a Wednesday night." Our Dave looks down at the envelope.

"You can take your friend," says Gaz.

"What friend?" asks Our Dave. He looks to Kate's

smooth, clever blue eyes, and her blonde hair. This is not a favour.

"That friend out at Willerby," says Kate. Our Dave gives them both a worried look. They will have been watching him. Gaz's quiet ways means that he spots things about people, that's what he's been trained to do as personal protection. Face will have noticed any details that stick out as well. Perhaps Our Dave is not as good at covering his tracks as he thinks.

"I'll see what I can do," he says.

"Who is she?" asks Kate.

"Nobody really. Just a friend." Our Dave does not like it when they know too much about him, even if they know everything about him already.

"Can I give you a lift anywhere, Our Dave?" asks Gaz.

"No ta, mate, I'm off into town to meet an old friend." Our Paul is going to meet Wendy, instinct instructs him not to say anything. He steps back away from the door and looks down at the envelope in his hand again. The odd feeling of being looked after comes over him – they are trying to repay Our Dave back somehow. "Thanks for this," he says.

"We had it going spare," says Kate as if to cover what she is really trying to do. Our Dave turns down the little path away from the two of them. He slips the envelope into his inside pocket and makes his way down Belvoir Street. Their eyes follow him as he goes.

Kate closes the front door after he's gone, and turns to look at Gaz. He is dark-haired and handsome in a quiet way. He smiles at her and is at once awkward standing in the long hall of her terraced house where he now lives. It has been difficult for both of them to adjust.

"I just want him to be happy," says Gaz. "The poor bastard has been through enough." Kate nods. He walks down the hall to get his shoes, picks them up and sits on the bottom step of the stairs as he puts them on. Kate leans on the wall and watches him. When he stands up and walks to the door, she pulls him close and they kiss. Her hand on the back of his head sends tingles down his spine and back.

Gaz is unlike any man she has lived with before. He's quiet. He cleans the shower out after he's used it. He washes their clothes and folds them neatly. He remembers to leave the wheelie bin out for the early morning collection and, when they sleep next to each other at night, he is motionless and she can hardly hear his breathing. She knows the territory; Gaz has edited himself so as not to be any trouble to anyone. It's how he learned to live in the care homes he grew up in. He can't tell funny stories at dinner parties or spark up conversations with strangers. He doesn't do quick one line jokes or wink at random girls. Gaz is not a cheeky chap. He is rock solid. Kate's friends do not understand him. When they ask why she is with someone so quiet, she answers that they love each other, and it quietens then with the truth of it.

Gaz has never let anyone get so close. Kate is self-aware; she listens to him and gives him space too. She rubs Gaz's shoulders when they're sore, even though he is self-conscious about the attention. She lets him look after her. On Friday nights they go to the curry house on Chants Ave or down to the Vietnamese place on Newland. Gaz eats food he's never tried before. When they walk down the street, Kate hooks her arm round his. It feels right to both of them. She's teaching him to cook. Gaz loves her so much that he worries something might happen to her.

There's someone who put them together when they should have fallen apart. Someone they owe.

Our Dave.

CHAPTER FIVE
Ultimatums

It's Sunday evening but not yet dark. Jerusalem wants a smoke and the night outside is warm in the late autumn. After Bev has spoken to her daughter, Chloe, on the phone, she and Jerusalem walk along Chants Ave in the early evening. With Hull Fair just round the corner, the street should be rammed with people, but it's Sunday and in line with tradition and the law, the fair is closed on the day of rest.

Autumn is setting in and the leaves on the trees that run down Marlborough Ave have turned a golden orange before they're due to fall off. They turn left and walk down Perth Street West – they'll go over the railway bridge and then down Spring Bank and back onto Chants Ave. Bev will buy the lass a pint in the Avenues pub before they go home. The smell of Jerusalem's cigarette makes Bev want one.

The girl doesn't say much as they walk but there's a sense of calm to her. The boots seem to fit her nicely and she's taken to wearing the Marx cap that holds her hair out of her face. It's deserted down the path to the little pedestrian bridge behind the houses, weeds and brambles grow over the railings and the sunshine is going down over the roofs in front. It's the kind of place teenagers come to drink cider or smoke a spliff, and there's the calm warmth of the autumn wind. Jerusalem and Bev climb the stairs of the railway footbridge, walk halfway down, and look out over the side at the train tracks stretching towards Cottingham in the distance.

It's been a funny summer.

In his flat on the corner of Park Ave and Chants, JT found a red and white striped snake under his broken guitar collection, and on advice from those who know, let it live under his fridge. The flat roof of the tattoo studio fell in after the heavy rains, and Mandy got the whole back room fitted out on insurance. Tess on Victoria Ave had her heart broken by that dickhead writer, for the second time, and then painted a six-foot collage entitled Power that she sold for three grand to Beverley Art Gallery. The four-piece punk band, Animal, picked up a stalker online. He attacked and bit the lead singer, Josh and while he was being treated for it in Hull Royal, he fell in love with his nurse. Although the punk band never gigged again, Josh at least found his soulmate and they moved to Scotland. Good things have turned bad and vice versa this summer.

Bev leans on the side of the bridge and looks at the railway line below them, weeds grow through the railings and the bushes are heavy with brambles. They have hardly spoken since they left the house, and the silence is easy, as if they've known each other longer than just a few days.

"Where is your husband?" asks Jerusalem.

"I got rid of him."

"Is he dead?"

Bev looks at her funny. "No, we got divorced years ago. I wouldn't be surprised if he was dead though."

"It's normal for European women to live without a man." This is a statement from Jerusalem.

"Honestly, living alone is better than being with the wrong one," says Bev. "Where's your husband?"

"I will not take one till I am older, if I take one at all," she says. "I'm not like the other girls from my country, I can do what I want." It sounds like a fact.

"Really?"

"My father was rich. I will be rich too." There's a train approaching down the tracks.

Bev wouldn't make a very good counsellor or a youth worker – she's prone to telling things straight. It has got her into trouble and it will again. "How come you're here then? How come I found you on the York Road with no trousers on? How come you say you belong to some bloke in Amsterdam?" Jerusalem gives her a withering look. "It sounds like shite to me, love." Bev enjoys saying this, especially when it's true.

The train thunders past under them and the little railway bridge wobbles with the whoosh of air. Jerusalem appreciates this honesty from Bev.

"Uncle George bought me," says Jerusalem, "and I will have to go back to him. It's like the story of Joseph in the bible. He was sold to slavers and he rose to become king of them." Jerusalem is repeating a sermon she heard in church many years ago. Once upon a time this story made sense but it's out of place here in the UK.

Bev stands up from the side of the railway bridge and folds her arms as she frowns. She's a Hull woman – she does not deal in waffle, and her face demands explanation. "You've been trafficked, doesn't matter who did it and if you think you belong to him. You'll have to tell someone because you can't go back. You know it." This is the drizzle of real life that falls on the streets of this city, there's no comfort in it, or poetry even.

Jerusalem looks out down the train tracks and breathes in through her nose. "It is the strong who survive this world, and they take what they want from it as well." There is drama in this young woman's conviction. "You told me you were attacked like me, what did you do?"

"I got on with it. There was nobody to go to."

"Like I will get on with it as well. Like I always have."

"It doesn't mean you're strong because you don't say anything. I wish I hadn't been quiet; that's just it. It's women like me who shut up, who thought it was their fault, who didn't say a word. It's me that let those men get away with it. It has to change."

"There is the difference between you and I," says Jerusalem. "The men who did ill towards me will not get away with it, as you say. I know the registration of the truck that took me. I know the name of the company they run and that they are from Newcastle. I found the address online. When I'm ready, I will visit."

"You'll get the shit beaten out of you," says Bev, "or you'll get killed."

"I do not mind if I die." It's the kind of thing teenagers say, it's all epic and final.

"You won't die," says Bev with just the right amount of scorn to not make it offensive. "In the end you'll just wither up like you've been in the bath too long, and all the plans you had for the future will wither up as well. You'll not go to Newcastle to sort those blokes out, just like you won't run away from whoever you say owns you. It's time to wake the fuck up, lass. You've been given a chance, a way to get off the merry-go-round. I can help you."

"This is down to me," says Jerusalem. "I've got this far."

"You can't do it on your own, not in the end," says Bev. "I've tried." This is what she has learned over the many years that she brought Chloe up as a single mum. "I live in that house on my own, I wake up alone, I watch the telly on my own, I raised my daughter alone and now she's gone. I'm lonely. You will be too."

"It is you who need my help then," says Jerusalem.

"You might think you know it all right now, lass, but time will show you that you have to accept a helping hand once in a while."

The yellow autumn sun is beginning to go down behind the houses on the horizon. There's the noise of someone coming up the steps at speed, and they turn to see a man with black rimmed glasses and a cycling helmet carrying his bike. He walks past with an 'ey up' and then goes down the steps at the other side. It has broken their discussion.

Bev looks up at this young, earnest woman with tattoos on her forehead and chin and her brown eyes that blaze with steady fire.

Perhaps they were meant to find each other, these two.

"Let's keep going," says Bev.

They walk in silence up Woodgate Road, turning left to head back to Chants Ave. The fair is already set up but won't open again until tomorrow. Outside the Halfway House pub, a lorry delivers beer, while a hand-painted white sign at the Kurdish car wash advertises: "Car Parking £10" – up from last year. Tomorrow, this will burst into life by four o'clock, so that when the sun goes down about half six, the lights from the fair will ignite the sky with oranges and yellows. There'll be the blaring and thumping of music from the rides and the throng of people.

Now, it's all quiet. The white shutters are down on the food stalls. A man in a flat cap and a cut-off denim jacket, revealing his powerful tattooed arms, walks between the deserted rides. Two coppers stand guard out front, and the carousel looks out of place in the still darkness of the overcast evening. Jerusalem and Bev pass by the entrance to the empty fair without going in. They both look at the spectacle of it, and the huge motionless Ferris wheel sticking up into the skyline.

"It comes every year," says Bev. "Pisses me right off as well." Like many people who don't have a business down Chants Ave, the fair is an annoyance. It brings hordes of people and traffic that clog up the street, tonnes of litter and there's the booming noise of the music. She is just about to turn to Jerusalem to explain more, when the girl stops and fixes her eyes on something she has seen over the road past the two coppers standing guard.

"What is it?" asks Bev.

"I saw something."

"What?"

"A man." Jerusalem reaches her hand up to touch her own neck with her fingers. This is where he held her down in the back of the truck in the darkness a few days before. Her face is pale. She did not expect to find what she was looking for so soon. "I need to see," says Jerusalem.

"See what?" asks Bev as she follows the taller girl. They cross the street to the fairground and at the entrance, a short female copper stops them with a raised hand.

"I'm afraid you can't come in," she says, "the fair's not open on a Sunday." She's being pleasant.

"How am I supposed to get to see my mother? She only lives on Anlaby Road?" this is Bev. The copper shrugs her shoulders as if she's not really bothered, and the two women walk into the deserted fair.

Jerusalem saw the man with the cut off sleeves go right past the boarded up stalls and closed down rides. They follow. The kid's roundabout is covered with a blue tarpaulin, and the faded helter-skelter has seen better days. Jerusalem stops when she sees the waltzer ride ahead. It's not spinning, but she recognizes the gaudy, badly spray-painted faces on the side, along with the galaxy backdrop featuring a blue-grey night sky and twinkling stars. The big man with the flat cap and tattooed arms walks around the side, facing away from them. Jerusalem turns to Bev and her face is pale.

"What is it?" whispers Bev.

"I thought I knew him," says Jerusalem. She does know him. It is the man from the other night who held her down by her throat. She won't do anything now, of course, she is with Bev. Jerusalem will have to give this a little thought, but not too much, she does not want to lose the poison that rumbles in her stomach for these men. It will have to be soon.

As they walk back past the copper at the entrance, the smaller one calls to Bev:

"How's your mam?"

"She was out," she calls back.

It's Sunday evening. This is Ye Olde White Harte just off the town centre. It's really called that and the atmosphere is quaint and quirky, with what everyone says is a human skull on the top shelf behind the optics looking down on the little room. Our Dave stands at the end of the bar. The landlord has just gone to change the barrel.

It's quiet like Sunday evenings are. The mess from Saturday night has been sorted, the roast dinners have been served, and now there are just a few of the regulars dotted round the pub. This is a coaching inn from way back in the day. The decision to begin the English Civil War is meant to have been made in the plotting room upstairs, it's supposed to be haunted as well.

The tall landlord returns to the bar and pulls beer through the pump. While he's filling pint glasses with froth, Wendy steps into the pub. She's wearing a thin neck scarf over her green dress. Our Dave thinks she has a touch of the movie star about her; she's glamorous but still ready to get her hands dirty if she has to. You can take Wendy for a hike down the beach and up the cliffs at Flamborough, to the chippy on Hessle Road or up to the posh gastro pub at Dalton called the Pipe and Glass. She fits right in wherever she goes. Our Dave's stomach turns over as she approaches and stands next to him at the bar. He gives her a smile and she returns it with one of her own. Usually, they hug. Something is off.

The barman sets two half pints of Frothingham's Best down in front of Our Dave. Wendy takes one of the glasses and they both sit down opposite each other next to the empty fireplace. Wendy has not yet looked him in the eyes.

"Thanks for the lemon drizzle cake," says Our Dave.

"Are you embarrassed about me?" she asks. Wendy is polite but to the point. Her lipstick is a subtle red.

"No. Why?"

"When I dropped the cake tin off that man with the scarred face didn't know who I was. I told him I was Wendy."

Now Our Dave realises why she is a little frosty. "I haven't told them about you," he says.

"Why?"

Our Dave takes a deep breath. He's not good at lying to people he thinks a lot about. "They wouldn't care, Wendy. The less they know about what I do the better, to be honest."

"It's been many months since we started this, Dave. If we're going to be part of each other's lives, then you'll have to meet my family, and I yours."

"They're just people I work with. They're rough types. Not the kind of folk you'd be used to."

She finally looks at him properly, and her blue eyes are clever and warm. "Please don't lie to me, Dave, will you? That's what my Harry used to do, like I was just some silly little woman who shouldn't be troubled by anything important. I've invited you on more than a few occasions to meet my son, and my friends, and there's always been some excuse." She looks down at her half pint. She has not raised her voice and this makes what she is saying more profound. "If you want this to end, Dave, we can do it right now, but if you don't, then I'm going to have to be added to your life. I'm too old to play games." She picks up the ale and takes a sip that leaves a tiny mark from her lipstick on the rim. Wendy was nervous before this date, knowing that she was going to say this. She likes this tall man and given a few alterations; he could well be the one for her.

Our Dave licks his lips and takes a deep breath through his nose. He will have to play this one carefully. He doesn't want Wendy to find out some of his business, especially as her son is an active policeman. It's not that she is nosey, but she is clever and she notices things. Our Dave gazes at her as he considers what he is going to say. Hazel was never concerned with his business at all, she had her own life and friends and what Our Dave did at work was not her worry. Wendy here is different. They are lovers more than man and wife. If Our Dave didn't think so much of Wendy, he wouldn't say this, but Face is trying to make the business legitimate, and he is going to sell it to him in the long run. A little bit of truth might not hurt.

"Not all of the taxi company is legitimate, Wendy. That's

why I've got that man with the scarred face in, he's putting it all right. You work for the coppers and your son is CID. I didn't want anything to happen." She looks at him with a blank expression. "I want to move on, Wendy. I want to move on from what I've always done, and Avenue Cars and everything that's happened there is part of the past, you're the future." He picks up his half and takes a glug that drains most of it. Now he has come to terms with the death of his wife, and the business is being put in order, he really does want to move on.

Wendy is pragmatic and sensible. "What are we going to do then?"

"Leave."

"Me and you?"

"Aye. I'd like that." Our Dave did not know he would say this. He certainly hasn't thought about it.

"Where?"

"Any place they don't know me, Wendy. Anywhere we could be together."

She cocks her head. "When we first started seeing each other I asked around. That's why I know you're a good egg, Our Dave. I don't think you're worried about me discovering your tax dodging, what would I do about it anyway?" Her eyes moisten. This is hard for Wendy. She did not know that men could be like Our Dave after being married to her late husband for thirty years. He is kind to her; he listens, he's never late. She does not at all want to lose him, but her sixth sense is telling her there is something else. "You'll need to be honest with me, Dave."

Wendy is getting closer to him than anyone has in many years. Our Dave defends himself with that ready smile. He would rather you talk about yourself. He drinks the rest of his half. "I'm afraid, Wendy. I'm not sure I can get close to anyone ever again." Men of Our Dave's generation do not speak like this. It is painful for him. "When I lost Hazel, it destroyed me, completely. What if that happens again?"

Over the last few months, she has done more with this man than she did with her husband. Among other things, they have walked cut cornfields in late summer, stopped at Wetwang for fish and chips, stayed the night in Scarborough, and walked hand in hand along the marina in the sunny evening.

"Is that the only time you've had your heart broken, then?" she asks.

"Aye." Our Dave is being more honest with her than he has been with himself. It is uncomfortable.

"You'll have to realise that it will get broken again. That's how it is if you're a person with feelings."

"You've had yours broken a few times then?"

"It's been turned to stone over many years," says Wendy. Her eyes are bright blue and keen. "When my Harry died, I cried at the funeral and I didn't think I would. Now he's gone I'm free. I think we should stop seeing each other for a while, Dave, just until you've figured out what you want. If you want to be with me, then I'll be here, but not for long. You'll have to let me in if you want to carry on."

Our Dave runs his big joiner's hand across his face like he does. "I just kind of fell into this with me and you, Wendy. I wasn't looking for it but now I've found you, to be honest, I don't want to stop seeing you. I like you."

"You just feel distant. My mum used to say that if you're not sure if a man likes you, then he doesn't."

"Is that what you think?"

"With you, I don't know." Wendy finishes her drink. This is not how this meeting was meant to go. She gives Our Dave a curt smile. "You know where to find me," she says, "but I won't wait long." Wendy stands up and collects her glass which she returns to the bar before she drifts out of the door in her long green dress with the silk scarf around her neck like a movie star.

Our Dave sits staring at his empty glass.

He doesn't know what he thinks.

CHAPTER SIX
Retribution

It's Monday. In the kitchen downstairs, Jerusalem has cooked pasta for the both of them. While Bev was at work, she cut the grass in the back garden that didn't really need cutting. She washed down the front and back doors, mended the gate hinges and weeded the front drive where Bev usually parks that big, white BMW. The house is spotless, and when Bev came home, she smelled the rich sauce that Jerusalem has cooked for the pasta. It is lovely to have her here.

"Please, sit," she orders. Bev takes a place at the little kitchen table while Jerusalem serves out the pasta in a bowl. It steams as she sets it down.

"Have you thought about what you're going to do?" asks Bev. Jerusalem has been on her mind all day.

"I have," she answers.

"Well?"

"I will get in touch with Uncle George in a few days. I have something I need to do first."

Bev is disappointed. "You'll go back to him?"

"Yes. Now I've had chance to think, I can see that is the only option. I must complete what I started." Jerusalem tucks into her pasta with her spoon.

"I know someone who might have a better idea," says Bev.

"There is no better idea. I will go back."

"I'll just have a word with him about you, is that ok?"

"Who is he?"

"He's the boss at the taxi office, a good lad. He's called Our Dave."

Jerusalem has been busy, not just on Bev's house and garden – she has been planning. In the toolbox that Bev has in the shed, the one that she used to fix the gate, she has found a good hammer that will come in handy. There's a length of garden wire and some gardening gloves. There's also a Stanley knife with a sharp blade that retracts with the sliding thumb button. Jerusalem will wear the gloves for sure – she is not certain about the wire. Hanging up in the cupboard under the stairs, she found a long, black coat with deep outside pockets, the hammer fits nicely into one. In the room she's staying in, Jerusalem went through the wardrobe and there was a wide black scarf. As a little girl in Ethiopia, she wore a headscarf like this all the time, it will be an excellent disguise.

After she'd weeded the front drive, Jerusalem used the phone she stole to look at maps of the area. From what she remembers, the waltzer ride is at the back of the fairground. On the map, there's a fence onto the railway line and then another fence that leads into a quiet looking street. It might be best to go out that way when she's done what she's going to do. After she's cooked and cleaned up for Bev, and as she is doing the washing up, she looks at the reflection of herself in the kitchen window with the dark night outside. All she has to do is wait.

Bev explained all about Hull Fair. She says it brings business to the area and some trouble, but not as much as in the past. Jerusalem has seen travelling funfairs in Amsterdam. Uncle George took her to one in Westerpark a year ago. He showed her the rides and the stalls, the lights, and the punters. There was the sweet smell of waffles cooking. He showed her the angles too, and how the only thing you really need to pickpocket someone is confidence, and that people who looked poorer were a better target than those who looked rich. Uncle George explained that wealthy people are generally mean and shrewd. He said he knew this because he was one of them.

It's just before nine when Jerusalem makes her move. Bev is in the front room watching a TV show with her face in her mobile phone. Jerusalem goes to the front door and puts her hand on the Yale lock:

"I'm going to buy cigarettes," she calls to Bev down the hall. "I won't be long." Jerusalem does not really want Bev to see her leaving. She is wearing that long jacket with a hammer in the pocket and she has the scrunched up headscarf in her hand.

"See you in a minute," calls Bev.

Jerusalem walks down Lynton Ave towards Chants, and as she goes, she fits the black headscarf over her head, pulls it tight and knots it at the back the way her mother showed her all those years ago.

Chanterlands Avenue is unusually crowded. Every car parking space is taken on the main street and the pizzas shops are all open even though it's Monday night. The Kurdish barber is open too, Maya Spice has the doors wide for walk ins. There are less families now because it's late, but you can still see little kids in prams wrapped up warm and clutching helium balloons. A man carries a giant stuffed tiger he must have won. There's the smell of chips, and the lights and noise from the fairground carry over the roofs of the normally quiet houses.

Jerusalem makes her way down Chants Ave. She waits at the lights to cross Spring Bank West with the crowd and then walks across the railway track past the carousel. Unlike yesterday, the ride is spinning and blaring music – there's a man and his girlfriend laughing atop a white plastic horse as it goes up and down and round. Jerusalem passes the gypsy caravan and the coppers, then goes into the packed street she and Bev went down the day before. The drum beat from the music pounds into the night sky and strangely, she feels at home in the noise and with the crowd around her, like it's Queen's Day in Amsterdam. She can lose herself in the multitude. She can be nobody at all.

She takes a left and goes past the game stalls, there's hook-a-duck and darts next to the hoop throw, on the left are dodgems racing round and round each other under the hammering boom of the music, and in front of her, with the carts spinning on the up and down movement of the floor, is the waltzer car ride. This is what she is here for, but there's no need to rush in.

She positions herself in the darkness next to a burger van and watches from underneath the headscarf. It doesn't take her long to work out who is where. The man with the cut off sleeves and a cap works the front of the ride beckoning people in with his right arm. There's a little booth where the punters pay. The fat man sits next to the mean faced woman, and she takes the money through an open window. The tall kid who was sitting in the passenger seat in the truck, is in the DJ booth at the back and yells something into his microphone at intervals. Gangs of enthusiastic teenagers pass yelling and whooping, there's a couple of thugs with shaved heads and a family with the little kid on his dad's shoulders.

Jerusalem can't wait too long, or she will back out, so it has to be quick but methodical. She knows where they all are and as the spinning ride comes to a halt, a few dizzied punters stumble out of one of the big seats down the steps with smiles on their faces. There's no one on the ride left. It has to be now.

In the darkness, she skirts round the back of the burger van and pulls the scarf up over her face leaving just her eyes visible. Her stomach rumbles as she approaches the front of the waltzer. With no riders, the man with the cut off sleeves and a flat cap has lit a cigarette and moved to the side to beckon more punters on board.

Jerusalem slips behind him and up the steps. She puts Bev's gardening gloves on as she is heading for the door to the little office. Her heart is thumping in her chest but there's the memory also of what these people did to her. There's no room for remorse or pity, she must be the agent that shapes the world. Jerusalem has learned that it is no good to wait for others to exact the justice she requires and like everything she wants or needs, she will get it herself. Life is for taking.

She puts her weight against the door as she turns the handle and it flies open. Inside, the hammering beat from the music is loud and the woman with the mean face at the window turns to her in shock. She is about to yell something when Jerusalem grabs her by the hair and yanks her backwards, so she falls off her stool and tumbles to the soggy ground below.

The fat man sitting next to her is in the middle of counting stacks of money and his eyes widen when he sees the figure come out of the darkness at him. His hand goes for the baton that he keeps under the desk, but he's too slow. A few nights ago, he pressed his flabby face against Jerusalem's cheek and licked along the side of her neck while the other two held her down – his hands grabbed and pulled at her sides as he humped her. She produces the hammer from her pocket without any pause and brings it down on his piggy hand. His yell is drowned out by the drum beat of the non-descript hip hop music. She pulls the hammer back and strikes him again across the face but without the same force she used on his hand – she's not here to kill him. He falls backwards off his chair and his head hits the back wall.

Jerusalem looks over to the desk and there, neatly stacked into piles are fivers, tenners and twenty-pound notes. This is a robbery after all. Jerusalem wants to make it as difficult for these men as possible. She collects the stacks and stuffs them into the inside pocket of her jacket under the long black coat.

She looks up. At the door is the man with a flat cap and cut off sleeves. His face is twisted in anger when he realises what's going on, and although he can't see it under the black scarf, Jerusalem smiles. This is the one who hurt her the most. She flings the hammer at him as she leaps up onto the table and out through the window where the punters pay. However much she wants to teach this man a lesson, her own preservation has to come first – she knows how strong he is. She has done enough work already to cause this little group harm. He grabs the bottom of the black coat as she moves through the window and yanks her back. Jerusalem turns and the blade of the Stanley knife slashes out across one of his forearms and the back of one of his hands. The cuts are deep and sharp and he lets go in shock. Like the fat man groaning behind, his yell is silenced by the hammering of that hip-hop beat. The one with the goatee beard stands outside his DJ booth and watches the dark figure disappear down the steps of the waltzer. He is too afraid to do anything but stand there.

As she moves round the corner, Jerusalem slips off the coat and pulls down the headscarf that covered her face and hair. At the railway fence, she throws the coat over first, for protection from the barbed wire, and then scrambles over, pulling it after her as she goes. She runs diagonal over the double railway line then repeats the process on the fence at the other side, and, in a minute or so, she is walking down a little street with the noise and light of Hull Fair blazing behind her. She is breathless and sweating, her heart is pumping. She has exacted revenge. It feels sweet, maybe.

Jerusalem squeezes through some bushes and is back onto Spring Bank once more. She's carrying the black coat rolled up under her arms and the headscarf is in her pocket. The crowds are thinner, but people still pour out of and into the fair. She waits at the pedestrian crossing to get back onto Chants Ave and moves with the crowd. She smokes a cigarette as she walks the busy street weaving her way through the people. Her hands are shaking.

At Lynton Ave she dumps Bev's coat in the green bin outside her house, it will be ripped to pieces and she will retrieve it tomorrow. Uncle George taught her never to leave evidence behind. She opens the front door and steps inside as quietly as she can.

Bev stands in the kitchen with her arms folded looking down the hall to the front door. "That was a long trip to the shop," she says. Jerusalem can't help but grin back at her.

"I got you something," she says, walking into the kitchen.

Bev steps back to let her through. "Where've you been?" she asks. Jerusalem beams as she fishes the money from the inside pocket of her jacket. First, she sets the messy wad of five pound notes on the counter, then follow the tenners, and finally, the much bigger stack of twenties.

"This is yours," says Jerusalem, "think of it as payment for what you've done for me."

Bev flares her nostrils. "Where did you get it?"

"It is payment for my suffering," she says. Bev looks at the money on the counter and then back up to Jerusalem's dirty face. She was wrong about this girl. She thought she was level-headed and sorted, the house cleaning and the cooking put her off the scent. Now she can see that Jerusalem is just as screwed up as those kids she drives to the special school, only the hurt is buried deeper, and she is capable of much more. She walks to the cabinet in the kitchen and reaches down two glasses, takes the bottle of gin Jerusalem brought back the other day, and fills each one half full. She returns and hands one to the girl.

"Drink this," she says. Her voice is calm and commanding. "Then, me and you are going to sit down at this table here and you are going to tell me everything from start to finish. Do you understand?"

Bev wants what's best for this young woman, even though she does not know who she is. Jerusalem looks down at the glass in her shaking hand. The memory of what happened to her in that truck on the side of the road that night comes back to her – she thought it would go once she had exacted her revenge. The tough front that she puts on slips every so often, especially when there is emotion involved.

"You'll have to tell me everything," repeats Bev with authority.

"I will," answers Jerusalem.

CHAPTER SEVEN
A plane.

Just off Newland Ave, there's a long path of greenery between the houses on Ella Street and the big double garages of the posh terraces on Victoria Ave. It's called the drain even though it isn't a drain at all. It's thirty foot wide with lamp posts running down one side. You can cut through here up to the Avenues, walk the dog, teach a kid how to ride a bike, fly a remote-controlled plane, or play football with two jackets as the posts for each goal. The big double garages are spray painted, some with commissioned pictures, and others with the scrawls of vandals.

Our Dave and Barry from Richmond Street Garage are here to look at something in one of these garages. There's a tall man with prematurely greyish black hair and wide shoulders leading them up the grass strip to show them the back of the property. This is David Porter. Ordinarily he's a joiner but he also prints t-shirts and makes short films on the side. He's not your stereotypical tradesman type, if there is one, he doesn't watch football in pubs or have questionable political views, he's got a snow-white West Highland Terrier called Jean, and two girls at three and five. He doesn't get out much. David's wife's grandmother left her a house in Brighton when she died and so, for the price of a two-bedroom house a long way from the beach down there, they are able to buy a huge six-bedroom terrace on the poshest street in West Hull. The building is run down and almost every part of it needs redoing, but David has time, the skills and the heart to do it.

There's something big in the double garage at the back, and David doesn't know what to do with it. Our Dave is good for advice on house renovations. Good people tend to find each other in this city. Our Dave has brought Barry from Richmond Street Garage because there's something mechanical behind the rusted double doors.

"Have you had the place long?" asks Barry as they walk round. He's dressed in his blue overalls and wearing round glasses under his bald head. Barry has a breathless quality when he speaks.

"Got it last month," says David. "I only just had a look in the shed a few weeks ago." He stops at one of the double doors and fiddles with a key in a rusting lock. "I had to spray it with oil to get it open first time round." He twists the key and then bends down to pull at the handle on the bottom, the huge garage door complains against the concrete as he does so, and the ancient mechanism screeches at the movement,

The smell of mould and dust billows out from inside the double garage. Barry's torch goes on straightaway and it illuminates the darkness. He can see the round shape of a car at the right-hand side. This is the kind of situation where Barry can make real money. If there's an old-style Volkswagen Beetle or a 1980s Capri, he could do it up and sell it on for a lot more than he paid. His educated eyes assess the shape of the car that's parked there in the darkness, it has a boxy roof and the long pronounced boot sticks out. He sighs. Barry already knows what it is.

"It's a Ford Cortina." It'll be worth fuck all. He won't say this to David though.

"Not that," says David Porter pointing over to the right of the garage. Barry moves closer and shines his torch over the long sleek nose and to the windscreen, he sees the landing gear underneath and notes that the wings have been removed or fallen off. The windscreen is covered with thick green muck and the paintwork is ruined with dust and filth. Spiders have made webs in the exposed engine work where a flap has come off the side.

"It's a plane," says Barry. Our Dave isn't going to make a clever comment at this. He doesn't really know Barry well enough.

"I couldn't believe it myself," says David Porter.

"Where are the wings?" asks Barry.

"At the side here," the tall lad points to long fiberglass blades under the aeroplane.

Barry's first instinct is not to have anything to do with this, but he's a mechanic and naturally loves anything that moves. His curiosity makes him step forward. "Who'd have a plane in their garage?"

In a few minutes, Barry has managed to get the front engine compartment open and is examining the wires and valves that make up the machine. Once he's done that, he opens the cab door and hauls himself up to look at the dusty dials and the joystick. He wipes some of the dashboard clean with his fat, dirty fingers. Barry is not the most gifted mechanic, but he knows how to treat the lads who work for him. He pays well and on time, and over the years he has run Richmond Street Garage, he has come to understand what can be fixed and what can't. He knows how much a working plane like this will sell for, it will be way above ten grand, perhaps more.

"I'll give you a grand for it," he calls out of the open door to David Porter. The tall man with greyish black hair looks to Our Dave. He was going to give it to Barry as long as he could get rid of it, this was the old man's advice.

"He wants fifteen hundred," says Our Dave. Barry glares through his mucky, round glasses.

"I've got a bad heart, you know." He always says this kind of thing when faced with a price he doesn't like.

"I'll take fourteen hundred," says David Porter.

"Twelve hundred."

"Done." Barry gets out of the airplane and walks over to David Porter to shake his hand which will seal the deal. "I was gonna give it to you for nowt," says the man.

"Like fuck you were," says Barry.

It's a 1973 Cessna and is more than fifty years old. Barry manages to get the body of it on the flatbed truck they have at the garage, and then comes back the next day for the wings. It's a lucky find. If Barry's lads can't fix it, someone will take it off his hands for a few grand.

David Porter offers Our Dave a hundred quid for his help and when he refuses, he buys a bottle of posh whiskey online and then delivers it up to the taxi office one morning when he's walking Jean. They have a chat, like you do, and neither of them can figure out who would have a 1973 Cessna in the double garage at the back of Victoria Ave.

Jerusalem started at the beginning and told Bev it all. She is from Tigray in the north of Ethiopia and a town called Mekele. Her father owned the cement factory on the outskirts to the west, and she lived in a compound in the green hills under the shadow of the Kokholo Johannes Church. Jerusalem was rich for an Ethiopian girl. She went to school up at the church and learned English, history, Tigrinya, and the ancient script of Ge'ez. She learned that Ethiopia was once Abyssinia and the only African nation never to be colonised by the Europeans. She was going to be a pilot and her father sent her to Mekele airport where she learned how to fly two seaters along the dusty disused track behind the main runway. She can see from Bev's eyes that she does not really understand, Europeans think that Africa is mud huts and lions bringing down zebras like they see on natural history documentaries.

Civil war came from the capital in 2020 and Eritrea, the country to the north, joined the fighting as well. Separatists from Jerusalem's region fought for their rights but were sandwiched between two forces. Tigray is rich in more than just history, there are gemstones and gold in the mountains, perhaps there is petroleum too. Jerusalem's father saw it coming and rather than putting her through the dangerous journey of going down to the capital, Adis Ababa, he paid smugglers to take her to Europe. They took her into Saudi

Arabia and once she was in Riyadh, the same smugglers sold her to a Dutch man named Uncle George. He promised her she would be safe in Amsterdam. In a way it was true because, just after Jerusalem left, the civil war came down on Mekele. It is called ethnic cleansing. There was looting, rape, and each side said the atrocities were the fault of the other. She has not heard from her father since then, nor anyone else from her family.

In Amsterdam, Uncle George made her work in the red-light district for a time behind a window. He took it upon himself to train her in the nitty gritty details. Bev can already guess what kind of a man he is. Prostitution is legal there, in a round about sort of way, but that just makes it easier to traffic young women into the business. Jerusalem was not cut out to be a working girl. She isn't naturally polite and of the couple of times she tried, the punters complained she was too offish, too boring or too aggressive. Uncle George had her staying in the top floor of a flat he has behind the main station in Amsterdam with three Eastern European girls and a Russian. It didn't take long for Jerusalem to assert her dominance over all of them so that they were afraid of her, and Uncle George saw more potential in this fierce, angry Ethiopian girl with tattooed crosses on her forehead and chin. Uncle George hurt her of course, but he hurt everyone, that was his business, and he made it clear that he was not being unfair at all. That was the way of the world.

He showed her how to pickpocket, got her to deliver packets of powder to some of his working girls and regulars, and, as long as he was respectful of her, she worked well. He had her spot for police when big deals went down. Jerusalem was worth more as an operative than a whore. She picked up Dutch, dressed like she was from Holland and slotted in like she'd grown up in Amsterdam, just like Uncle George himself. Sometimes they went for dinner in the steakhouse on Nieuwe Hoogstraat and he would call her little sister in Dutch, and unlike other girls he used this on before, Jerusalem did not even smile. Uncle George told her that he loved her as well, like he does, and though Jerusalem didn't seem to care, he could see that she did.

In the summer this year, after Uncle George paid for her to get her Dutch pilot's licence, she began to run people over to the UK and to the airfield just north of Pocklington at night. She did a run a month and her passengers were high end, people with wealth who wanted to get into the UK and couldn't do it through legal means because they were Iranian diplomats or Russians with money. Uncle George had something set up in the UK so they could get their citizenship quickly enough.

Jerusalem tells Bev the detail of the last flight, and the man with black hair who took over the plane and left her stranded. She glosses over the events in the back of the showman truck because she does not want to think about it, and this is where Bev picked her up. Jerusalem explains how she saw the man with the flat cap at the fair and the waltzers ride too. Her eyes are wide as she recounts her preparations, and then how she robbed the ride and attacked the men. Her dark skin is pale.

Bev has barely touched her glass of gin. Jerusalem has had two. The time on the kitchen clock reads one in the morning and the dark October night is cold outside. Bev is horrified by what she has heard from this tall, spirited young woman but there's a part of her that is proud of what she has done too.

"You're not going back," says Bev. She means to Uncle George and her life in Amsterdam.

"I have to."

"Why? Because you belong to him? Because you're too frightened to do anything else?" Bev leans forward. "You'll have to make a stand somewhere, Jerusalem, because if you don't, you'll be pushed and pulled around like a rag doll till there's nothing left of you."

"I am going back to Amsterdam, this whole trip has helped

me see something. You have helped me see it." Her brown eyes are level and serious.

"So, you'll go back to flying his planes over the North Sea, will you?"

"Not at all," says Jerusalem. "Now I know what I'm capable of, I'm going to do something else altogether."

"What?" asks Bev.

Jerusalem sees it clearly now. The revenge against the men at the fairground was never going to make her feel better. She has to strike at the heart of the problem.

"I'm going to kill Uncle George," she says.

HULL FAIR FOUR

You hear all sorts of stories about the people who work at Hull Fair. Taxi drivers say that the workers are dangerous thugs who you shouldn't pick up. Blokes at the bar in the Avenues alehouse will tell you that car thefts rise when the fair is in town. Mobile hairdressers say you'll have your wallet and phone pinched by some pickpocket in the busy crowds. Shop assistants in town record an increase in shoplifting. It's all hearsay of course.

Showmen and women run these travelling fairs. They're members of a guild and there are rules they have to follow. They pay for the privilege of membership to such a club, and they pay the council too for the rides they bring, and rent for each caravan and car that parks on Walton Street too. They're on the road from March to November and have places they stay and pitch up as regularly as the seasons change, so that in early October they are here in Hull, and by the third week are in Middlesbrough, then back down to Darlington for November, then Leeds and so on. Each ride and group travel as a separate unit. There are schools they set up for their kids in the winter months, and some on the road as well. They have a parliamentary presence, and the Showman's guild has been on the go since 1910 to protect those who work on these travelling fairs. It's a serious and honourable business.

It doesn't mean they aren't tough, savvy folk. They deal with the public day and night. They hear people whooping on the spinning rides year in, year out, and like rock stars might treat their fans with some indifference, that is how some of them treat the punters. Travelling folk have always been vilified by those who do not know them or the world they live in, so every year people complain. They say that the rides are ten pounds a go, and the chips are four quid a tray. They natter that the dart game is fixed and the sights on the guns at the shooting range are off, yet they still go. Old and young still walk the narrow alleys between the rides with the smell of steaming vinegar on chips, and the wind with a nip of cold in it that says winter is on its way.

Showmen police themselves, it's part of the way they live. They don't steal from or screw each other. They help out if the mechanics on your ride need tinkering with, they'll lend you money if you're on your arse. They've got an eye on each other's kids.

The waltzer ride in the corner has been robbed. This is why the coppers are here tonight now the fair is all shut up and closed. Someone reported this to the police. Mally would rather that hadn't happened but it has; the coppers are here and as the man who looks after the fair, it is his job to deal with it. The owner of the waltzer is a Geordie called Rob, he's had his hand broken up with a hammer and his wife, Joan, cracked her hip when she fell off a chair. The muscle they take with them, a guy in a flat cap and a sleeveless denim jacket called Pat, got his arm and hand cut open with a Stanley knife. Three coppers fan out around the silent ride with their long, hi-vis coats and powerful torches scanning the ground.

The plainclothes officer stands in front of Mally and has a shitty, angry look on his face. He is overweight in a dark brown suit and a long overcoat with flabby jowls, and a bald head.

This is DI Brian Wilson and his father was a copper too, so are his cousins. His mother works for Humberside Transport Police and his ex-wife is a control room operative back at the station.

"Once they've seen the doctor over at the hospital, they'll have to come to Clough Road Station," he says to Mally.

"It's Monday night of the fair, you'll ruin their business if you keep them away from this ride." Mally puts his vape to his lips and takes a big toke so the light glows. With his red braces over his black jumper, he looks like he's stepped straight out of the 1930s. His brow is creased. "We don't want this getting out," he says, "if people think there's robbings here then they won't come."

"People will already be talking about it, Mally, you know what it's like these days with their smartphones and social media. It'll be all over Hull."

Mally blows out air in a huff. This is the worst kind of thing to happen at a fairground, and for the police to be involved as well makes it even more of an issue. He looks up to the copper who is taller than he is and whispers through his teeth.

"You promised me there'd be police all over this fairground to stop this kind of thing."

"There were, just like last year and the year before that. We don't get trouble here anymore, Mally, that's why all this seems off for me. You sure you don't know who did it?"

"You don't know travelling people, Officer. If they'd wanted to rob someone, they wouldn't have made a song and dance about it like this fella has. This job wasn't just to rob money, it was to humiliate them."

"So, you do know who did it, then?"

Mally rubs his chin as he calculates. He doesn't know who robbed the fat man from Newcastle, but he is sure he could offer someone up. That way they could all get back to normal. They could say it was within the fairground community and the punters wouldn't be put off coming. "Do you want me to sort this? Then we'll have your man with a snap of our fingers," says Mally. "It'll all be put to bed."

"That's not how policing works."

"Of course it is, that's exactly how policing works. You find someone who fits the bill and you bang them up till the trial and you've done a top job." Mally moves closer yet to the flabby copper. "You haven't got time to turn this into an investigation before the whole fairground goes back to being a car park. Let me sort this, and it'll all be done within the hour."

DI Wilson considers the request. There will be a ton of paperwork to fill out anyway even if they do arrest someone, but there will be more if they have to investigate. Wilson also has a low opinion of these travelling types and believes it really will be one of their own who has done it. The copper narrows his eyes in thought at the man wearing braces in front of him. "You say you know who did it?" he asks. This is his way of agreeing.

"I do. I'm certain of the very lad. I'll have him here in ten minutes and you can take him down to the station."

DI Wilson nods. Best to get this wrapped up as soon as. The copper watches Mally slip away into the darkness of the fairground. No doubt, there will be some lad he can persuade to take the rap. Then, after the coppers have questioned him, the man who was robbed and the people who were attacked won't want to press charges, and it will all blow away in the wind.

DI Wilson isn't going to lose any sleep over this one.

CHAPTER EIGHT
Wendy, again

It's Tuesday afternoon. Our Dave sits in the coffee house on the corner of Park and Chants Ave. Before COVID, it was a hairdresser and now it's a community café. It's empty at this time on a Tuesday and Our Dave looks out the window at Chants Ave in all its October glory. A middle-aged looking spice head shuffles by and there's an old dear dragging a shopping cart on wheels, then a blonde woman dressed in a grey trouser suit. You get all sorts down this street. How many years has he been here? It's the same but different. Our Dave remembers when the petrol station across the road was just a pump with two hoses off it, he remembers the old pet store that was opposite, and the doctor's surgery on the corner. This street has grown and changed in front of his eyes. Maybe it is time to see somewhere new now the business is moving on – maybe he can become someone new as well.

It has been some time since he has had to win a woman's affection after making a mistake. He used to upset Hazel when he was married, especially in the early days. The best thing to do was give her time and then apologize, they were together after all. Wendy is a different beast; she will want some sort of gesture that shows he is serious about her. He takes a sip on his cappuccino and sets it back down on the saucer. She'll want the truth and so that's what he'll give her. He has arranged to meet her in the car park at the back of the petrol garage and he is going to walk with her all the way down Chants Ave. As they go, he will introduce her to every single person that he meets. When they get to Avenue Cars, he'll give her a sweeping tour, introduce her to Face properly, and then walk back down Chants again. The car park at the back of the petrol station only allows you to stay for one hour, so this will give Our Dave a time limit to gauge how well she deals with the folk down his street. This coffee was just to collect his thoughts.

Wendy is on time. Our Dave watches her white, sports-injection Fiat drive across the petrol station forecourt and into the car park at the back. She gives him a wave and a big smile with her perfect white teeth as she goes past. She parks up, gets out, and they greet with a kiss and a hug. Our Dave isn't going to mention what they spoke about the other day. Wendy isn't either. He invites her to walk down the street with him, and it begins.

There's a man outside the expensive chip shop next to the petrol station with a ragged beard and missing front teeth. He smells rotten too. Our Dave stops for a chat because he knows the lad, he introduces Wendy, but they don't shake hands. Twenty yards on, Our Dave stops for a natter outside the pet charity shop and the middle-aged lady who volunteers on Tuesdays, Sheila, takes him inside to look at some new cat calendars they got in ready for Christmas. He introduces Wendy. They stop at the estate agent, the post office, they chat with the poet Jim and his curly haired dog. They walk on past the tanning studio and Casa Della Pizza, Our Dave waves at someone who beeps their horn. They pass Dixons the butcher, the closed down booze shop on the corner, the medical centre, Bengal Pride and the bookie across the road. A man with a porkpie hat and wispy beard stops Our Dave to tell him that he's been sober for eleven months.

Our Dave knows people down here.

At Avenue Cars, they go round to the car park and through the back door. There is nobody downstairs so they go up to the office that was once a front bedroom where Face is working on his laptop with the radio on. Our Dave makes his introductions although they have already met, and Face is suitably charming as he begins to explain the taxi and the property side of the business. He's tactful of course, he won't mention anything criminal to Wendy. She nods as she and Our Dave stand in front of Face's desk in awkward silence.

Downstairs, Our Dave reminds Wendy that there is the

time limit on her car parking space and she'll be charged if she stays there more than the hour. He will make her a quick coffee and then walk her back down the street. It has gone well so far. He is pleased with himself, and Wendy is all smiles as they stand in the galley kitchen and he boils the kettle. Perhaps he has managed to win her affection back after all. She touches him lightly on the arm as if he is winning.

The back door opens and in walks Bev. Our Dave does a sharp intake of breath. She has a dark look on her face as she stares at Our Dave next to the boiling kettle.

All bets are off now.

"I need a word," she says as if he's done something wrong. Behind her there's a dark-skinned girl with cross tattoos on her forehead and chin. Our Dave gives her a weak grin.

"This is Wendy," he says as he presents the older blonde lady with her flowery perfume and freshly washed hair.

Bev gives her the once over. "Is this the lass you've been seeing?"

"Aye." He was not aware anyone knew about her.

"You've finally come to introduce her, have you? It's been months. We all know about it, Our Dave. Gaz tailed you to find out where you were disappearing to all them afternoons." This is how she is. Bev does not alter her behaviour depending on who she is talking to – it's a curse and a blessing at the same time. It means you can trust her to tell the truth, but she's a nightmare at times. Like now.

"You could say hello, then," says Our Dave. "You could try and be nice for a change." His jaw tightens in anger.

Bev catches herself. He is right. She turns to Wendy and gives her a smile. "I'm sorry. Our Dave here looks after us and so we have to look out for him too." Wendy grins because her suspicions have been realised in this one sentence, she had an inkling that Our Dave was trustworthy and now she knows that he really is. "Nice to meet you," adds Bev. She looks back to Our Dave. "I still need a word."

"Can't it wait? I'm a bit busy."

"It can't, I'm afraid," says Bev. She beckons the dark-skinned girl behind her to come inside the kitchen, she's carrying a plastic Heron supermarket bag in her left hand. Our Dave gives her a friendly grin too, but Jerusalem has no expression on her pretty face. "This is Jerusalem, Our Dave. I picked her up the other day on the main road near Bishop Burton. She'd been attacked. She says she's a refugee, and she was trafficked to Amsterdam." Jerusalem blinks at the man in front of her, he's taller than she is and has a degree of wisdom in his blue eyes.

"I can't deal with this now," says Our Dave. "I've got to make sure Wendy gets back to her car."

"I need your help," says Jerusalem. It's the first time she has spoken in front of them, and her voice is smooth and calm. She holds open the yellow supermarket bag so that Our Dave can see what's inside, it's the money she stole from the fair workers last night in a mess of twenties and tenners. Wendy looks over and sees the money inside as well. "I want to get rid of this," says Jerusalem. "I need you to help. Bev says you know people."

Our Dave does know people, but this is the worst time they could have asked for his help with Wendy standing and watching the whole thing. Bev must imagine that anyone who comes into Avenue Cars is trustworthy; it's naive. Wendy's husband was a sergeant at Clough Road Police Station, her son is an inspector there, she works for the transport police herself. She is not a fool. She'll know there's something not right here.

"You'll just have to wait here for me," says Our Dave. His tone is darker than usual. "I'll see Wendy down the street and I'll be back to sort this out." He glares at Bev. The one time she could have kept her mouth shut, and she brings some stray lass with a carrier bag full of money into the office. She can see the look of anger in his eyes.

Wendy and Our Dave stride back down Chants Ave together. They've been going a few minutes and neither has said a word. Dave nods hello to people, he greets George from Chants DIY, a fella in a tracksuit with smart, business shoes, and two middle-aged women jogging, but doesn't stop for a chat. He is conscious that Wendy has seen too much of what he does already. She walks at a quicker pace than she did previously.

When they get to the car park behind the petrol station, Wendy has got a few minutes on the clock before she has to get going. She unlocks her sporty Fiat by pointing the key fob at it, there's the click of the mechanism.

"Just so you know, Dave," she says. "I don't care what happens in your office. I just care about me and you. Do you understand? I know what goes on. I know it's not all roses round here. I've worked for the police for the last forty-one years."

"People come to me for help sometimes. I just do what I can. I don't know where that lass will have got all that money, but I'll see it gets put right, if I can." Wendy examines him. You can tell when someone isn't telling the truth. The wind catches her blonde hair as she fishes her sunglasses out of her handbag ready to put on against the autumn sunshine. She's smart and together, Our Dave likes her.

"Thanks for coming today, Wendy. Bev's got a right tongue on her, I'm sorry."

"I didn't ask for your family to be perfect, Dave. I just wanted to know about them, and for them to know about me."

"Looks like they already figured out what I was up to."

Wendy puts on her sunglasses. "I liked that. You can tell a lot about a person by how much their friends care about them. Are we going to carry on with this, Dave?"

"I want to," he says without thinking.

"I do as well." Wendy gets into the sports-injection Fiat

and closes the door. She puts the key in the ignition and the engine fires up as she winds down the window. "I'll call you," she says. Then, like that movie star she is, Wendy takes off out the petrol station on Chants Ave and into the Tuesday afternoon traffic.

Back in the office at Avenue Cars, Jerusalem and Bev sit in front of the yellow supermarket bag on the table. It's still full of money. Opposite is Our Dave. The October sun is streaming through the front windows into the waiting room next door that nobody uses anymore. Once upon a time, when taxi offices were a thing, people would just walk in, approach the little window, and order a taxi with the receptionist. It could be three o'clock in the morning or three in the afternoon. It doesn't happen at all these days with the mobile technology folks have in their pockets and the taxi drivers that work on apps. Our Dave locked the front door a few months ago, he'll probably never open it up again.

"I'm tired of helping people, Bev," he says into the silence they've been sitting in. He didn't expect to say this. It's the truth. He always felt better listening to someone else prattle on about their issues, it made him feel like he was doing something good. Times are changing. Perhaps Our Dave should start looking after himself.

Bev's smooth blue eyes made up with mascara stare back at him over the yellow supermarket carrier bag full of money. She is not convinced. She's always trusted this man, whatever he might say. "Wasn't so long ago, Our Dave, that you sat in the chair in the far corner and needed my help, more than you'd ever needed anyone's help before."

He had forgotten this.

A year or so previous, Our Dave was at the mercy of a thug right here in this office, and it was Bev who took the handgun out the drawer in the kitchen and put a bullet through him. The mess from a gunshot wound and a dead body is horrific.

That's why they had the whole back room refitted and painted. "You owe me," she adds. He does owe Bev, but he is still angry at her big gob that almost cost him the relationship with Wendy.

"This is it though," he says. "By the time Christmas comes, I'll be out of this taxi company." Jerusalem does not like it when people speak and she is not included, especially when it concerns her, it makes her feel like a child.

"I will pay for your services," she says. She pushes the plastic bag full of notes she robbed from Hull Fair nearer to him. For the first time he examines her face, he sees the proud, high cheekbones and the brave eyes. It's his nature to help.

"What do you need?" he asks. Bev begins. She dispenses with anything that is not important.

"She's a refugee, trafficked to Holland. I picked her up one night on the way back outside Bishop Burton. She'd been attacked and dumped on the side of the road."

"You told me that already," says Our Dave.

Bev's eyes flash with anger before she continues. "I took her home. Turns out the ones who attacked her were with the fair, so, and I didn't know this, she went and battered them and stole their takings."

Our Dave listens. He heard the waltzer ride was robbed Monday night, and that the coppers were involved, but he's also heard that it was someone from the fair who did it, and a young lad has been nicked already.

"What do you want me to do?" he asks.

"Get rid of this money she nicked from them. She says the man who she belongs to in Holland will find her. She needs to disappear."

Our Dave examines the young woman again with the big cross tattoos on her forehead and chin. These are Bev's words.

"Is that right?" Our Dave asks her.

Jerusalem shakes her head. "I need safe passage to Holland, not with a passport and not so anyone will see me coming." Bev looks at Jerusalem but the young woman does not take her eyes off Our Dave. Turns out that Bev is the child in this conversation.

"I can do that," he says as he pulls the bag towards him. "How much is in here?"

"Four thousand, maybe." Our Dave peers inside. He's looked at bags of cash before and she's about right, it might even be more.

"When would you like to go?"

"Now."

"Do you have any ID?"

"No."

"I can put you in a truck Friday afternoon," says Our Dave. You'd be shut up in the back for the whole journey though, pretty much twenty-four hours."

Jerusalem shrugs as if this is nothing. "Okay with me."

Bev cuts in: "She wants to go back to the man who trafficked her, Our Dave. She says she's going to kill him." Bev does not want this brave lass to get hurt and the conversation has not gone as she planned it at all.

"Looks to me like she's a grown woman, Bev. I can help her, it's her decision, not yours." There's the sense in Our Dave's voice that he knows her idea is flawed and that revenge will not work out as well as she imagines, and neither will it give her any peace.

"I would like to go on Friday," she says.

"What about this money?" asks Our Dave.

"It's yours," she says.

"How about Bev takes it, for looking after you?"

"She already refused."

"You keep the money then. Pass some of it to the truck driver on Friday." Jerusalem gives Our Dave a slow nod. "Friday then," he adds.

"This wasn't really what I had in mind, Our Dave," says Bev. "She's only a lass, look at her."

"It wouldn't be my choice either," he replies.

Face enjoys a run most mornings, but as it was raining early on, he decides to go in the afternoon when his sandwiches from the mid-priced supermarket have settled. Even though the fair isn't open till four, Chanterlands Avenue is still much busier than usual. Face crosses the road in front of the estate agent and runs all the way down Perth Street. As he turns left into Hardwick Street, he has to pull up to stop himself crashing into a fat man in blue overalls. Face tries to carry on jogging but the man with round glasses and a piggy nose calls to him:

"You that lad who works for Our Dave?" Face nods. This is Barry from Richmond Street Garage. "Have you got a minute," he asks. Face shakes his head:

"I'm on a run," he says. Barry gently grabs his thin arm to stop him starting off down the road. Jogging is not a thing any person would do for fun in Barry's mind, so he thinks he's doing Face here a favour by stopping him. They have met before, neither of them can remember the first time, but Barry's lads fixed his camper van before he sold it. Barry begins:

"It's about that plane at the garage. Did Our Dave tell you about it?" He doesn't let Face get a word in before he starts up again. "It's that plane I bought from your Dave's mate on Victoria Ave, the one that was in his garage and was all knackered."

Face heard Our Dave talk about this. "You bought it, didn't you?"

"Well, I did, yeah, but only on the say so of Our Dave, see." Barry got the work experience lad to clean out the very back garage and stored the 1973 Cessna Skyhawk there with a tarpaulin over it. The wings are neatly packed up down the side. Barry contacted Hull Aero Club who operate out of a tiny airfield east of Leconfield. He called Beverley Air Society and the airfield at South Cave. Turns out nobody wants a 1973 Cessna Skyhawk even if it might be in good nick. Barry wants to salvage some of the twelve hundred quid he spent on it and he knows Our Dave is a good lad. He'll take this opportunity with the ugly man who works with him to lay some groundwork. Barry continues in his breathless voice:

"Only, I wouldn't have bought it if Our Dave hadn't been there, so I reckon the deals partly down to him."

Face knows how Barry works, he's not a thief but he doesn't like to lose money either. "If you bought it, Barry, then it's your problem. Can't you fix it?"

"We can fix it, but there's nobody wants to buy it?"

"That's not Our Dave's problem, is it?" Face is anxious to get back to his run and uses his clipped, lawyer's voice.

Barry thinks about the angles of the situation and his clever brain clicks and whirs. "Didn't you used to go out with that Spanish lass, the one with a short hair cut?"

Face is suddenly more interested. "We were married," he says. "What about her?"

"That bloke she's shacked up with is trouble, isn't he the chiropractor?" Face frowns as he listens. "He came into the garage the other day with his Range Rover Sport that's on finance, and he was swearing and blinding at my work experience lad about a scratch that was there when he brought the car in. I heard she's left him already; you know."

Face raises his eyebrows at Barry when he hears this. Surely his son Alex would have told him. He thinks about Inma a lot. After she came to visit him at the taxi office the other day, he has seen her in his dreams. He has questioned his AI chatbot in the office, and apparently, it is normal to think about your ex-partner after you have split up. It's normal to fantasise about them as well. Because he's blocked her on social media, he had to open a fake account so he could look at her pictures. "Oh really?" says Face.

"I shouldn't say anymore."

"Why not?"

"It's not my place to, mate. I mean all that I've heard is probably rumours. I don't like to gossip." Face is quick to understand.

"I could make a few calls about that plane you've got there, Barry. I could find a buyer for you maybe. I'm good at that sort of thing and I've probably got more time than you." Barry grins. He delivers the goods straight away.

"I heard she left him and has gone back to her mother's." Face nods and inwardly feels happy.

"I wonder why?" asks Face.

"The work experience kid lives in the house behind his flat." Barry is subtle and playful with his offer.

"He'll know it all then."

"He probably would."

"Shall I call you for the details about that plane later? Then I'll see what I can do for you, Barry." The fat mechanic gives him a big beaming smile.

"Why don't you wait till tomorrow afternoon, that'll give me a chance to get the paperwork together and chat to the work experience lad."

"That would be really helpful," says Face.

Barry watches the man run down Hardwick Street and turn into Marlborough Ave. He's good with people is Barry, probably better than he is with cars. He knows the full story of the half-Spanish woman already. Fixing people's motors gives mechanics an insight into their lives: when they look for the logbook in the glove compartment they find condoms, there's a spliff in a cig packet in the passenger side door, and a pair of knickers under the seats in the back. Barry knows that the dark-haired chiropractor is an arsehole, and that he wants what he can't have, so he has been chasing other women like he chased Face's attractive ex-wife. It was only a matter of time before he did it again, and then only a matter of time before she found out.

HULL FAIR FIVE

It's Wednesday night at the fair. It's in full swing. Some residents along Spring Bank and down Chants Ave are getting used to the heavy booming of the music, and others are just starting to get sick of it. Those people who don't like the fair are begrudgingly taking their families on Wednesday because they think it will be quieter. The police are getting used to the crowds, the chip vans have taken another huge load of potatoes to fry, that young fox who lives next to the railway fence is full to bursting with scraps, and the show workers are already looking forward to packing up and leaving next week,

This business with the waltzer has been forgotten already. Mally offered up one of the lads who works on the mega spin ride. He gave him a thousand pounds to say he did it, and he'll give him another thousand when he gets out of custody because nobody will press charges. It's good money for the lad and he doesn't care about his criminal record.

Mally has had a steady few days. By Wednesday night they have usually ironed out all the main technical issues and anything broken has been fixed. Pitch disputes between showmen have been sorted and the money is beginning to pour in. By now, the punters have usually become braver as well – they don't try to nick prizes like they used to back in the day, but they still act cocky and try to get on rides without paying. Though everyone else might have forgotten about the robbery and attack the other night, Mally Kemp hasn't. It has worried him.

He stands behind the waltzer ride in the corner of the fairground. Here in the darkness behind the bright lights and the smell of cooking hotdogs, where the punters never go, the generator hisses and coughs out diesel fumes. In front of Mally is Geordie Rob, the man who had one of his hands broken up by a hammer two nights ago, he's the bloke who owns the waltzer. He is also one of the men who raped Jerusalem. Mally has called him into the darkness here to have a chat about the incident the other night. Now tempers have cooled, he hopes to get a better idea of just what happened.

"Who was it?" asks Mally.

"I dunno," says Rob. This is the real investigation. The coppers walk around in their hi-vis jackets with crackling radios strapped to their chests and frown like birds pecking in the soil, but here is where Mally will dig out the truth.

"Don't play shite with me, Robbo," he says. "You'll have to tell me what happened here or you'll not be pitching up at this fairground again." Mally does not mean he will hurt Rob, he need only whisper in the right ears that this fat man is a troublemaker and some other ride will take his place.

"It was a woman," he says. Mally gives him space to explain more, but the fat man is struggling. Rob isn't given to introspection or explaining details. He isn't good at looking backwards or letting show his emotions. It's a defensive thing. He enjoys hurting people because people hurt him.

"You'll have to start talking," says Mally. "How do you know it was a woman?"

The fat man begins: "The eyes. She wasn't strong enough either, if a bloke had hit me with that hammer, it would have broken my hand and face as well."

"Did it not? That's what you told the coppers?"

"It's not as bad as I made out. I saw her eyes as she looked at me. They were brown. She's a black lass."

"That's not what you told the police, you said they had a scarf around their head, and gloves."

"She did, I could still see her eyes."

"Do you know her?"

"Not really." Rob here does not want to say how. He goes back to that defensive training he learned as a kid, if you feel frightened – you should attack. "It's not my fault I got robbed, is it, Mally? Here I am behind my rig answering questions like I've done wrong. That's not fair, is it?"

"Yes, but you're a nasty piece of works, Robbo. I knew your dad and I've known you for as many years as you've travelled. Things happen for a reason, whoever this person is, they came to find you and they attacked you, and only you. In my mind that means you must have done something. You'll need to start explaining it to me, or I'll have you off this ground by tomorrow morning and I'll have my lad out that police cell who said he did it." Rob has been pushed into a corner and Mally can hear the fat man breathing in the darkness with the noise of the fairground on the other side of the ride, and the waltzer cars spinning round and round.

"We stopped to pick someone up on the way." Rob feels like he has to justify himself. "My dad used to do it…he'd stop at the truck station south of Middlesbrough and pick up a lass, or sometimes two, you know, working lasses. Then all the lads would have a go in the next layby."

"What have you done?"

"We picked up this black lass on the way here, it was nearly the middle of the night and she was hitching on some main road. I just thought she was one of them working lasses."

"Was she?"

Rob stalls. He knows she wasn't. Jerusalem did not go down easily. "I thought she was," he answers.

"So, you all had a go on her, did you?" asks Mally. It's not just the smell from the generator that's making him feel sick.

"Aye."

"What about your missus?"

"She was there as well."

"You're a sick man, Rob. Like your old man was sick too. What did you do with her?"

"When it was done, I paid up. I paid up and dropped her in a layby." Rob didn't actually give her any money at all.

"How bad was she hurt?"

"She wasn't hurt at all, Mally." Again, Rob is going to attack. "What kind of man do you think I am?"

"I know what kind of man you are, son, a greedy, sick arsehole who gives travelling people a bad name." Rob is frightened of Mally here, the little man has influence and respect. He'd never hurt you, of course, but there are people loyal to him who most certainly would. "That was it, was it? You just dumped her by the side of the road?"

"Aye."

"And you think the person who robbed you was her?"

"It was."

"How the fuck do you know?"

"The eyes, Mally. The way she looked at me when she was taking the money from the office here; it was the same way she looked up at me from the backseat of the cab."

Mally swallows. Whatever he tells Rob here, the man will not be working any fairground from now on in. Mally will make sure of that. Right now, he has to limit the damage done and get that money back as well. It's not just Rob's reputation that is at stake here. If Mally can't keep the working folk of the fair safe from thieves then it will be he who isn't working a fairground again. "What does she look like?"

"A black woman, five foot eight I should reckon, tall for a lass. She's got fierce eyes and tattoos on her face. There's a big cross right in the middle of her forehead and one on her chin, they're faded, not like you get in a tattoo shop."

"You'd know her if you saw her, would you?"

"Oh aye," answers Rob. "What's gonna happen?"

"I'll find her."

"You'll get my money back as well, will you?"

"It'll be sorted," says Mally.

"Does that mean I'll get my money back?" asks Rob again. Mally steps closer to the fat man who is taller than he is. He whispers through a snarl. "You'll be lucky to leave on Monday with your balls still hanging between your legs, Robbo."

"What are you gonna do?"

"I'm gonna find that lass."

CHAPTER NINE
Uncle George

This is the Avenue's pub. It's six. With Hull Fair on, the pub is not as busy as it might usually be. The big screens on the wall blare out green football matches with muted commentary that nobody is watching, and Bev stands a few inches shorter than Jerusalem at the deserted bar while they wait to be served. Bev cares for people who need her too quickly, and when she picked up Jerusalem from that dark road near Bishop Burton, she left herself wide open. Those who present as tough on the outside are the most vulnerable after all. She does not want the girl to go back to Amsterdam and to the life she has there. Bev is here to talk Jerusalem out of it. Alcohol will help.

Lilly returns to the bar from collecting glasses and is about to give them her customary wide smile to show the bright white veneers. When she sees that it's Bev, the smile disappears. This is Lilly who also works at the cheap supermarket a few doors down. Her and Bev always have a little run-in when they meet.

"Started working here have you now?" asks Bev to the dark-haired woman.

"I do a couple of evenings a week," says Lilly. Her face is stone. By now, Lilly and Bev should be friends because of their connection with Our Dave. They are more alike than they are different.

"What can I get you?"

"Two large white wines," Bev doesn't add please.

"Not on the vodka tonight?" asks Lilly. She glances up at Jerusalem, sees the tattoos on the forehead and chin and gives her a genuine smile.

"Obviously not," says Bev. "It must be a change for you working here though, must be better than being flat on your back." Bev refers to Lilly's old job as a working girl. It's unnecessarily rude and not nearly as clever as Bev's usual barbed put downs. Lilly gives her a smile before she turns to fill two wine glasses. She will not bite back.

Lilly has come a long way since she entertained men in a house just off Beverley Road. Our Dave tried to get her work in Avenue Cars, but there was nothing for a girl who couldn't drive, so she got a job at the cheap supermarket a few doors down. She's been there a good few months, but she's also started working at the pub. The long nails have gone because they get in the way of pulling pints; she still has the false eyelashes and heavy mascara. Lilly serves drinks with efficiency and she remembers everyone; she has an ear for their stories but is not afraid to share her own. The landlord has already tried it on with her and been rebuffed in no uncertain terms. Lilly will do well in the pub game. She's brave and hardworking, perceptive and warm. Once upon a time, the comments from Bev would have sent her into spiralling anger; now she gets the upper hand by giving the woman a kind smile. It belittles Bev, as it's supposed to do.

Bev and Jerusalem sit down in a window seat in the conservatory at the side of the pub that looks out over Chants Ave. It's dark already. Along the street are those going to or coming back from the fair; there are kids wrapped up tight in big coats, dads holding hands with their daughters, a middle-aged woman wearing a thick scarf, and two younger teenagers with balloons in their hands in woolly gloves.

Bev picks up her glass of wine and takes a sip, it's cold and bitter. Jerusalem has been largely silent since they had their chat with Our Dave a couple of hours before. Bev sets her glass down. Her eyes burn with anger just beneath the surface because she knows that Jerusalem here is making a decision based on her gut instinct rather than her head – just like Bev did at her age when she got married.

"Why were you rude to that woman?" asks Jerusalem.

"She's a nasty cow," says Bev.

Jerusalem's face is flat and cold. "You're a nasty cow, too."

"I know, but I'm meant to be the nastiest one round here, it's time she realised that." Bev is pleased with this comment.

"I didn't think you were like that," says Jerusalem.

"I'm not. You have to stand up for yourself sometimes."

Jerusalem looks across the dark wood furniture of the Avenues pub to the flashing gambling machine against the far wall. When she blinks, she gets a flashback of hitting the fat man with a hammer across his face. It did not make her feel as good as she thought it would. She wonders how it will be when she does worse to Uncle George.

"I can get you a job round here," says Bev. The Ethiopian returns her brown eyes to the blonde woman opposite her. "You could do any sort of work you like; you could go off to college if you wanted."

"My passport is in Holland. My visa is Dutch. I wouldn't be able to work here." Jerusalem knows how Europe likes to follow orders and rules, to some degree. Even if she wanted to, she couldn't stay.

"I can get you out of here then, somewhere safe."

"I've made my decision," she says. Bev takes another glug of her wine. Jerusalem hasn't touched hers.

"I just don't want you to do something you'll regret later. You're still young. You could do anything with your life."

"I told you what I'm going to do already," says Jerusalem. Bev scoffs at this, looks out the window, and then back to the young woman.

"You're not a bloke. You don't have to pretend you're some sort of tough nut." Bev likes the build up to a row as much as an actual row. Jerusalem leans forward and cocks her head, she whispers as she looks into Bev's face:

"I'm all I need, right here, I'll will get myself out of this situation."

"You can't fight the world. It'll chew you up and then shit you out, lass. You have to let go of it. Move on." Jerusalem reaches out and takes hold of Bev's hand on the table, she grips it tight. The movement is earnest and suddenly, it's Bev who feels like she is the younger woman listening to the advice of someone who knows.

"I will not forget what you have done for me, sister," whispers Jerusalem. "You helped me when there was nobody else. I'll pass that on, one day, I promise." The two of them look at each other. They are a world apart.

Bev takes another gulp of that white wine because she does not know what else to do. Jerusalem lets go of her hand and stands. She hasn't touched her drink. "I'll meet you back at the house," she says. "I need a walk and cigarettes."

"What about your wine?"

"You finish it." Bev takes a shallow breath. This young woman is beyond her reach.

"I'll leave the door unlocked for you," says Bev, her face is flushed red under all her make-up as if she is about to cry. She watches Jerusalem walk down past the tables and round the corner to the front door. It leaves her alone with a half full glass and the busy evening street outside. She glugs the rest of the wine. This is the story of Bev's life, when she falls in love, they leave. It never changes.

Lilly walks into view and collects glasses from the next table. She can't help herself as she approaches Bev.

"Lover's tiff?" she asks. There's no clever response to this so Bev picks up Jerusalem's glass and looks out of the window into the dark, busy street. She makes a mental note that Lilly can give as good as she gets.

Hull Fair brings so many people to this street that it feels like a big city. Normally on a Wednesday evening, the traffic would be light with almost no footfall. Tonight, Bev has to dodge the gangs of teenagers and pushchairs as she walks back towards her street. It's not very far.

She goes down Lynton Ave and sees that the light in her

hall has been left on behind the frosted glass. She is critical of herself, as if she has money to waste to keep lights on when she's not even there. She goes to the door, puts her key in the yale lock and stops suddenly as if she realises something. Perhaps the girl has to return to Amsterdam after all. What has it got to do with Bev? She is just a middle-aged woman who is lonely. She turns the key and opens the door.

In the hall, Bev sets down her handbag and takes off her jacket. She hangs it up and pauses to look at herself in the little mirror on the wall. Her face is wrinkled under the make-up, her blue eyes don't have the sky in them anymore, and her blonde hair needs the roots doing. She is exactly where she was always afraid she would end up – old and alone.

In the kitchen she puts the light on and hears something click behind her. There's a smooth and deep voice:

"Don't turn around," says a man. The accent is European sounding. She feels something touch the back of her head very lightly, and tingles go down her spine in fear. "That's the end of a pistol," he adds.

Jerusalem likes the busy street. It reminds her of Amsterdam and it's good to get lost in the faces. She buys cigarettes from the supermarket on the corner of Marlborough Ave and then stands outside to look at the lights coming from the fairground. There's the boom of competing dance tracks out of different rides, and the smell of chips and roast chestnuts mixed. Jerusalem has no intention of going back into the fair, it would be too dangerous. She is pleased with herself for finding the men and for dealing with them as well.

She will return home to Europe in the lorry with the help of the old man who Bev introduced her to. In Amsterdam she will go back to the apartment, collect cash she has hidden, and visit someone she knows in Bijlmermeer who will sell her a weapon. Then, with the pistol in her handbag, she will visit Uncle George in his apartment overlooking the river, and blow open his chest, and that will be it. Jerusalem will be free. She will go back to Mekele and find her father. She takes another pull on her cigarette and feels strong, like young people do when they see the world ahead of them, and the road is straight to the horizon without any curves or bumps or accidents.

She is sorry for the blonde woman, Bev. She is sorry that she is lonely and that the world has made her cruel. Jerusalem will not fall into the same trap. She won't wait around for the world to give her what she wants because she'll just take it. It starts with Uncle George, and once he's dead, she'll see a new path.

She walks back towards Lynton Ave and the takeaways are busy with fair goers. The traffic is thick, and she turns up the collars on her denim jacket against the cold. The short walk doesn't take her long. Jerusalem turns the handle, pushes open the door, and steps inside. The heating has come on because the temperature has dropped. The light from the kitchen illuminates the hall.

"I'm back," she calls. There's no answer.

Jerusalem wanders through into the kitchen, and as her boots step on the laminate floor, her stomach drops. There is something wrong. She takes a sharp breath in through her nose.

She's too late. He's already found her.

Bev sits in a chair at the round table. Her eyes are wide and there's a mark on her left cheek where she's been hit. It will bruise up in a few hours. She stares straight ahead as Jerusalem enters, as if she's in some sort of trance. Behind her, melting out of the darkness, is a white, middle-aged man with a bald head and thick, dark rimmed glasses. His glossy leather jacket is boxy and smart – it's nineties style. He is smiling to show a gold tooth.

This is Uncle George.

There's a matt black pistol held loose in his right hand. He looks more like a middle manager in an office than someone involved in organised crime – Uncle George specializes in logistics after all. That's how he operates. It's spreadsheets and underhand payments rather than brute force and intimidation. The world doesn't run like a gangster film, and those who do well pay attention to details and are boring, like Uncle George here. He's still got that mean streak though, or else he wouldn't be in this business at all.

"Where have you been?" he asks, and his accent is thick and Dutch sounding.

Jerusalem does not show her shock. "I went to get some cigarettes."

"She's a nasty one," says Uncle George as he nods to Bev. "She tried to bite me. I thought I was going to have to shoot her."

"What do you want?" asks Jerusalem.

"I'm here to save you. I'm missing a pilot. I've come to take you home."

Jerusalem folds her arms. "I already arranged a lift back to Amsterdam."

"What happened?" he asks.

"You tell me," says Jerusalem. "The men who collected my passengers took the plane from me. This woman picked me up. It's thanks to her that I'm still here."

Uncle George looks down at Bev in mild disgust. "She's menopausal. I told her to be calm but she came at me. I think she's got the message now." Bev sits staring at the kitchen wall. Her face is beginning to swell where Uncle George hit her with his pistol.

"How did you find me?" asks Jerusalem.

"You're not nearly as smart as you think, friend. You logged into your email account, one that you didn't think I knew about. Someone was monitoring that, and it was a matter of a few clicks to trace you right here to this house, in this street, in this town." Uncle George is good at details. "You should have contacted me straight away, friend. I could have arranged you passage immediately."

"I liked the time off. I wasn't sure if I was going to come back." Uncle George smiles to reveal that one gold tooth. He steps up as he examines Jerusalem standing in front of him.

"You don't get to choose, friend."

"Everyone gets to choose," says Jerusalem.

"They think they do. It keeps everyone happy. Like the Albanian kids who took that plane from you, they probably thought it was their choice. They thought they could make a quick dollar stealing from another thief. It doesn't work that way." He turns to look at Bev sitting on the dining chair in front of the round kitchen table with that vacant look on her face. "You'll be ok, my darling," he says. "The bruise will go in a couple of weeks, and we'll be gone in a few minutes." The 'my darling' doesn't sound right. He turns back to Jerusalem. "I have a car and a driver as well. They'll be outside."

Jerusalem doesn't need time to think about this. "I'm not going," she says.

Uncle George cocks his head and his big forehead frowns. "Who says?"

"I say."

He takes a deep breath. "I've invested a lot in you, friend. I've given you a place to stay and got you a licence to fly. I pay you well and you don't have to work like the other girls. I intend for you to be more of an asset in the future, so, you are coming with me."

Jerusalem feels the fire in her. The stomach tenses, she shows her teeth as she stares at this man, she should be very afraid of. "You'll have to shoot me," she whispers. It shows her innocence.

"No, I won't," he says. "I'll have to shoot her." He lifts the pistol so that the end rests against the side of Bev's head. His finger goes to the trigger. "Is that what you want? The blood will be on your hands and it will be your fault."

Jerusalem is disarmed. The fire within is doused by fear and worry. Bev does not deserve any of this. She's been through enough already and just because she took the time to help a stranger, she finds herself in front of Uncle George. The warrior part of Jerusalem, the one who traces her ancestry all the way back to King Soloman – she would tell Uncle George to shoot Bev and then shoot her as well. The real part of her, however, the one who cried herself to sleep when she was taken from her home, the one who covers the frightened child with a mean scowl, the one who would rather run and hide than face the world, that Jerusalem does not want him to hurt Bev. In all this, she was the only one to show her any kindness at all.

There are two light taps on the front door.

"That'll be our driver, Tony," says Uncle George. "We're not staying. I've got a meeting with someone in the morning. Looks like we might have a more secure airfield to use, and now we can't work with those Albanians anymore, I need a new partner. You don't think I came all this way personally just for a skinny African girl, do you?" Jerusalem lowers her gaze. There's another tap on the frosted glass of the front door.

"Be a darling and let him in, would you, friend?" Jerusalem has no choice but to comply, and she walks down the hall then opens the front door. A wide, tall man in a heavy, tailored overcoat with the collars up, steps in without invitation. He has a clean-shaven, square jaw. He's Dutch. She knows it straight away.

"Tony will take you to the car, while I finish up here," calls Uncle George. The big man takes Jerusalem by the arm, not at all forcefully, but she has the sense that it could be. Her lips are dry. How quickly fortunes can change, half an hour ago she had her life laid out before her with her plan to get rid of Uncle George. Now, she realises it was childish as she is bustled out of the front door by this big man.

In the kitchen, Uncle George leans down to whisper into Bev's ear. "No need to tell anyone about our little meeting, miss. It is your fault that I hit you," he says. Bev knows this line of argument. Her ex-husband used it on her when he had too much to drink and he belted her. He said it was her fault because she wound him up. Bev turns to look up at the man with her blue eyes. Uncle George adds more:

"Mention this to anyone, and I'll be back. I'll have Tony do something unpleasant. He goes for women your age. He likes the pale washed-out look with lots of make-up. It gets him going… and he's a big man too."

Uncle George stands up straight, puts the pistol into the inside pocket of his nineties style leather jacket, and walks down the hall with his sensible black shoes clicking on the laminate floor. He doesn't slam the door as he leaves.

On the main road to Beverley just outside Cottingham, there's a posh, Moroccan style hotel and restaurant with a few acres of land to the back. It does weddings and expensive Christmas dinners, corporate events for local businesses and the council. It's not cheap. Our Dave would never come here if he wasn't with Wendy – she's definitely not the stuck-up sort, but she likes going somewhere upmarket once in a while. She has invited Our Dave here, just like he invited her to Avenue Cars. There is someone she needs Our Dave to meet.

In the little bar at the side of the restaurant they stand and chat before being shown into the main dining room. Wendy's son is called Brian. He is a plainclothes police officer out at Clough Road Station and like his late father, he has only ever been and wanted to be a policeman. DI Brian Wilson shakes Our Dave by the hand and the grip is limp and his copper's hands are soft from office work. He's flabby and dressed in the shapeless, dark brown suit that he wears for work. From his nodding and occasional checking of his phone, Our Dave can see that he doesn't want to be here. Wendy is fussy with him. She has explained to Our Dave already that Brian is six months divorced and that he now lives alone in his modern residential house overlooking the Humber on Victoria Dock. They have made small talk and Brian has explained that he is seeing someone, but it is too soon for her to meet his mother.

After they're seated and given menus, Brian orders a sirloin steak with triple fried chips, Wendy has the salmon and Our Dave goes for the risotto. The waiter takes the menus and they sit in the half full restaurant with their drinks in front of them. DI Brian Wilson has examined Our Dave already, he sees the well-kept beard and teeth, the thin but still powerful forearms, and the checked shirt that has been ironed. Brian noted the Ford Galaxy in the car park and the non-flashy phone Our Dave looked at to check the time. He sees what Our Dave wants him to see, a good-natured, steady man, not as worldly wise as he might think, but honest.

Brian explains that there's been a robbery at the fair. It's between the showmen, he says. He tells them about the character of Mally Kemp who looks after the whole thing. Wendy listens patiently as does Our Dave, even though he knows that DI Brian Wilson won't have solved the case as quickly as he makes out, and there will probably be more to it than he realises. Brian Wilson continues to expound on his talents, how he also does consultancy work for businesses, and how he is now working with a Dutch company out of Amsterdam who are thinking of setting up a business here in Hull. Our Dave has heard about this copper, he's heard that he's not the most pleasant to work for and that he likes the sound of his own voice. He wonders if anyone took the piss out of him at school for being a Beach Boy.

The meal begins. Wendy reverts to the woman she was before her husband died. She defers to Brian's opinions and listens to his stories about policing, hears how the people of Hull are robbers and drug addicts and how they will tear each other to pieces if not controlled. Brian has already decided that

Our Dave is a pushover, and so, he doesn't have to hide his opinions. Wendy shoots Our Dave a sideways, apologetic glance as Brian looks down on his phone after it has pinged. She is sorry that she brought them together, but she is reciprocating the visit that he gave her to Avenue Cars, warts, and all. Our Dave looks back into her clever eyes. Her son is an arsehole, and she knows it, but she wants to show Our Dave that the people she loves are in no way perfect. Just like Bev shouted her mouth off, DI Brian Wilson here, glugging down his lager is rude and ugly, in an official sort of way.

Our Dave reaches his hand out under the table and Wendy finds it with her own. He gives her a squeeze there. The policeman stands up from the table looking down at the phone in his hand.

"I've just got to take this call," he says. Wendy smiles up at him as he puts the phone to his ear and walks out towards the little bar area away from the restaurant. It leaves Wendy and Our Dave alone and the table is peaceful without him there.

"He's a busy fella," says Our Dave.

"Just like his father," she answers. "He likes to talk a lot, but he's a good man underneath it all, Dave. He does a good job and wants to do the right thing."

Our Dave's phone buzzes in his pocket. He pulls it out but doesn't accept the call right away. First, he looks at the caller ID to see that it's Bev. He checks the time – it's nine thirty in the evening. She wouldn't ring if it wasn't something.

"I have to take this," says Our Dave.

Wendy flutters her eyes. "You might be more like my son than you think."

Bev said she was in trouble. Our Dave left Wendy with her son in the posh restaurant to drive back to Hull. While he is worried about Bev, he is also relieved to be away from Wendy's copper son, DI Wilson.

In the backroom of Avenue Cars, they stand in the

darkness of the kitchen. Bev leans against the sink and Our Dave rests his back against the counter. Bev has covered the mark on her cheek with concealer, she used to be an expert at doing this when she was married.

"I don't know what I can do," says Our Dave. "How would I find her? How would I be able to get her back?" He means Jerusalem.

"You know people."

"Yeah, but I'm not a magician. You just told me she's been driven off into the night in a car that you didn't see, by someone you didn't get a look at. The only information you have is that he's called Uncle George and you don't know where they're going."

He took her call back at the restaurant and she wept down the phone so he said he would come. Wendy looked troubled and he hugged her tight before he left. He whispered something in her ear that perhaps he shouldn't have. It was only three words long, and it softened her greatly. She said it back to him too, so that his stomach made noises as he drove back down to Chants Ave in the darkness when he thought about her.

"There must be someone you can call," says Bev.

"There is, but they wouldn't be able to do anything on just that. What is this girl to you anyway?"

"She's in trouble, Our Dave. That's all you need to know, she's in trouble and there's not another person in the world who'll help her. I thought you'd do something."

"You expect me to just drop everything for some woman I don't know and I've never really met? She's got into trouble, Bev, and a million people get into trouble. It's not your job to help everyone of them, just like it's not mine."

"So that's it, is it, Dave? You're just going to give up?"

"I don't know her, she's nothing to me, and that's how it should be for you. You can't pick up every stray you come across and put it upon yourself to save them."

She wrinkles her nose in disgust at this. "That's what you do, Our Dave. That's what you did with me all them years ago. That's what you did with Dilva too. You remember when she first came into this office, she was shivering like a shitting dog, and look at her now, all loved up with that Ryan and settled. Just like you wanted it. You did it to Gaz as well. I know you set him up with the lass from Belvoir Street, I know what happened. And then there's Face, he sits up here like some lord, but it wasn't six months ago that he was a piss-head loser who'd lost his wife. You help people, Our Dave. That's what I'm asking you to do now."

"I can't do the impossible, Bev," he says softly.

"You can't, or you won't now you've got your bloody fancy lass."

"It's not like that."

"It is like that. You lost your wife, and you're dealing with it, and you're moving on. I'm so happy for you. Now you don't have anything to prove by being everyone's saviour anymore." She is cruel and sharp. Bev knows that the truth hurts.

Our Dave takes a deep breath in worry. He is sorry about this. "You'll just have to leave it, Bev, there's nothing you can do."

She puts her hand over her eyes and her thumb touches the bruise that Uncle George gave her in the kitchen back on Lynton Ave. The roar of Hull Fair is quietened this late. She can still smell the man's aftershave from the kitchen. It's not fair that women like Jerusalem always have to lose and that bastards always win. It never happens that way on the Sunday night police dramas, maybe that's why Bev likes them.

"I need your help to find her, Our Dave," she whispers. "I need it, not her. This is for me. You told me once you'd see me right."

"I will"

"Then I need this girl found, and I need you to help her get away from the man who's taken her." Our Dave can't help

Jerusalem, she's just another poor lass caught up in the shite of the world, but he has to help Bev. She's been there for him when nobody else has. They are family almost.

"You bloody owe me, Our Dave," she continues, "after all these years, that'll be it. You help me find that girl, and I'll be done here. I won't bother you ever again. You can find someone else to drive the kids to their special schools. You're selling up anyway, and I'll step out of your way, no bother at all."

Our Dave licks his dry lips. Bev has a soft spot for hard done cases, but she's as wise as they come. He is going to get rid of the business after all. Even so, he does not want to get involved in all this – but he will, one last time – for Bev, the woman who saved his life right here in this taxi office.

"I'll make those calls," he whispers.

"What can I do to help?"

Our Dave darkens. "You can stay out of it."

CHAPTER TEN
Uncle George, again

Our Dave has all the details from Bev. He sits in the office at Avenue Cars. It's just after half nine in the morning and he has the laptop screen open in front of him. Chanterlands Avenue behind is settling down to the business of early Thursday; rush hour has just finished, the kids are all in their classrooms for the day, the Kurdish barbers across the road are doing their first haircut, and Sam from the butcher's shop has hacked up all the beef he got from the cash and carry early this morning.

Our Dave already made a call to find out who he's dealing with. There are people who know people in the bigger towns and cities across the UK, and Our Dave has contacts in the underworld that go back to the eighties. It didn't take long. If he still smoked, he'd definitely have a cigarette now, or maybe a cigar even. It's not good news.

The man Bev described to him is unpleasant indeed. Uncle George traffics people. He's many steps up from the gangs that operate off the French coast with their small boats, and he deals with those who have money and influence. He can ship wealthy Russians to America and get them a green card, he can organise for Turkish diplomats and their families to relocate to somewhere quiet in Germany or in the UK. Uncle George also runs girls through Cologne and Amsterdam. They come from all over the world and are tricked with a job offer as a nanny – by the time they get to western Europe they're in debt so heavily to Uncle George, he can put them to work on their backs. He's not particular where he gets the women. They come from the Philippines, the Baltic states, Ukraine and further afield as well – some of his customers like a taste of the exotic.

Our Dave has been warned off him straight away. He is a big fish. He is not to be messed with and his operation dwarfs

Our Dave's little booze smuggling enterprise. He explained to his contact that Uncle George has kidnapped someone, and the response was deadpan – he is a people smuggler, that is what he does. Our Dave's contact has advised him to leave it alone if he values his life and the lives of his friends and family.

In the kitchen he boils the kettle while he looks out of the back window at the little car park with his grey Ford Galaxy parked in the corner. Bev and Dilva are off doing their taxi duties, and there's the dull tick from the kitchen clock in the silence. Our Dave won't be able to do anything against this man – Bev will have to let it go. The conversation he will have with her will be unpleasant. She will not take it well.

A bicycle moves round the corner in front of the window and stops. Face gets off, takes his lock from the handlebars, and secures his fixie to the drainpipe before he walks through the back door and into the kitchen. He gives the old man a big smile. He is much changed in these last few months; a bit of confidence can do wonders.

"You're late today," says Our Dave.

"I was on the phone." Face takes off his bike helmet and puts it on top of the tall fridge freezer in the corner. "I've got someone interested in the business."

"Oh aye? I thought you wanted to take it on."

"I'm not saying we should sell, it's just there's this fella who's been asking questions."

"Who is he?"

"A Dutchman," says Face.

Our Dave turns to him. "Where's he from?" He doesn't want to hear the answer.

"Amsterdam."

"His name isn't George, is it?"

Face gives a wide smile as he hears this. The scars all over his cheeks and down his neck don't even look that bad. "Yes, do you know him? He's called Mr George, he runs an import export business out of Amsterdam, seems nice enough, excellent English. He's looking for someone on the east coast of the UK to take deliveries direct from his base in Holland. He sells medical devices. There's a good profit on items of that kind."

Our Dave takes a deep breath. This is not the sort of pickle he wants to get into, especially when he is so close to getting out of the business altogether. It can't be the same man, but Bev did say she heard he was in Hull on other business apart from the girl he kidnapped. "So, what did you tell him?"

"I explained a bit about our furniture imports and he seemed keen to know. I said he could chat to you anytime to get a better flavour of how it works." Our Dave frowns at this. "Turns out he's in the UK at the moment. I said he could visit today."

"You didn't?" Our Dave's face drains of colour.

"He said he'd be here mid-morning, between ten and eleven. The name's Mr George," repeats Face, "he seems really friendly."

Our Dave feels a lump rise in his throat. "How did you get into contact with him?"

"He called me, actually. He said a friend of a friend gave him our details."

"You should have asked me first before you set anything up." There's that darkness to Our Dave that Face has seen before.

"What is it?"

"I want you to call him and put him off. Tell him that I'll get back to him myself."

Face narrows his eyes. "This could be a quick way out for you, Our Dave. I'll keep the property side of things afloat; it might be good for you." The older man shakes his head.

"You're too cocky, Face," he says. "You already think you know without looking properly. Like those lasses you've been seeing – you think you've found something you might like, and by the time you've stuck your toe in the water you realise you've made a mistake." This is too close to the bone. It's not Our Dave's style at all. "If you'd have run it by me first, I would have made some calls. I could have found out who and what he is before you invited him here for a catch up."

"You can do that now." Face is defensive. "You have to take chances sometimes, Our Dave."

"Turns out I do know him, and I've made those calls already. He's a bigger fish than we are in lots of ways, and the very best thing we can do is steer clear of him."

"Who is he?"

"It's organised crime."

"That's what we are."

The taller man shakes his head. "We just bend the rules, this bloke takes the piss. If he asks you to do something and you don't do it, you end up floating in the river face down. If he wants to buy our business then he will, for whatever price he feels like paying, and that might be fuck all, by the way." Face swallows. He feels like a little kid. "You've been played."

"How was I to know?"

"Experience," says Our Dave. "He's a people smuggler. Nothing at all like we are. He deals in misery."

"I'll get on the phone now," says Face.

"You better had," says Our Dave. This is a side of him that few will usually see. He is angry with Face. The man is a lawyer by trade, he can check if a contract is watertight, compose correspondence that threatens litigation, speak in court, and understand written Latin; but that sixth sense that tells you something is not quite right is lost on his academic brain.

There's the crunch of tyres on gravel from outside and a large, matt black Land Rover Discovery pulls into the car park. The paintwork is spotless and there's a big man in the driver's seat wearing dark glasses. The vehicle is ominous, as if it's just driven out of a gritty, low budget early noughties gangster film. It stops dead in the centre in the most inconsiderate spot so that nobody else will be able to get in.

"Too late," says Face. "Looks like he's already here."

"How do you know it's him?"

"He told me about his car. What do we do?"

"Pretend we don't know anything about him."

"I don't."

"Don't tell him any of what we do here. How good are you at lying?" asks Our Dave.

"I'm a lawyer, and I've been married," Face replies.

Uncle George seems like a reasonable man. His first name is Ulco, and he says it's a fairly common name where he comes from in Enschede on the Dutch, German border. Dealing with so many foreign people as he does, they assumed his name was Uncle, as a term of endearment. It stuck. Our Dave pretends to smile at this. Uncle George and his big driver, Tony, are warm Dutch men with self-deprecating humour and simple tastes. Uncle George takes his tea black and big Tony, with his tailored jacket and the collars up, has a mug of hot water. They sit in the back office of Avenue Cars and Our Dave is glad that Bev is not around. He sends her a text asking her not to come back to the office because he's got someone there. She thinks it's the business that she's asked him to get involved in but she'd shit herself if she knew Uncle George were here, sitting on the green swivel chair she uses every morning.

Turns out he and his driver are in the East Riding on a few bits of business. George has a haulage company with contracts linked to factories in Utrecht and Amsterdam. They make medical equipment like thermometers and needles and then ship it around the world. The business is complex and George needs a UK firm he can partner with to help deliver the products around Britain. Also, George is into aviation and he's got his eye on a plane at the airfield just south of Withernsea, it's a P28–200 Arrow II, a classic from the 1970s. If it's what he wants, George will have it flown back to Holland.

It all sounds very plausible.

Like the majority of people in business, George is pleasant and easy to chat to. The charm is disarming. His bald head and slightly beaten-up shoes give him that everyman kind of appearance. The gold tooth looks a bit off but doesn't make him seem sinister. Our Dave knows what he is up to because it's the game he himself has played for so many years. You don't get what you want by putting the frighteners on people, you do it with good humour, trust and decent business sense. Our Dave knows already that the man who Bev told him about will go a lot further in business to get what he's after. Despite how affable Uncle George and his driver, Tony, seem to be, there's still a lump of worry at the back of Our Dave's throat as they chat.

They talk about football, the weather, English traffic, and a smattering of politics. Uncle George is trying to build rapport – this is a good way to begin a deal. He hasn't explained exactly what he wants from Avenue Cars, but he will. Similarly, Our Dave hasn't mentioned that his import business doesn't really bring Dutch furniture into the docks here, and that the trucks are full of spirits. He is fairly certain that Uncle George will already know what Our Dave gets up to anyway.

Tony steps out into the car park for a go on his vape and, after a nod from Our Dave, Face says he has an important call to make then disappears upstairs. It leaves Uncle George and Our Dave alone in the back office sitting at the round table with their chipped mugs in front of them. Our Dave will have to nip this in the bud, quickly, before it can get out of hand.

"I don't exactly know what Face has explained to you, but our import company is not for sale at the moment."

Uncle George leans back on his chair and crosses his little arms over his lap, his tubby stomach stretches at the buttons on his reasonably-priced blue shirt under his nineties style leather jacket. He gives a kind of half grin, and the wrinkles on his bald head move as he does. "I didn't say I wanted to buy your company, only that I was interested in it."

Our Dave's heart drops. This is worse than buying it. He already knows the angle before Uncle George here explains.

The bald Dutchman continues. "I'd really like you to run some of our trucks through your operation. I mean, there'd be our product inside, but you'd be bringing it into the UK under your control, maybe even with your drivers." This means that Our Dave will take all the risks, have all the headaches, and do all the work. Whatever Uncle George intends to bring into the UK, Our Dave doesn't want anything to do with him.

"I don't think so," says Our Dave. He has to be careful here. He has no real idea what Uncle George knows about him.

"You don't want extra business? You don't want to expand, friend?"

"Not at my age. You're a young fella." Uncle George is probably in his early fifties – so this is a mild piss take. "You want to do the best you can, but I'm thinking about retiring. It's the end of the game for me, so I'm not interested in doing business with you, Mr George."

The Dutchman adjusts himself in the green swivel seat as he considers this. "I'd be paying you good money. Imagine what you could do in your retirement?" This is the first offer.

"I have enough already."

"What about the people around you, wouldn't they want to go into partnership and expand? What about that Face? He could afford to get plastic surgery or something?"

"I'm the boss, not him. I make the decisions. I build the contacts and the network."

"You could really make something out of this place," he says, glancing around the room at the paint job that looked okay for a couple of months last year. The cheap carpet is fraying at the doorway, there's the smell of mould and a damp patch on the wall near the stairs. It's as if the old Avenue Cars is trying to push up through the decor, like weeds through a new patio. "This is an opportunity, Dave," says Uncle George.

The Hull man gathers his thoughts. He will have to make this very clear to the Dutchman and in doing so may provoke him. "We don't want your business," he says. "That's it. There's nothing to understand or discuss. Face may sound like he knows the world, and he does in some ways, but he should never have set this meeting up with you. It was not his decision to make."

"Don't blame him. I set the meeting up," Uncle George swats the air as if to forgive Face and his inexperience. "If we're going to be honest with each other, Our Dave, then I will lay all my cards on the table. I know what you bring into the country. I have little eyes all over. I'm impressed at how clever it is, and how small it is too. I want you to work for me. You can use all the people you bribe at the ports and all the tricks you know, all the contacts and all the experience too. I want that for me."

"I'm saying no," says Our Dave.

"You did your homework on me, right? Or have I got you wrong? Someone with a sneaky, little network like you, will have their ears open."

"I did my homework."

"I thought you would. So, you know what kind of a man I am?"

Our Dave doesn't answer this. It would only play into George's narrative. "I'm retiring. This place is getting closed down. None of my people can handle the operation after I'm gone."

"People don't say no to me, Our Dave. I've been as nice as I can."

"I'm saying no to you."

Uncle George sits forward slowly and puts his hands on the edge of the table. He takes an effortless deep breath through his nose. "You boomer generation have always had it so easy, you know. You always had a job, you got to buy property that was cheap, you got government subsidies, you got everything you wanted…but sometimes, you just don't get to choose what you want, you have to suck it up and get on with the job."

Our Dave sighs. He's not going to argue with this man, there'd be no point. He knew as soon as the Dutchman walked through the door that he would lose to him; all this palaver, the handshakes and the coffee, the warm jokes and friendly smiles would all come down to Our Dave saying no to his offer. Our Dave is not big enough to stand up to George, but he won't give in. "I'll not work for you."

Uncle George waggles his finger at Our Dave in admiration. "I like you, and I like your people. You're no nonsense, just like we are. I'll give you the chance to think about it and I'll come back to you in a few days. I'm not here long, like I said, I've got to look at that airplane. I don't want you to say no to me, Our Dave, I don't want to have to do anything." Uncle George is earnest when he says this, as if somewhere in his heart it's true. As if all the things that he has done over the years have just been in the service of some greater good. "You sound like you've been in the game long enough to know what I mean."

"What will you be bringing in on the lorries I use?" asks Our Dave.

Uncle George does not hesitate. "People," he answers. Our Dave narrows his eyes. "Not many, and with your reputation and contacts, they'll sail past any problems. The money will be good."

"We won't do it."

"I'll give you some time to think."

"My folk won't do it, and neither will I."

Uncle George stands up. Our Dave does too. They face each other and the Hull man is taller and thinner with the arms on his checked shirt rolled up. Uncle George has done a lot of business, and he has worked with, and ruined, more people than he can remember. He knows how it goes:

"They will work for me in the end, Our Dave." Uncle George does not sound like he is threatening the man, more just stating a simple fact. Tony has entered the room from the car park, and his big shoulders in the smart coat fill the doorframe. He gives Our Dave a friendly grin.

"Tony and I are staying just outside a little place called Tickton," says Uncle George. "He's a bird watcher, you know. He says there's all sorts of things to see here that we don't get back at home." Tony shrugs his shoulders in apology for his geeky pastime. The attempt at humour makes the situation awkward. In truth, Uncle George likes it that this man is prepared to stand up to him, it shows backbone, and it means his business enterprise will be rock solid.

"I'll be in touch then, Our Dave," says Uncle George. Tony steps out the way to let the man pass and then follows him out the back door to the carpark.

They get into the Land Rover Discovery, start the engine, and then back out into the side street and are off into the stop start traffic of Chants Ave at this time.

Face appears at Our Dave's side.

"What happened?" he asks.

"We're about to get shafted."

CHAPTER ELEVEN
Our Dave gets set

In the office upstairs, Our Dave sits opposite Face looking at his scars. The lawyer has his brow creased in thought. Our Dave has explained everything – the coincidence with Bev picking up Jerusalem, her abduction, Uncle George's brutal reputation as well as the stark reality of one crime organisation swallowing another. Face may be a lawyer and a stickler for the rules but he is from Hessle Road stock, his grandfather was a trawler skipper, and so were his father and grandfather before him. It's where Face gets his charm and his robust sense that the universe is only a few steps from screwing you over. Six months ago, he shot someone in the chest, a woman, and watched her bleed out in Our Dave's kitchen. He weathered it then, and he'll weather this now, that's why Our Dave can trust him.

"What do you suggest?" asks Our Dave.

"Sell him the whole business."

"You'd all be done in if I did that. Maybe I should pay him a visit."

"And do what?"

"Something old school." Face screws up his features as if this is a stupid idea.

"You don't know where he is."

"He said he was at Tickton." This is a tiny place on the road out of Beverley towards the coast. There's a pub on the little river there and moored up boats in various states of disrepair. It's not the kind of place Dutch gangsters would choose to stay.

"Tickton?" repeats Face.

"There's a big Georgian house just outside," says Our Dave, "posh folk hire it out for weddings and the like. It's a hotel as well. He'll be there. His minder is a bird watcher." The old man furrows his brow in worry. It's a good job Hazel isn't around anymore with what he's thinking about doing. He doesn't have the shotgun under the shed in his allotment anymore so he will have to source something else. He hasn't got the connections he once had.

"Well, what will you do when you find him? You've told me what kind of man he is. What could you do to him?"

"Something stupid," says Our Dave. "At least if I do that, he'll leave this place alone."

"He won't." Face sits back in his chair as he does when he's thinking. "You'll have to be tactful. Heavy handed won't cut it, not if you want Bev's friend out of there as well."

"He won't expect us to do anything, not when he hasn't actually threatened us yet. I'd say the best plan is to get rid of him." It has been a long time since Our Dave has done anything in cold blood. "Sometimes you have to belt someone first, before they hit you."

"The best way to win a fight is not to fight at all," says Face.

"Sounds like shite to me, kid." replies the old man. Our Dave knows a thing or two even if he might not look like he does. His mind is whirring already about what equipment he can get his hands on and from where. What will he drive? He's not as young as he was and he's not sure how it will play. That big lad, Tony, will be a hard one. What if Uncle George has a bigger team even? "I'll deal with it," he says.

"There you go again, like before, Our Dave. As soon as it gets rough the walls go up."

"What's that supposed to mean?"

"It's how you used to operate." Our Dave forgets that he and Face here went through difficult times together a few months back. He forgets the man knows who he is. "I can almost see you thinking. However much you'd like to pretend this is a street fight, it isn't. We can approach this with a bit more sense and planning, we can do it together." Face is right. Our Dave likes to tackle jobs on his own. "You're not the hero anymore. Think about it, Our Dave, we already have someone who specialises in this sort of thing."

"What sort of thing?"

"Violence."

"Who?"

"Gaz."

The old man looks down. He knows this. He takes a deep breath. There's that sinking feeling in his legs. Young Gaz is ex-security. He's got experience of protection work, he's quick, brave, and in the past has handled situations that neither Face nor Our Dave would have the skills to cope with.

"I don't want him involved."

"You've involved him plenty in the past."

"Only by accident."

"What's wrong with this time?"

"He's a good kid. I don't want him doing what I do."

"But it's okay for you to drag me and my family into it?"

"You could have backed out anytime, Face. You're tougher than he is. You couldn't finish a fight if you tried, but you've got that quality – you can do what has to be done and not let it bother you, like when you shot that Kasia. You didn't even flinch."

"I wasn't always like that, Our Dave."

"Yes, you were. Me and you are the same. We'll get our hands dirty. Gaz isn't like that. He's all heart. His missus is pregnant as well."

Face raises his eyebrows. "When did he tell you that?"

"He didn't. It's the way he looks at her. You can read Gaz like a book."

Face gets up and turns to the window overlooking the street. He puts his hands in his pockets as he looks down at the street below. It's nearly lunchtime. He can see Steve from Steve's Cycles next door showing a parent and kid a new bike, the chippy across the way is just opening and there's a little queue forming outside the library with people taking books back.

"You know if Uncle George gets to you, he'll get to me, and then Bev and then everyone else. When Gaz finds out, he'll do something about it. You know he will."

Our Dave looks down at the floor he has not stopped staring at. "I know," he whispers. It would be much better if Gaz had not become involved with Our Dave at all.

"So better to use him to get the result you want, "says Face. "Once we get over this business with Uncle George, we'll go legit, or at least I will, and you can go wherever you want, with your fancy woman if you like."

"Who said she was a fancy woman?"

"Bev did."

"She's got a gob on her," says Our Dave.

Face goes back to looking out the window. "You'll have to talk to Gaz," he says like he's barking orders to a secretary. "You'll have to ask him to do whatever you're thinking of doing. He'll have Uncle George and his driver dealt with in no time."

Like he explained, Our Dave does not want to get the man involved. "I'd be putting the lad in danger."

"You'll be saving him in the long run."

Our Dave stands up and he is taller than Face, he can't remember the last time he had to look up to someone. "I'll have a word with him now," says Our Dave.

"We'll need this all sorting before it gets dark."

"I'll be back."

"And we'll talk about it together. We'll work it out. That's how it's done. If you go it alone, we'll fail. We stand as a team on this, and we use our best people, that includes my brains, Gaz's muscle and your experience." Our Dave nods in agreement.

He walks out of Face's office and down the stairs, through the kitchen, then out into the carpark behind Avenue Cars. The sky is bright and the smell of autumn is in the air, it's apples rotting in the graveyard a few streets away, the falling leaves from the trees along the wide streets behind, and the sweet doughnuts from the fair nearby. Whatever he said to Face, Our Dave is not going to get Gaz involved in this. All this working together nonsense is for superhero comics. He's going it alone. Like always.

That's how he knows it will get done.

Back in 1983, in the second half of December, Our Dave was given an envelope with a name on a slip of paper inside. There was also a photo of a man's head cut out of a newspaper. The face was smooth shaven and chubby with a Trilby hat over black hair. It was Our Dave's first job; turns out it was the last of that kind as well.

He feels the same kind of trepidation now as he did back then, a mixture of fear and nervousness. Just like in 1983, Our Dave must find the means to complete the job himself, as well as the transport. It's hard these days. He's got a lot more to lose. Back then he was just an apprentice joiner fitting trawlers out on the docks.

There are still people Our Dave knows in this city. He's on foot because it's quicker, and he goes past the supermarket on the corner then turns right. This is Westbourne Ave West, a small dead-end street just a few minutes' walk from Avenue Cars. It's a while since he's been here. There's someone he wants to see.

He goes up the path of the second to last house and taps at the frosted glass on the red door with his knuckles. There's foreign sounding music coming from inside. A woman with dark hair opens up and she gives him a bright and wide smile.

"Dave?" she says. This is Dilva. She's worked for Our Dave for the last year and it's she who ferries the foreign kids around the city. She's from the Kurdish part of Iran and speaks Arabic as well. In the short time he's known her, Dilva has gone from being an afraid outsider to part of the furniture. Our Dave can rely on her.

"I'm looking for Ryan," he says. He has not visited this house for some time. There's been no need. She beckons him in with her head and he steps inside, closes the door behind him and follows her down to the kitchen.

Ryan comes in through the back door. He's wearing a khaki vest that shows off his once powerful arms that have gone to fat, and he's clean shaven with dark black hair. Like Dilva, Ryan was a lost soul a year ago. You would never put them together but here they are, getting on with it. Ryan used to live next door and he moved in soon after Dilva's husband passed away. Ryan has grown in this last year as well. Where once there was an angry, arrogant cock, who could only talk about his time in the army, here stands a shorter man who has his ears open. He's given Dilva confidence and protection and she's given him stability. He's even got a job working in the DIY shop on Chants Ave. It's going well.

"What can I do for you, Our Dave?" asks Ryan. He knows that this won't be a social call.

"Can we have a quick chat in the garden?" he asks.

Ryan seems worried suddenly. "What about?"

"I need a bit of advice."

Ryan feels his throat tighten. The appearance of this man could mean he has to go back to his old ways, and he does not want to. "Step this way," he says and the older man follows him outside. Our Dave just hopes that Ryan hasn't totally given up his dodgy activities since he moved in with Dilva.

In the shed at the bottom of the garden here, wrapped in an old towel, Ryan has a sawn-off shotgun, a box of shells, and some wire wool for cleaning it out. He wanted to get rid of it a long time ago, but he didn't know where, so the safest thing to do was just to hide it. Ryan is happy to give it to Our Dave – it means that it's no longer his problem. The sniper rifle that he had previously has been sold on to a Geordie out of town. Gone too are all the replica handguns, the crossbow, and even his katana sword. Dilva doesn't like weapons in the house, and

Ryan gets his fix of fighting these days by playing squads on Call of Duty with her eldest son, Mohammed. They each have their Xbox consoles in different rooms and shout instructions to each other across the landing. In many ways it's the comradery that Ryan missed since he left the army many years ago. He goes on long walks with Mohammed out past Cottingham, they scoff at superhero films together and talk about World War Two history – he is as good a stepfather as any, despite what he was in the past. Responsibility has matured him.

Ryan doesn't ask what Our Dave needs the weapon for, it's none of his business and there's no suggestion of money because in days past, Ryan has been paid very well by the man for minor jobs. He keeps the shotgun wrapped in the old towel and puts it in a garden refuse bag. Our Dave adds the box of cartridges to the pocket of his bomber jacket.

In the kitchen, Dilva has made them both a cup of tea and there's a Tupperware box of homemade biscuits open on the table. She's sprayed air freshener all down the hall to hide the smell of Ryan and Mohammed's feet, and she is sad when Our Dave says that he can't stay to finish his tea. Dilva makes him take the whole box of biscuits and gives him a hug at the front door before he leaves. She likes Our Dave. She wishes she could do more for him. She looks at the garden bag that he is carrying tucked under the arm of his bomber jacket.

"He's not going to be in trouble?" she asks. "I mean Ryan. What do you want with him?"

"I just picked something up, Dilva." She smiles and her eyes twinkle above the straight white teeth. Like Gaz and Kate, Our Dave does not want anything he does to affect these two. They've found a way to be happy.

"I don't think Ryan is ever going to be in trouble again. Not now he has you," says Our Dave.

CHAPTER THIRTEEN
Let's go to Tickton

On the allotment off Raglan Street behind Newland Ave, Our Dave's plot is in the far corner. Behind the rows of neatly planted beetroot plants and late blooming potatoes, he stands in his corrugated iron shed at the bench where he keeps his seedlings in spring. He's closed the door and unwrapped the sawn off shotgun. It's been a while, but Our Dave knows how they work. This one is a Welton from the early nineties. The conversion is a pretty good job with a clean cut along the barrels. The safety and the mechanism have been well looked after and Our Dave oils them, then gives both barrels a good clean with the wire wool. The shells smell old. He cuts one open to have a look at the pellets and powder inside. They're out of date for sure, but he thinks they'll be ok. He could do to test the weapon, but however deserted the allotment seems, someone will be around to hear the boom – especially since Our Dave's plot backs onto the big, posh gardens from the houses on Newland Park.

There's a wax jacket hanging on the back of the shed door that Our Dave uses when the rain is bad sometimes. It's seen better days but it might be perfect for the job in hand. He tries it on, and the right-hand pocket is just deep enough for him to hide the shotgun. He will look suspect with a big bulge. It's no good. You have to hide things in plain sight and he wishes he still had his fishing bag that he carried his old shotgun in.

Our Dave does a rummage round the shed, there are plastic bags, cardboard boxes and netting, but nothing suitable. In the back of his grey Ford Galaxy, Our Dave removes his yellow tool bag and brings it inside the shed. The shotgun fits snugly if he removes his cordless drill and puts it at an angle. He loads it up with two smooth red shells, makes sure the safety is on, and adds more shells to the pockets of his bomber jacket.

Back in 1983, Our Dave was given that envelope by a man in the Queens in December. There was a separate number to call from a phone box; the woman on the other end told him he had to get to the Grand Hotel in Scarborough. It's the big one that overlooks the seafront. The man in question would be staying there from the twenty-first to the twenty-third. That was his window.

Our Dave managed to buy a pistol from a man off the docks along with a case of whiskey that he didn't want. That was it. He caught the train up to Scarborough on the twenty-first, and it went from there. The pistol was a small snub-nosed revolver with a rotating barrel that held six bullets like a cowboy shooter. It was black with age. Our Dave cleaned it up. He remembers standing with it pointed at the mirror in the bedroom he shared with his brother and hearing the mechanism rattle as he shook with fear. Back in those days, Our Dave had got himself into something that he couldn't quite get out of. A bit like now.

He concentrates on the road as he drives the grey Ford Galaxy through the traffic towards Bransholme. He'll cut through the back of the estate and go through a few little villages to get to Tickton. He knows the Georgian house where Uncle George will be staying because he's been to a few weddings there over the years. He'll park out front and just hope that Uncle George is at home. The time on the dashboard reads half two. He needs this done by the evening.

That's not it, of course. Our Dave is not going to park on the gravel outside Tickton Grange, walk into the hotel there, find Uncle George's room then blow his head off. That might be how he played it in 1983, but life has taught Our Dave the value of preparation.

Bransholme here has a bad reputation. It's a huge council house estate on the northern edge of the city where jerry built maisonette houses from the nineteen sixties are already crumbling. It's not all that bad. There are pockets of troublemakers, but there are worse places to be in Hull. Some of the maisonette terraces come with lines of little garages behind the houses but they're a bit too small for modern cars. Our Dave has had two of these lock-ups next to each other since the nineties. They're in the far north corner with the countryside a street away. Up here the houses are mostly boarded up these days and the last couple of residents are the elderly who like the quiet.

Our Dave parks his Ford Galaxy on a bigger road a few minutes' walk away from the lock-ups, gets his yellow tool bag from the passenger seat and goes the rest of the way on foot. At the white door of a little garage, he fits the key into the middle of the handle then pulls it up. Inside, is a 2008 Mini Cooper registered to an elderly lady in Manchester. Our Dave reverses it onto the street and leaves the engine running as he gets out to close the garage door. The place is deserted around him, and he looks to the boarded-up windows and the couple of cars parked on the street. He might have been spotted, but it's a chance he has to take. If he had more time, he'd do this at night for sure and he would probably use the black van he has in another lock-up near the car lot on the river Hull in town.

From here, there's a little road through to the village of Wawne, and then Our Dave can cut out across the fields to Tickton. Once he's out of the estate, the country is flat and open with a big blue autumn sky rolling into the late afternoon. The Mini is too small for Our Dave's big frame even though he's adjusted the seat. He won't be able to get the girl and the two men into here so he'll have to use that big Land Rover that Uncle George has... if it all goes to plan. He looks over to the yellow tool bag on the front seat and then back through the windscreen. The road is thin between these little, flatland villages and the fields are freshly cut as autumn rolls into winter.

Our Dave is not sure he's ready for this. His hands on the

steering wheel look wrinkled and old and his stomach is turning circles. Like all those years ago on the train to Scarborough for his first job, he thinks about running. He could turn right at the main road and be off the other way. He could return home for his passport and a kit bag and then be on a flight out of Humberside Airport by this evening. These are the same kinds of feelings that washed over him as he sat on the rattling train in Dec 1983 with that snub nosed revolver in his pocket. Then, just as now, it was never about Our Dave. He has people to think about. Uncle George has threatened him by insinuation but back in the eighties, Our Dave was told that his mother would be going on holiday to the intensive care unit at Hull Royal Hospital, if he didn't get the job done. He was to get paid for it of course, but the added bonus was just so he didn't bottle it when he got there.

Our Dave turns the Mini onto the main road heading towards Tickton. There's no getting out of this. At least, if it all goes tits up there are capable people who'll handle the business. Face will use Gaz if he needs muscle. Dilva will be fine with that Ryan. Bev will get another job somewhere else and this will all seem like a bad dream. Our Dave isn't sure about the Ethiopian girl; she'll probably go back to whatever life she had in Amsterdam. He doesn't like to think about Wendy.

Before the village of Tickton itself, Our Dave turns right into a slip road and slows down as he approaches the house. On one side there are a couple of well-to-do bungalows and then there's Tickton Grange itself. It's not the grandest old house in the East Riding of Yorkshire by any means, but it's big enough to hold events and small enough to be profitable. He turns into the gravel drive and goes slow all the way up to the white Georgian manor with the added period features, sash windows and a gleaming red front door. Parked front ways is the same matt black Land Rover Discovery that visited Our Dave a few hours before. He backs the Mini up next to it, so it will be easier for him to drive away, turns off the engine and grabs the tool kit from the front seat before he gets out. He has a vague idea of what he'll do. Nothing cocks up situations more than too much planning.

His shoes crunch on the gravel as he heads for the red front door and his heart is pounding in his chest. Our Dave's throat is dry and his stomach rumbles. He steps inside. There's a smile from a dumpy receptionist with her blonde hair scraped back in a ponytail.

"Good afternoon," she beams.

"I'm looking for a Mr George," he says. "I've come to do some work on his vehicle, that Land Rover outside." Our Dave nods to the tool bag in his hand and the woman grins back at him.

"Would you like me to give him a call?" she asks.

"He said to come straight up, so we can sign all the forms. It's an insurance thing." Although he's nervous, Our Dave delivers this without any sign of it. Nobody suspects an older white man with a light beard and a big smile. It's a privilege.

"He's in the granary," she says, "it's just out the door and down the path next to the willow tree. It's a separate building."

"Thank you, Miss," says Our Dave as he gently rests his hand on the counter. She gives him a wider grin. She likes her job here; the people are lovely.

"I'll just bob round then," he says.

Our Dave goes back out the red door and to the side of the manor house. Sure enough, there's a block paving path next to a willow tree leading to a red bricked building just ahead. It's a converted granary with a traditional stone facade and smooth arched windows along the bottom under a low roof. Uncle George probably has enough money to stay wherever he wants, so, he might as well rent out a whole suite. Once upon a time houses like these would have been home to minor aristocrats and those born into money, now, it's Our Dave who stands in front of the heavy brown door with the words 'Granary Suite' on a silver sign. He is West Hull's finest and carries a sawn-off shotgun in a yellow tool bag by his side.

He pauses before he knocks. It will not go as planned – it never does, this he knows from experience. Just like back in the Grand Hotel at Scarborough all those years ago, he feels his skin prickle with terror. He's just got to get this sorted and come out of the other side, then it will all be okay, like it was back then.

He taps on the wood and steps back. There are voices inside and the door opens to reveal the big shape of Tony, Uncle George's driver. He's taken off his heavy, tailored jacket and is wearing a blue business shirt unbuttoned at the neck, he gives Our Dave a smile when he recognises him.

"Dave?" he asks.

"Aye. I just wanted to have a word."

Tony shrugs his shoulders and opens the door a little wider as if Our Dave is some sort of boy scout who has come to sell clothes pegs. "You better come in," he says.

The suite is a posh, open-plan kitchen cum dining area and lounge. The bedrooms must be off the corridor at the back. At the far side, under the arched windows are two couches facing a glass table. Jerusalem sits in one of them staring down at her phone. She looks up as Our Dave enters, and her smooth face does not give away emotion but she is surprised to see him. She gave up on the idea of being saved a long time ago.

Tony stands beside Our Dave and Uncle George walks through the kitchen towards him with his shoes clicking on the expensive off-white tiles.

"Dave?" he asks. Like Tony, he looks mildly amused at the old man with a black bomber jacket and his tool bag in one hand.

"I thought I'd come and say hello," says Our Dave. Both Dutchmen smile at this.

"You've brought your tools, I see," says Uncle George as he motions to the bag. There's light sarcasm to his voice.

"Aye."

"Put the bag down, please," says Tony standing next to him. Our Dave turns his head to look at the big Dutchman – his demeanour is still one of amusement, but there's a touch of mettle in his voice. "Just set the bag down, nice and slow." Tony has a sense of the unexpected and he can smell something is off about this. The room bristles.

Our Dave does not comply straight away and remains staring at the big man for a few moments. He has to make this look good after all. Tony cocks his head and raises his eyebrows and then Our Dave sets the bag down on the floor next to him. There's a light clink from the tools within.

Uncle George approaches. He bends to pick up the tool bag and then holds it open with both hands as he looks down. He sees the sawn-off shotgun and closes it up again.

"I'm not shocked, Dave, and I'm not disappointed either. I would have done something similar in your position. I actually respect this. It means you know what kind of man I am and you know I always get what I want. This gun here would be the only way to stop me." The Dutchman means this. He likes the old school honesty of Our Dave, and that, despite his age, he is ready to do what is necessary to defend his business. "Would you sit down and have coffee with us, Dave? We've just had a tray brought in from the hotel. Perhaps this time we can talk about things seriously."

Our Dave has flushed red. His heart is still pounding and he swallows back his fear. It has not quite gone as he thought it would. From the couch in the corner, Jerusalem gives a sigh and goes back to looking at her phone; he's just an old man after all.

In the other corner of the kitchen, there's a dining table with four chairs. On a round tray there are cups, a pot of coffee and a teapot as well as cakes on a little stand. It's all very quaint. Tony shows Our Dave to one of the seats with an open hand and the mild amusement has gone from his face now. Like Uncle George, he's required to show some respect to a man who has been hopelessly outclassed even before he got started. They sit him in the corner seat with Uncle George at one side and Tony at the other. Jerusalem hasn't looked up from her phone. Uncle George sets out cups and saucers in front of each of them.

"Coffee, isn't it, Dave?" asks Uncle George as he reaches for the pot.

"Aye."

"Will you have a cake?"

Our Dave shakes his head.

"I like the look of them but they repeat on me," says Uncle George. As before, this is all very friendly. They could be old mates as the Dutchman pours black coffee from the white designer pot into Our Dave's equally designer cup and saucer. The old man looks at him with a blank expression. Uncle George does not want to upset Our Dave, he is clearly someone he could use in the long run.

"Don't go looking at me like that," says Uncle George, "it's just business, it's nothing personal. You've been in the game long enough, you should know this. Organizations take over other organizations, big fish eat little fish, it's just the way of the world. I don't want there to be any hard feelings between us." Our Dave nods. "I've got some papers I want you to have a look at, they're just figures for now, but they'll give us an idea of how many people we expect to bring in through you, and I need to discuss the actual process of getting them across the customs checks on your lorries." Our Dave still wears that same blank expression. "Now we've got through that shotgun nonsense, perhaps we can get down to actual business, Dave. What do you think?" Our Dave lowers his eyes. He will have to take this. He will have to make it look good as well.

Uncle George stands up and walks over to the kitchen

counter where there's a laptop bag with his notes. "It's all a very simple model, Dave," he says as he turns his back.

This is it.

It's actually gone better than Our Dave had expected. From the knock on the door to the defeated look on Our Dave's face; this was all the lead up to the actual show. It's easy to like Uncle George with his pleasant, affable manner. Our Dave reminds himself of the misery the man will have engineered with his trafficking business. He is justified in this. Tony would do the same to him if he had to. Like Uncle George said a moment ago, this is just business.

As soon as Uncle George turns his back, Our Dave goes for the snub-nosed revolver in the inside pocket of his bomber jacket. The art of deception is in showing the obvious and not concealing the hidden. This is the same gun he took to Scarborough all those years ago and the one he has kept hidden in a tin box on a shelf in the shed on his allotment.

He pulls the weapon out in a smooth movement, and before Tony has time to do anything but let his mouth hang open, Our Dave squeezes the trigger and the end of the pistol erupts in a blaze of fire and noise. The bullet hits Tony in his collar bone, it is cruel of Our Dave but then again, these men are here to do him and his business harm. He went for the shoulder because he doesn't want to kill the Dutchman – moving the body would be a massive pain in the arse, especially as he'll have to have this operation all wrapped up as quickly as he can. The big man falls backwards off his chair and Our Dave follows with the snub-nosed revolver pointing at his head. Uncle George turns in shock.

"Stay right there, fella," whispers Our Dave down to Tony on the ground. "Let's not make this any worse." The big man's eyes flash for an instant as he realises what's happened. Our Dave has seen this kind of look before – it's the telltale sign that someone is about to react, so he squeezes the trigger and the gun recoils in his hand. The second bullet goes through

Tony's neck just above his chest and makes a splat sound. His nostrils flare in shock – the pain will come later.

Our Dave steps back and levels the gun at Uncle George standing at the counter. The Dutchman appears dumbfounded with the laptop bag in his hands. This he did not expect. He has misjudged Our Dave. He now senses hubris.

"You've got about an hour before Tony here will bleed out," says Our Dave as he looks at Uncle George. Tony grunts on the floor as he realises the gravity of the wound and the danger he is in.

"You'll pay for this," mutters Uncle George, and at once he understands that it is the wrong thing to say. He has underestimated the man. He's not in Holland now. He doesn't have friends on every street corner. These people drive on the wrong side of the road. They put milk in their tea. They can't speak a language they invented. He's out of his depth.

"Lass," calls Our Dave to the Ethiopian girl. Jerusalem is now standing with her eyes wide and her mouth open. There's Tony on the floor with his left shoulder a bloody mess and blood issuing from his throat. Uncle George stands like a stone statue in front of Our Dave who has what appears to be some sort of revolver.

"Go inside the yellow bag," calls Our Dave. "There's something there for you." She sees the tool bag on the floor and bends down to open the handles up, inside is the sawn-off shotgun and she pulls it out. Uncle George raises his eyebrows as he looks at her with the weapon in her hands. Now he sees it. The shotgun was not for Our Dave at all.

"You'll have to take the safety catch off, it's on the top," says Our Dave. She looks down and pulls the switch.

"Now, you better be careful, friend," says Uncle George to the girl. "I've been good to you, and I expect more from you as well. All that I've put you through this last year was not so you could betray me like this."

She gives him a wry smile from the corner of her mouth. Our Dave steps forward. He has to get this all sorted as quickly as he can. "On your knees, George," he says. Our Dave no longer sounds like the friendly, lost old man he presented a few minutes ago. Uncle George does not take his eyes off Jerusalem, her eyes twinkle in a way he has not seen before.

"I will not go easy," he says.

"It doesn't matter to me," says Our Dave. "You're only not dead right now because of the mess it would make. As soon as you get into that Land Rover you've got, I'll shoot you. If you yap and take the piss, I'll do it slowly and you'll be in unimaginable pain. If you shut up, I'll put one right through your skull and you'll go to sleep straight away." Our Dave is actually lying here. He will shoot him in the head as soon as possible anyway. "Now get on your knees," repeats Our Dave.

Uncle George's eyes begin to water. He has been in tricky situations before, but not for a long time. "You're making a mistake," he says.

Our Dave shakes his head, he does a double step, moves in, and brings one of his knees up into Uncle George's groin. It's an old trick. If you've ever been kneed in the bollocks, you know how to do it back. Uncle George grunts in pain and his hands go to his stomach.

There'll be no small talk. Like all the way back in 1983, Our Dave is just here to do a simple job and that's what he will do. As Uncle George begins to go down, Our Dave draws a yellow supermarket bag out of the pocket of his bomber jacket. He shakes it open and pulls it over the man's head. His free hand goes for the garden twine in the other pocket. He has clever fingers, does Our Dave, and he pulls the bag tight and fits the string round the neck to hold it on. The knot is unnecessarily tight. Uncle George swoons, and, like he's done it a thousand times, Our Dave drags one hand then the other around the Dutchman's back and ties them together at the wrists.

Jerusalem thought she would enjoy seeing her boss suffer

but now it is here, she does not feel anything at all. She is more impressed with the coldness of Our Dave and how he deals with George. It's as if he works in a butcher's shop.

Our Dave does not want to kill Uncle George yet because his dead body will be difficult to move. The bag is over his head so that when he does shoot him, most of his brains will be caught in the plastic. Jerusalem holds the shotgun light in her hands and it is trained on the Dutchman. She misjudged Our Dave as well.

"Someone will have heard the shots," she says.

Our Dave looks up. "They won't all the way out here," he answers. This is Tickton village just outside Beverley, the most exciting thing that you can do here is leave. Our Dave glances over to the body of Tony on the tiles behind them, he is groaning. They will have to carry him into a vehicle. It will be a massive pain. However, it has gone much better than he expected so far.

"Where are the car keys?" he says to Jerusalem. "I'll take the Land Rover, you can take the Mini I arrived in."

"The keys are on the table," she answers. "I can't drive."

"Then you'll come with me. I'm going to back the Land Rover up as close as I can to the door, pop the boot, and then you'll help me get them inside.

Jerusalem nods. "Did Bev send you?" she asks.

"Kind of,"

"She said you were someone to trust."

"I am, if you're a friend."

She smiles. There's a double tap at the heavy front door.

They freeze.

Jerusalem blinks back at Our Dave, and he takes a deep breath. On his knees next to the breakfast bar, Uncle George groans as he recovers from being struck in the balls. His arms are tied behind his back, and he has a yellow Heron bag tight over his head.

There are another two sharp knocks on the front door. The

timing couldn't be worse.

"I'll get it," says Our Dave. "Keep the gun on him." At the door, he looks through the peephole in the centre and to the two people standing outside.

His heart drops. There's an overweight female copper in uniform next to a familiar, doughy looking man in a dark brown suit. It's someone he didn't expect to see here. It's DI Brian Wilson, Wendy's son who's a plainclothes copper. He did tell Our Dave he was doing some consultancy work for a Dutch company.

Our Dave steps back a few paces and looks at the scene around him. There's Big Dutch Tony bleeding out from his shoulder and neck onto the off-white tiles, and Uncle George on his knees while the autumn sunshine glints on the yellow plastic bag tied over his head. Our Dave turns to see Jerusalem holding the sawn-off shotgun.

"Is there a back door?" he whispers.

CHAPTER FOURTEEN
A rescue

"Where's he gone?" asks Gaz. He's sitting opposite Face in his office at Avenue Cars. It's mid-afternoon Thursday.

"He told me he'd gone to see you," says Face as he taps at his computer screen. It's not at all unusual for Our Dave to disappear, but he'd arranged to meet Gaz this afternoon to talk about lending him the money to get that taxi van. It's ten minutes after two and the old man is not here. If he has an appointment, he will be there or at the very least he will call. Gaz has sent a text message and rang him as well; there's been no contact. Face here is a good liar but Gaz can see the worry behind his eyes. You get a feeling when something is wrong, like just before a punch-up when the air bristles with electricity and energy. Face ignores him as he types into his laptop.

"What sort of job has he gone on?" asks Gaz.

"I don't know, he's a busy man but it's not like Our Dave to miss an appointment."

"Is anything wrong?"

Face stops typing to look at him. "Nothing we can't fix," he says and then goes back to his screen. He's not sure how much to tell this man.

"What's that supposed to mean?" asks Gaz.

"It means that Our Dave doesn't want you involved."

"So, there is something wrong."

"Like I said, nothing that we can't handle." Gaz examines Face across the clean desk. He's learned to take things slowly these days. Once upon a time, his mind would rush to conclusions, but now he lets the truth come slowly to the quiet surface. Kate has taught him a lot in the time they have been together, she is brave and honest with herself so that he has to be as well. Gaz has told her everything, even things that he never admitted to himself and just the same, she has shared herself. It makes Gaz strong.

"I'm here to help," says Gaz. "If Our Dave is in trouble, I need to know." Face continues to type into his laptop.

"It's beyond us I'm afraid, Gaz."

"How so?"

"I can't really say. I'll let Our Dave know that you came. I'm sure he'll give you a ring when he gets back." Face points at his laptop screen. "If you don't mind, I'm actually pretty busy."

"Is he in trouble?" asks Gaz.

"It's nothing to do with you, and it's out of my hands anyway."

"You've told me there's a problem by telling me not to worry, mate. It's pissing me off. Our Dave is a friend of mine. I thought you were as well." He doesn't sound angry but Face looks across at Gaz with his smart, nondescript black suit and dark tie. "I need to know where Our Dave is."

Face might as well tell him. "Someone is trying to take over his operation. Two men from Amsterdam. Seem like decent enough sorts but Dave thinks they're nasty. He said he was thinking about sorting them out?"

Gaz narrows his eyes. "Sorting them out?"

"I don't know what he meant. I think he changed his mind anyway." Face turns back to his computer screen.

"Look at me," says Gaz. Face stops typing. The young man's voice is commanding but not loud. "You're going to tell me the lot, Face. I mean all of it."

Face is succinct and precise with his explanation, then, Gaz makes a few phone calls on his mobile downstairs. He calls people Our Dave is friendly with. Bev is picking someone up from the hospital and she doesn't know where he is. Terry, who he plays snooker with sometimes, hasn't heard from him. Dilva picks up and says that Our Dave came round to speak to Ryan and collected something. Gaz knows what kind of man Ryan is, or rather was, before he got all loved up.

In the office above Avenue Cars, Face explains that the Dutchmen might be staying at Tickton Grange near Beverley. Gaz knows it. He did a security course there a few years back. They guess this is where Our Dave will have gone. It's not hard to put the pieces of the puzzle together now that Gaz has set them out in front of Face – he is surprised that with his lawyer's brain he didn't see it himself. He should have realised that Our Dave is not going to change, not at his age. He was always going to try to take them on his own.

The old man's truck must be parked up outside his house on Westbourne Ave. They'll need a car and not one that can be traced to them. Gaz is more organised than Face expected and the young man makes more calls, anyone who could help is too far away to supply him with anything. He'll have to source something else, but they have to move quickly.

Face locks the office and they begin walking down Chants Ave and then turn left into Perth Street West. Gaz's stride is brisk. Face keeps pace.

"I thought you said we needed a car?" he asks.

"This is the quickest way to get one," answers Gaz as they walk past the terraced houses. At the end of Perth Street West, after you go under the little railway bridge, there's an industrial estate. On the corner is one of those big children's indoor play areas and there's a huge car park. Gaz walks through, scouting for something that might be useful. He doesn't want anything fast or too small, something battered will be good enough. Against the back wall of the next building is a black plumber's van with the words 'Pell and Williamson' written on the side in big letters. There's a red stripe under the front of the bonnet and across the back. It's got some wear on it, and like any workman's van there are newspapers, empty chip boxes and half crushed cans of pop along the windscreen inside. This is perfect.

Gaz approaches and tries the handle before anything else. It's locked. He looks around him quickly, removes a metal tool from his inside suit pocket, extends it and then, like a professional lock smith, he sticks one end down the side of the window and jiggles it. The button on the door pops open to show it's unlocked.

"Are you stealing this?" asks Face.

Gaz opens the driver's door and hops up. It's obvious that he is. "Get in," he says.

Under the steering wheel, Gaz pulls away a plastic panel and searches for the right wire. The tool he has is also a penknife and it takes him a minute to find the correct cables and cut them. Face gets into the passenger side. In another thirty seconds, Gaz touches two wires together and the van starts up beneath them with a rumble. He puts her in first gear and looks around to make sure nobody is approaching. They pull off out the car park and drive off down National Ave. The tyres could do with pumping up and the tracking on the steering wheel is off. That's all ok for Gaz.

At the traffic lights half a mile down the road, Face breaks the silence. "Did that place have security cameras?" he asks.

"No. That's why we went there."

"Where did you learn to steal vehicles that quick?"

"They teach you on the level five personal security course." Face looks around at the muck of the working plumber's van. There are three seats in the back, and beyond, in the large boot space, are shelves full of plumbing bits and bobs, washers and taps and whatnot. There's the smell of sweat and plastic.

Face turns back to Gaz. "You're full of surprises," he says.

They go through Cottingham and then down Dunswell Lane. There's a phone that has been left on the front seat and it rings frantically. They ignore it but it keeps ringing, making Gaz feel more guilty than he already does. Face switches it off.

The traffic is light and Gaz keeps to the speed limit on the road towards Beverley, out of habit more than anything else. He's just pinched this van so he won't be liable for any ticket that he picks up via the speed cameras.

Face looks out of the window at the big bungalows. "What are we going to do when we get there?"

"Depends on the situation," answers Gaz.

Face doesn't like to do activities that he has not planned. Now he no longer drinks, his life is full of comforting routine, there's the bike ride to work every day, the three-mile run down to Pearson Park and then up to the railway bridge. He cooks something healthy for him and his son at six, they have a natter, and then Face gets his head back into the laptop for Our Dave's business affairs. As they drive along the new ring road then past the new Aldi, Face feels nerves biting at him. Losing the drink has given him clarity, but also the ability to feel emotions that previously did not worry him.

"Our Dave will be okay, you know," he says. "He can look after himself, and he's been in the game a long time." Face is saying this for his own benefit.

Gaz keeps his eyes on the road. "I'm just backup in case something goes wrong."

"What do you think he's doing up here?"

"He went to visit that Ryan, you know?"

"So?"

"You do know what he will have picked up from him, don't you?" asks Gaz.

"What?"

"A gun."

"He doesn't like guns," says Face.

"That doesn't mean to say he hasn't got one."

"I thought I'd talked him out of doing anything stupid,"

"He'll be there to kill him, Face. Our Dave might seem like a nice old man to you, but he's not above getting his hands dirty if he has to. You were there in the kitchen of his house when Kasia got shot."

Face nods. "It was me who shot her, Gaz. Not Our Dave."

"He'll need our help now, just like he did back then."

They are unlikely colleagues, these two. Gaz here doesn't

know a single word in German, he's never read Aristotle, he's never had guacamole; but he has the level street intelligence that comes from dealing with people in stress and situations for so many years. Likewise, Face has never done a day's boxing training in his life, he's never driven faster than eighty-five miles an hour either, he's never had a fight in a pub, but he has shot someone through the chest, and Gaz has never done that. Both these men have known despair, however, and both these men owe Our Dave. Without him, they might not be sitting in a stolen black plumbing van as they keep to the speed limit on the road out of Beverley leading towards Tickton.

DI Wilson stands at the Granary Suite door behind the Tickton Grange Hotel and taps on the door again. He's here to meet Uncle George at the Dutchman's request and he's not alone. In the car parked around the corner in front of the main house, is another plainclothes copper and next to him is a slightly overweight female officer in uniform. She's called PC Grace. The man in the car is DI Harris, a Scotsman.

They're all on the payroll for Uncle George, for various reasons. DI Wilson is sick of being paid less than a doctor or lawyer – people who don't even risks their lives. Back in the car, Harris the Scot is just a greedy bastard, and PC Grace here has rather fallen into this whole situation because of her position – she overheard Wilson and Harris as they discussed the matter, and rather than try to cover it up, they added her to the group. She gets a way smaller cut of the big bribes that Uncle George pays them, and DI Wilson gets the feeling that she'd rather not be involved, but she is neck deep in it now. It's Wilson who organised the airfield up at Pocklington, and it's he who helped clear the way for Uncle George to bring the high-end migrants there. There's no paperwork of course and it isn't actual police work, but he did have to look at all the angles, and it's he who pays to make sure the sergeant up at

Pocklington police station and his units never notice anything that goes on there.

Wilson raps on the door again. The Dutchman has asked him to come because he needs to explain his plans, and more importantly, he said he would dish out some money. Wilson is losing patience as he taps again. He looks across at PC Grace with her big face and black hair in a bun. She struggles with her weight and has big doughy jowls with light make-up. In the car on the way here, DI Harris suggested that she get onto that slimming drug, Ozempic.

"I'll have a look round the side and in the windows," she says. "He might be listening to music or in the shower."

DI Wilson frowns at her. "Let's not treat this like an investigation, PC Grace," he cocks his head slightly when he speaks. He taps again and they hear something that sounds like glass smash from within. He gives her the nod and PC Grace moves round the side of the renovated granary building to get a look through one of the big windows. She doesn't see anything at first but as she moves, she spots the motionless figure of Tony laid on his back below the dining table with blood all over his head and shoulders. PC Grace is about to report this into the radio on her jacket but catches herself – like Wilson said, it's not an investigation.

"We've got a problem here, boss," she calls round the corner. "Looks like there's a man down in there."

DI Wilson is rightly cautious. He would rather handle this than have anyone else involved, especially after the conversations and business he has been discussing with Uncle George. He tries the handle. It's not locked and he is first inside. He's radioed Harris from the car as backup and he orders PC Grace to stand at the front and make sure nobody follows. Wilson will assess the situation before he reports anything to anyone.

He notices Uncle George first, the man has been trying to use the breakfast bar to stand up – that's how he smashed a glass. He's got a yellow plastic bag over his head with his hands tied behind his back. Wilson looks round before he rushes to his aid. Someone has shot big Tony, twice, it looks like. As he approaches Uncle George, his heart skips a beat. This situation could prove fatal for DI Wilson's career. If the big man dies there will be questions asked.

"DI Wilson here, George," he says as he goes to the man. "What the bloody hell's happened?"

"Get this bag off me," calls a muffled Uncle George. Wilson sees the knife block set on the counter and goes for the smallest one. He cuts through the knot at the back of the Dutchman's head and then through the bindings on his wrists. They're tied tight. Once he is free, Uncle George pulls the bag off his head, then gasps and drools from the side of his mouth as his eyes swim back into focus. Plastic bags have holes in the bottom so you can't suffocate in them but it's still not pleasant.

"That klootzak," he whimpers. "He was just here. The bastard was just here."

"Who was?" asks Wilson. Uncle George seems disorientated and so Wilson walks a few steps to see the big figure of Tony laid out on the floor, with his shoulder a bloody mess. The smell of him is rich and sickly. The DI looks back to the door and there is the Scottish policeman DI Harris who has joined them from sitting in the car up front.

"Step in and close the door," says Wilson.

"Who did this?" asks Harris.

Uncle George has come to his senses and leans on the breakfast bar, he bellows out at the two plainclothes coppers: "He's called Dave, they call him Our Dave, and he's got a girl with him too, a black girl. They were just here. They'll still be in the area."

"They armed?" asks Harris.

"Yes."

Wilson swallows. He doesn't need this shite. The last thing a copper like him wants is a crime scene. This is too big to contain, they will have to radio back to base. "We'll have to call this in," says Wilson. "There's a man been killed here."

Uncle George has regained his wits but he is still clearly in pain. "Hold your nerve," he barks. "All you people need to do is find him, and we can sort this out."

Wilson looks to Harris in worry. It would be better if nobody else was involved, there'd be no paperwork and no reports, no suspicion that any of the police here were involved in anything either.

"Did you hear me?" calls Uncle George, his face is still beetroot red from being tied up in a Heron bag. "He'll still be here…you'll have to stop him." Wilson dithers.

The correct procedure would be to radio this in, and if he doesn't do that, he's not sure what to do.

"Let me put it this way," snarls Uncle George, leaning on the breakfast bar with his gold tooth showing through the clenched teeth. "You find that bastard, Our Dave, or you'll get what's coming to him."

Our Dave and Jerusalem are in the back bedroom on the other side of the double bed, crouched down with both of them looking over the flowery, mauve duvet to the closed door. There is no rear entrance to this place.

Our Dave saw that there was a policewoman. He knows what they are like. If this is an investigation there will be more of them stationed at the exits. That's why they haven't made a run for it just yet.

This must be the room Tony is staying in because there's his oversized, smart jacket hung up. Jerusalem has left the sawn-off shotgun under the bed. Our Dave has put the snub-nosed revolver back into the inside pocket of his bomber jacket. He holds his finger up to his mouth to stop Jerusalem speaking but there's no need, he can see from her demeanour that's she's relaxed and quiet already, even though her eyes are on the door as well.

They hear groaning from Uncle George in the kitchen, then a minute later the glass smash, and then the door opening, and footsteps. Then there's the overly loud, dickhead voice of DI Wilson, and then Uncle George as he barks orders.

Our Dave and Jerusalem look at each other. He checks behind at the period sash window, stands up, undoes the catch, and slides it open in silence. Jerusalem moves behind him; they should have done this straight away. There's a sense of calm in these two, as if they have been working together for years.

Our Dave gestures to the window and Jerusalem clambers through first without effort. He struggles a bit more with his aged hips – he was too old for this sort of thing ten years ago. Outside, Jerusalem edges down the side of the building. It's a good job she's shielded by trees so the other residents can't see her creeping to the corner.

At the edge of the building, Jerusalem pops her head around the corner to look at the front door, and there's the big female copper standing with her arms folded. PC Grace is a single mother with two children aged six and nine. Her mother helps with the childcare when she is on a shift for work, but otherwise, it's just her looking after the children – it means she has eyes in the back of her head. She sees Jerusalem's body pop out and go back around the corner. The Ethiopian lass darts back down towards Our Dave. Like she's running after her youngest, PC Grace bellows loud enough for the people inside to hear her:

"Police!" and she gives immediate chase with her hand going to the taser in a holster at her side. When she reaches the corner, PC Grace sees Jerusalem disappearing under the line of trees next to the building at speed. Her finger goes to the trigger, but there isn't a clear shot – it's not a gun and the wires will get caught on the low branches. PC Grace goes after them; her heart is already on fire in her chest.

Jerusalem and Our Dave make a break from the back of

the building. There's a wide path flanked by trees that leads down to a field. Our Dave is not as quick as Jerusalem, but he can still manage a fair rate for an old fella. In the field, it's still set up for the summer weddings. A path leads to an empty white tent with a pulpit in front. This is where people get married outside.

Jerusalem runs down the aisle first and Our Dave follows. She goes through the tent and out into the field behind where there's a fence with an open gate. She stops, then looks back to see Our Dave struggling to keep up. She does not want to lose this man, it's he who came to rescue her after all.

There's the female officer's voice not far behind, shouting the word 'police' at the top of her big lungs. It's getting nearer. Through the gate is the obvious way for them to run, but Our Dave and Jerusalem dash to the right and into the thick undergrowth of the forest behind the wedding ceremony tent. They hope they'll give the chubby copper the slip. Sharp branches nip and scratch at them as they push on through the hedge, their feet trip at the roots below, but this is worth it. The two of them go for another minute until they get to a little path in the forest. Our Dave takes out his phone to see the missed calls from Gaz and Face. There's a message too from Gaz. It reads: '*At Tickton Grange, out the front.*'

Our Dave responds straight away, typing with two thumbs like Bev taught him. He pumps in: '*Drive down the track on the right hand side.*' Our Dave sees the two blue ticks to show that the message has been read and puts the phone away.

He and Jerusalem move quickly along the path between the trees and then out into an open field behind the manor house. They can't hear the policewoman shouting anymore but that does not mean they are out of danger.

"If we cross this field, there's a lane on the other side. Gaz will meet us there."

Jerusalem looks at him with her natural mix of arrogance and mistrust. "You know this place?"

"At my age you know everywhere," he answers.

"Who's Gaz?" she asks.

"A friend of ours."

Gaz puts his phone on the seat next to him and starts the engine by touching the two wires under the steering wheel. They have been parked here a few minutes and he's just got a text from Our Dave. A face appears at his open window. This is DI Harris with his thick beard and piercing, serious eyes. Once PC Grace lost the two suspects in the bush she radioed to him, and like the trained coppers that they are, he returned to his vehicle to check all exits.

Harris noticed a black works van with a red stripe. He noted the men inside – the driver has a nondescript dark suit and a black tie, the passenger's face is scarred. They don't look much like plumbers from Hull. He decided to have a word.

"How can I help?" asks PC Harris. Gaz gives him a sideways glance and hits the accelerator to drive away. Now he's read the text from Our Dave, that's his priority. The tyres on the plumber's van churn up the gravel as it speeds off round the car park and in front of the manor house. There are angry shouts from Harris as they go.

The ginger copper races back to his car, and there standing beside it waiting for him, is Wilson:

"PC Grace is staying with George," he snaps. "She's got her first aid training. Is that vehicle anything to do with this?"

"It must be," says Harris. The van is already driving away round the property and towards the main road. Wilson looks at him over the roof of their black Mondeo. This is exactly the kind of thing that they didn't want to happen. Wilson assured Harris that this was easy money and it would just be a matter of pulling a few strings and making sure Uncle George didn't get bothered by anyone. Neither of them expected murder, or blood, or car chases, and the more extreme this gets, the more trouble these men could face.

"Let's call it in," says Harris in a moment of clarity. "We can radio the station and have them bring back up. A man's been shot for God's sake."

The senior officer shakes his head. He is in this way too deep to get out. "You'll be the one gets shot next, Harris, if we don't get the people who did this," he whispers.

The two jump in their black Mondeo and Harris guns the engine so they burst after the van that has disappeared round the corner in a spray of pebbles. They get around the side of the house just in time to see the black van leave the driveway and head down a side road to the right of Tickton Grange. According to the sat nav picture on the dashboard in front of DI Harris, the road is a dead end. They follow, and the little road is flanked on both sides by bushes and fields of stubble. Harris sees the black van up ahead and slows the Mondeo as they go up the single, country track.

"This has gone too bloody far," whispers Harris to Wilson as he drives. "I'm a police officer. We need to call this in."

"You need to hold your fucking nerve," says Wilson. "This is what policing is these days. It was you who agreed to take the money and it's you who'll stay with it now the going's got a bit rough."

Harris takes a deep breath. He wishes to God he'd never agreed to this. Every second the big Dutch man bleeds out on the floor of that hotel suite behind them, the more trouble he is in.

Wilson snarls in his ear: "You can think about it when you're on holiday in the Caribbean next year." There's something sarcastic in his throaty voice. Harris slows the Mondeo down as he drives into the little lane and then stops – there's no way round him on either side. Wilson opens up the glove compartment and pulls out a black holster. He removes the gun. It's a Glock 17 and standard issue to the British Transport Police.

Harris checks the time. It's ten past three. His shift has

already ended. He looks up to the little road ahead and sees two figures get into the van. Then it begins reversing back down the lane at speed. He grabs the gear stick and puts the Mondeo in reverse.

"Don't you bottle it, Harris," snarls Wilson next to him. The van is two hundred yards away. It's not moving as fast as it could, but it shows no sign of slowing down. "I'll handle this," says Wilson. He gets out of the car and like he's just come out of an eighties police TV show, aims the Glock at the plumbing van as it reverses down the country lane. "They'll shit themselves," he says under his breath.

A hundred yards off, the plumbing van turns and crashes backways through the hedge into the field beside them. The back doors take a battering, but it doesn't stop. Once the vehicle has backed up into the field proper, the driver puts it into first gear and turns it around. The wheels skid on the mud below. It's a slick move.

DI Wilson sees the van struggle to get any real speed over the stubble of the cut wheat. The suspension will probably be knackered after this. Wilson gets a look at the people inside. There's a man in a black suit driving, someone with a face that looks like it's been burned off in the middle, and next to the door, a bald older man wearing a bomber jacket who seems somewhat familiar. Wilson curses under his breath. It's Our Dave. He'll have to have a word with his mother about the company she is keeping. He watches the van bump over the cut wheatfield and at the far corner is an open gate that will lead them out onto the main road. Wilson gets back into the car and slams the door shut. His jaw is tight with anger.

"Back this car up and get after them," he snaps.

CHAPTER FIFTEEN
A chase

It's twenty past three, they are about a mile north of Tickton. Gaz drives the van he stole from a car park in Hull earlier this afternoon, and he is carrying passengers. Face sits in the centre seat and Our Dave is next to him by the door. In the back is Jerusalem. They are driving at speed. It looks like they are being chased by a black Mondeo who, according to Our Dave, is being driven by two coppers.

"You should've got in the back," says Face.

Our Dave has a big frame and he's pushed the lawyer to the middle seat of the van as it rumbles over the tarmac. "I like to be in the front," he says, "Gaz might need some help with the navigation, as well."

"Can you put your belt on?" says Gaz over his shoulder to the dark girl. She keeps putting her face through the headrests so she can look out of the windscreen and see what's going on. She looks at Gaz driving with her big brown eyes and examines his face; she sees the clean collar of his white shirt, the black tie loose at his neck, smells the light aftershave and sees his strong hands on the wheel. There's a sense of togetherness in this man, like Our Dave. Ordinarily, Jerusalem doesn't take orders, especially from someone she has never met before, but she sits back down in the seat in the plumber's van and finds the seatbelt to put over her. The same as with Our Dave, she feels like she's in good hands.

Gaz picked up Our Dave and Jerusalem at the far end of that lane and then reversed back down towards the main road. When he saw the car parked in the way behind, he reversed through the hedge to avoid them. The bumpy surface of the field has affected the wheel alignment on this van. After driving through an open gate, he joined the thin traffic on the A1035 out of Beverley towards Bridlington.

Gaz gets to the fifty speed limit straight away and looks in the rear view mirror to see if they are being pursued. Sure enough, far back into the traffic, is the black Mondeo that tried to block them on the lane next to Tickton Grange. Gaz thinks he can see the beard of the driver.

"We're definitely being followed," he says.

"How did you know I'd be here?" calls Our Dave.

"I phoned Dilva," answers Gaz. "She told me you collected something from Ryan. I guessed what you'd be up to after Face told me what went on."

Our Dave shrinks a little when he hears this. It isn't the first time Gaz has saved his skin. Our Dave is the old man with all the money and the experience and there is Gaz, in his early twenties with nothing at all but his hard work, bailing him out. If Our Dave gets through this, he needs to evaluate himself. Perhaps it really is time to sell up and disappear. It is humbling.

"Well, ta," says Our Dave.

"You get yourself into all sorts of shite," answers Gaz. He glances over at Our Dave and their eyes meet, just briefly. There is something between these two men. Our Dave hoped he could protect Gaz from this kind of world. Turns out it's the other way round.

Gaz looks into the driver's side mirror and sees the black Mondeo overtaking a car behind to get closer. The passenger's arm comes out the window and fits a magnetic red light to the roof. This police siren sounds into the afternoon. Gaz winces. This is not a good situation to be in.

"We'll have to lose them," says Our Dave.

"It's the police," says Face. "You don't lose them. We'll be all over every camera in the East Riding. We should pull over as soon as we can, Gaz, this is only going to get worse if we don't."

"They'll be bent, Face," answers Our Dave. "Why else do you think they were there with that Uncle George? We pull over and we'll end up with a bullet through the back of our heads, all of us." Gaz accelerates and moves to overtake the car in front. The plumbing van rattles as it speeds up.

"He pays the police," calls Jerusalem from behind them. "I heard him on the phone this morning. They were coming over to talk to him about money. You cannot let them catch you." Gaz winces again as he overtakes the next car, and an oncoming silver BMW beeps in anger at him. This is getting worse. He thinks of Kate back on Belvoir Street off Princes Avenue. He does not want a life of criminality, and he is not interested in the money or what it can buy him. He just wants her, and without thinking, he's been dragged into this shite.

"There'll be back up," yells Face, "helicopters, more cars, roadblocks, we're best pulling over."

"They'll be alone if they're bent," says Our Dave. He scans the landscape ahead; they are approaching the little village of Routh on the main road. The traffic is thin, and the landscape is flat and green with fields stretching out either side. Behind, the sound of the siren on top of the black Mondeo wails out into the autumn afternoon.

There's a turn-off to the right that leads onto quieter village roads, and Our Dave thinks this might have been the best way to get rid of the men in the car behind. Gaz is going way too fast to turn, he thinks. Twenty yards in front of the junction, Gaz hits the brake and skids so that the van slides and turns at the same time, with the tyres painting two fat black lines on the pale tarmac as they screech. The drawers full of plumbing equipment rattle in the back. Jerusalem is thrown to the side but held tight by the seat belt. Our Dave is crushed against the passenger door with Face pressed against him. Gaz is going to make that turning after all. This is one of the manoeuvres they learned on the level five security course that he did.

On this thinner track, Gaz accelerates into the countryside. There'll be no cameras out here. In his side mirror he sees the black Mondeo made the turn as well, but with less skill than he did. The van handles well enough round the bends and the twists, they go past a run-down farm, round another corner and then onto a straight single lane road between two fields. Gaz floors it, and the engine roars and complains below.

"Where are you taking him?" calls Our Dave.

"Mappleton. If we don't crash before we get there." Gaz is angry he is in this situation but he will keep it in his chest. It won't do any good to let it get to him, so he grips the wheel, and the van zooms down the little East Riding lane towards the coast. Jerusalem clings onto her seatbelt as they rattle round one corner and then another.

"Left here, then a hard right, Gaz," calls Our Dave. The driver obeys the orders and the van screeches between the hedges as it thunders along the road. Behind, the black Mondeo follows yet with the angry siren on the roof blasting out noise. There are no houses, and precious few cars out here. This is the East Riding of Yorkshire proper.

"You're not going to drive this van off the cliff, are you Gaz?" calls Our Dave. He watches the road in front disappear around a blind corner.

"Not with us inside," replies Gaz. He accelerates hard and takes a sharp right. Through the rear view mirror is that same flashing blue light and siren, and whoever is driving the police car has some skill at this sort of thing. Gaz looks down at the fuel gauge that shows the van is nearly empty – he will have to get this over with quickly.

The Ethiopian girl has the beginnings of a grin on her smooth face. She likes Gaz already and Our Dave too. They're brave, like people should be, and they are prepared to stand up against injustice. Jerusalem has not met anyone with these qualities since she left her father all those years ago. In the back, with the seatbelt tight over her shoulder, she feels at home somehow as Gaz accelerates towards the sea and the plumbing tools and spare parts rattle behind.

The siren calls yet into the autumn afternoon as Gaz takes the van back up to sixty with his left hand on the gear stick and his body hunched over the wheel. The Mondeo moves closer on the single lane track, and Gaz eases off the accelerator as he considers the way – he can use the size of the van to prevent the Mondeo seeing the fork coming up in the lane ahead.

This is Sigglesthorpe Road, just after Little Hatfield, and the corner is too tight to take at any sort of speed. The copper with a beard can't see it coming, so as Gaz turns the van and takes off down the lane, the black Mondeo continues onwards and ploughs into a wooden fence. The crash is loud as the bonnet splinters the post at near enough fifty. The wheels hit the mud and this snaps the front axels and shafts the suspension. The airbags in the front seats go off with a hiss, and the bonnet rises up like a concertina in the impact. This will write the black Mondeo off.

The car comes to a hissing halt and DI Wilson roars into the airbag in anger – it's not just that he's lost the van and Our Dave, it's the shit he will have to go through with Uncle George, then the paperwork for the Mondeo and the web of lies it will force him to spin. He bellows swear words out into the silence of the East Riding field as the van in front roars off into the distance.

Gaz drives up the coast to the lonely car park at Mappleton and they are subdued now the Mondeo is far behind them. Jerusalem looks out at the flat lands and the green fields as they zip by.

Mappleton is a coastal village that has been falling into the North Sea since the nineteen nineties. It's deserted as Gaz drives up to the car park overlooking the cliffs and the beach down below. Just to the right is a bungalow that looks like it's been chopped in half, the front garden and porch have slid off down onto the beach leaving the brickwork exposed and the patterned wallpaper open to the elements. It's like the apocalypse has happened to half of this little village.

Gaz presses the parking brake pedal down and turns off the engine. The silence is eerie after the noise of the chase some twenty minutes earlier.

"Everyone out," he says.

"What now?" asks Face.

"Time to put it off the cliff here," says Our Dave. Gaz nods. Once they are all out and standing in the car park, Gaz uses a rag from the glove box to wipe down the dashboard as well as all the handles on the doors and the steering wheel. He is thorough. Then, he leans in and pulls the lever to release the parking brake and closes the door. The black plumbing van that was parked just off Chants Ave a few hours earlier, begins to move as gravity takes hold. Gaz gives it a push to get it going a little bit faster, and the momentum carries the van rumbling along the grass before it goes over the little cliff edge front ways. It won't blow up; the drop is probably only two hundred yards. There's a crunch as it hits the beach on the other side out of sight.

Gaz puts the rag into his suit jacket pocket and his face is creased with worry. At least the owner of the van will get an insurance pay out in the end, even if it will take ages. Our Dave approaches.

"He'll get a new van on insurance," he says as if he's repeating Gaz's thoughts. "Might take a while, but he won't be out of pocket." They both look across at the North Sea stretching out in front of them; it's flat and vast and in the distance, they can see the white waves dancing against themselves and the sky is a brooding grey. It's a good job the car park is empty.

They're a funny little group these four, standing together at nearly four o'clock on an October afternoon in the deserted village of Mappleton. Jerusalem wears a black Marx HU9 cap over the curls of her afro with jeans and Bev's boots. Gaz is in his black suit with slim fit trousers and his top button is undone underneath the loosened tie. Our Dave puts his hands in his bomber jacket pockets, and Face zips up his thin biking kagoul. They could not be more different. Gaz has his phone in his hands and looks at the time:

"Let's walk," he says. "It's a couple of miles to Hornsea, we can catch a bus from there. The longer it takes us the better."

"I'll give Bev a call, she'll pick us up," says Our Dave.

"Let's not get her involved if we can. People will be looking for us, and it'll be best if we keep off the road for a while. Nobody will expect us to walk and they won't expect us to get the bus either." The older man agrees.

This is Gaz's game now.

There's an old road down to the sand with black tarmac that disintegrates as it gets closer to the beach. It reminds Our Dave of picnics and afternoon strolls with his wife back in the eighties. This is probably the last time he'll walk this way. They begin across the slippery rocks and sand towards Hornsea. The sky darkens and there's a sharp wind from the sea.

Jerusalem walks on first with Face. A little while behind and out of earshot, Our Dave and Gaz stride side by side. They're silent as they walk, and Our Dave realises that he needs to keep this capable man closer to him in the days that will come. The beach brings back memories of Scarborough in 1983. The breeze off the sea is cold.

"I think I knew your old man," says Our Dave. Their feet now crunch on the wet sand below. Gaz looks at him as they walk but does not alter his expression. The sentence is impossible. The young man's brain can't process it.

"Oh aye," he answers. This is the standard response if you think someone is talking a load of shite. Our Dave is not kidding. There's none of the easy humour to his voice or the twinkle in his eyes. Face and Jerusalem are already a good distance away. They won't hear any of this with the wind.

"I knew him a long time ago, Gaz." The younger man lifts

the collars on his black suit jacket towards the cold. "He saved my life back then." Gaz shrugs his shoulders as he walks. He didn't ask for any of this. "I'm not taking the piss, Gaz."

Our Dave stops, and Gaz turns back to him. He examines the expression on the old face, the blue eyes with laughter lines and the well-trimmed white beard.

"We just saved you from getting nicked, or worse even. Whatever you've got to say, now isn't the time, mate."

"I'm sorry Gaz, it's just come to me." It really has. Pieces of the jigsaw that Our Dave could not fit together previously are now joining up. "I knew your old man, Gaz."

"My mam was a working girl, Our Dave. I don't know who my dad was, and you don't neither, and probably she never did. My old man could be any fella in Hull." Gaz does not like to think about this. "Why would you say that?"

"He looked after me, once. He did something for me. He changed the road that I was on a long time ago."

Gaz shakes his head, not in anger, but in light-hearted disbelief. He has come to terms with who he is after all this time. A sentence from an old man about a father he never knew will not rattle him. Not right now anyway. "How can you be so sure he was my dad?"

"He looked like you. He had the same ways as well, he had that sense of security about him, like he knew what to do."

"You've got that," says Gaz.

"I robbed it off him."

"I don't need you to fill my head with a load of bullshit Our Dave, I didn't think you were like that."

The older man steps forwards. The wind from the open and wide North Sea blows fresh along the beach from Hornsea. Our Dave thinks back. "It was a job I did in 1983, my first one. I got an envelope with a picture cut out of a newspaper and a name. I was to go on up to the Grand Hotel at Scarborough and do him in. It was just before Christmas. I was nineteen. There was a skipper there at the bar in the hotel, a Hull trawler skipper from St Andrew's dock. He had a few quid and he was having a drink. We got talking while his girlfriend went and powdered her nose."

"What good is telling me this going to do?" Gaz looks down the beach to see that Jerusalem and Face have got a lot further away.

"I had a man to kill, Gaz. I was nineteen years old with a revolver in my jacket pocket. I'd sneaked into the hotel bar and I was waiting for the bloke. I was going to shoot him when he went to the lav." Our Dave takes his hands out of his bomber jacket pockets. He's not really dressed for a bracing beach walk. "I nearly killed him. It was your old man set me straight. I never got chance to thank him either."

Gaz narrows his eyes yet. "How do you know he was my dad?" he repeats.

"I can't be sure, kid, but when you get to my age, you know things, you start to see patterns. His name was Skipper Bird, a trawler captain off the docks, black hair like you, and the same eyes as well."

Gaz feels his jaw tighten. He does not need this now, not when he's in a better place than he's ever been. "What's the point in telling me this, Dave, now?"

"It only just came to me. I owe him, and I owe you as well, Gaz. I'd be dead back there if it wasn't for you. I'd have died in that house fire off Beverley Road as well a few months back."

"What am I supposed to do with that?"

"I want you out of all this, Gaz. You and Kate, I want you as far away from me and Avenue Cars as you can get." Our Dave's eyes have begun to water. Maybe it's the sea air. "I'll have Face transfer money to your account when we get back, enough for you and Kate to get away somewhere, a holiday maybe, just until all this blows over. I never wanted you in on all this."

"I've got stuff to do back in Hull, so has Kate, she's got

clients and her course at the uni."

"It'll have to wait, Gaz. There'll be a shit storm coming after what happened with that Dutchman back there, and I won't be able to outrun it, neither will you. That's why I'm telling you this."

Gaz looks down the beach to see the figures of Jerusalem and Face, they are waiting further along. "What about those two?"

"Face is neck deep in this with me. He's tougher than he looks as well. The girl: she's built for this sort of thing, and it's for her sake we're here. It was Bev who picked her up and she told me what had happened to her. We're meant to be involved, Gaz. You're not."

"Who says?"

"I say. I owe your old man."

Gaz shakes his head and looks at the sand under his sensible black trainers that you'd never realise have steel toe caps. "I don't know who my old man was, Our Dave, and neither do you. I'm going to forget about what you said, and I don't want your money either, so you can forget about that as well."

"Richard Bird, that was his name, a skipper off St Andrew's Dock. You can find out about him. Ask around."

"You said his name already. I didn't expect this kind of thing from you, Our Dave." He really didn't. Gaz usually trusts the man's instincts, he has good business sense and is fair, he doesn't deal in gossip or drama, and perhaps this is why information from Our Dave is worth listening to. Gaz will take this seriously however much he would rather forget it. He turns away from the older man and begins down the beach towards the other two. His face is dark in the sea breeze.

"He could have been your uncle, or your granddad even," calls Our Dave. It stirs long forgotten emotions in Gaz. This will affect him later when his brain gets to thinking.

Our Dave feels guilty as he looks at the young man

trudging across the sand.

He has played this badly, as he does most things these days. He's gone in too heavy without thinking what he was going to say. Maybe Our Dave is wrong, maybe the man who saved his life all those years back at Scarborough was someone else, maybe his old brain is confused. Like he explained to Gaz already, the patterns he sees in life are beginning to repeat like waves in the ocean; he is starting to see where they are going. It is the benefit of some sort of wisdom.

CHAPTER SIXTEEN
Back to Hull

In Hornsea, Our Dave bought them all a drink in one of the cafés on the seafront. Gaz had a water. Face went for a black coffee. Jerusalem had an ice-cream with a flake, and Our Dave had a cappuccino. They were overpriced, but this is the coast; you're paying for the view, and the fact that the whole town is dead over winter.

After they finished up, they sat in silence waiting for the double decker to Hull in the red bricked bus stop. It took a while. On the top deck of the bus, Face scrolled his phone while they rumbled through the flat East Riding landscape. Jerusalem sat next to Gaz and looked out the front windows. Our Dave sat behind them. He regretted what he said to Gaz on the beach. That's what stress does to him – it makes him talk shite.

They get off the double decker at the bus stop outside the Station pub on Beverley Road and it's just getting dark. They'll walk the old railway line that's now a bike track behind the houses to Pearson Park. It's not far to Chants Ave from there. Next to the old station house and the disused railway platform, Our Dave stops just outside the glare of the streetlight. Usually there are drunks here but the early evening is cold so it's deserted. He wants to have a word with all of them together before they disappear back into their lives. Gaz looks cold, Jerusalem seems despondent, Face has zipped his biking jacket up to his neck.

"We can't go back to the office," says Our Dave. He has not really spoken to the three of them since the chase. "And you can't go back to Bev's house, lass," he says to Jerusalem, "Uncle George will be all over this place now, if he's not already here – same for all of you. It'd be much better if you contacted your family and went somewhere else till all this blows over."

"They've no idea who I am," says Gaz.

"The copper would have seen you."

"For a few seconds."

"Police remember faces, they're trained to do it."

"Maybe in your day," Gaz is overly rude to the man. It's a defence mechanism. What was said on the beach has soured him somewhat.

"I'd sooner you and Kate went off somewhere."

"I'm not a part of this, Our Dave."

"I don't want anything to happen."

"Nothing will, not as long as I'm there and not here." It's not usual to see this simmering anger from Gaz. His face is serious as he stands there in the half darkness.

"Thanks for your help today, Gaz," says Our Dave, "and I'm sorry for what I said before. My blood was up and it was just rubbish, you know how it is. Adrenaline must have got to me."

"It's all ok," says Gaz. He manages to say this as if it means the very opposite. "I'll be on the end of my phone if you need me. I'm gonna go on ahead, if you don't mind." Gaz takes a few steps back into the darkness of the path.

"I'll message you," says Our Dave. Gaz disappears.

"I'll call my lad and tell him to stay with his grandma." This is Face.

"Will that be okay?"

"I guess it'll have to be."

"Where will you go?"

"I've got a friend over in Beverley. I'm meant to be seeing her tonight anyway."

"Don't go home," repeats Our Dave.

Face pulls out his phone and begins to pump something in. "I'll get an Uber to pick me up," he says. It's ironic considering he partially works for a taxi company.

Our Dave looks over to Jerusalem. He'll have to look after her from here on in. "You can't go back and stay with Bev."

The girl shrugs her shoulders as if she doesn't care. "I know a place," adds Our Dave.

This is one of Our Dave's safehouses.

Behind the main building of Richmond Street Garage and squashed up behind St Cuthberts Church on Marlborough Ave, is a long building with a flat roof. It's been many things over the years: it was a ping-pong room in the eighties, then tyre storage for the garage, then a tool shed. After the roof fell in, Barry would have knocked it down but for a lanky gardener affectionately known as Big Steve who transformed the place because he didn't have to pay any rent. Over a period of six months during the COVID lockdown, Steve cleaned it up. He put in a bed and a little cooker, added a toilet and a tiny shower. He even fitted a window on the side and although the view is just the weeds growing behind St Cuthbert's Church, it was at least a place Steve could hang curtains. Big Steve fell in love with an American architect called Robby – they met on Facebook during lockdown, and he moved over to Florida to tend to the gardens of his dreams. The combination to the huge padlock on the door ended up with Our Dave, of course. Steve needed to pay for his airfare to Miami somehow. At the time, Our Dave felt like he was losing the best part of a thousand quid, but it has come in useful in the end. It's right that good people are happy as well.

Our Dave has another safehouse to the east of the city which is bigger but this will do for now. He took a photo of the combination on his phone and Our Dave finds it, then tells the numbers to Jerusalem as she fiddles with the big padlock. Our Dave goes in first, he puts the lights on. There's a single bed against one wall and a couch against the other. It's dusty but clean apart from that. At the little sink, he gets two mugs out of the cupboard. He rummages around in another and brings out a kettle which he fills. Jerusalem stands behind him.

"Uncle George will find us," she says. "He'll want me, but he'll kill you. What will you do?"

Our Dave plugs the kettle in and switches it on without looking at her. "I missed my chance," he says. "I should have put him to sleep back in that hotel." He makes it sound like he forgot to pick up something from the DIY shop.

"He will be organised straight away," says Jerusalem. "He will be looking for us as we speak."

Our Dave goes back to the cupboard to search for teabags while the kettle rumbles. "It's not Holland, he won't have the contacts he's used to over here."

"He has money, that will help." Jerusalem stares at the back of his head as he's looking into the cupboard. "You should be running," she says. "He will kill you, and he'll do the same to the people you love as well."

Our Dave has found a box of tea bags. "This is my home, lass," he says. "I know my way round here better than he does, and I've still got a few friends left."

"Just who are you?" asks Jerusalem.

Our Dave considers this but he doesn't turn to look at her. "An old fella who runs a taxi office."

"Why did you come for me?"

"I didn't do it for you. I did it for Bev. Uncle George threatened me as well. I was trying to shut him down."

"You could have killed him there. Why didn't you?"

"Bodies are hard to move when they're dead. Better to let them walk where you want, then do what you have to do."

"Are you an expert?"

Our Dave opens the box of tea and adds a bag to each of the mugs. He wants the normality of it to offset what they are discussing. "An expert at what?"

"Killing people."

"I've done it before. Only because I had to," says Our Dave down into the mugs.

"That's just what Uncle George would say as well. If I get

close to him again, I will kill him myself." Our Dave lifts the handle of the kettle.

"Let me do it, lass," he whispers. "That kind of thing changes you, and not in a good way." He fills both mugs with water and sets the kettle down, then turns to face Jerusalem.

"I will have my revenge," she says and her teeth are clenched under her smooth lips. "He poisoned me. He poisons women. I will snuff him out like a match flame." Jerusalem does not know why she is telling this man. Perhaps she is afraid. There's the smell of the mould from the damp walls and fresh tea brewing in the mugs.

"So, why didn't you kill him already, you had the chance?" asks Our Dave.

"Fear." Jerusalem has clearly thought about this. On the long bus ride back from Hornsea that very afternoon, she had the time to organise her thoughts. "I could not have done it before. I needed someone to show me how it could be done, someone cold and without feelings. I watched you shoot Tony today, like he was nothing…like meat hanging from a hook. Now I see how it is done. There's no joy to it, or fear either, it is just work." Our Dave does not like this side of him, and he can see the murderer reflected back in this angry young woman. He does not want to create another monster like he has been at times in the past.

"I'll kill him when the time comes. I'm already ruined, lass, and there's no reason for you to be as well. If there's fighting to be done, you'll leave that to me. Do you understand?" She does not agree or disagree, and her brave brown eyes blink back at Our Dave with a mixture of confidence and curiosity.

"I'm not afraid anymore, if that's what you think." Our Dave passes her a mug of tea and she takes it by the handle.

"You're shitting yourself," says the older man. "You might as well be honest. It's much easier in the long run, I should know." He gives her a smile.

"Is it funny to you?" she asks.

"It's how we deal with the world around here. We take the piss out of it. It makes the shadows less dark. You should try it. What's your name again, lass?"

"I am Jerusalem."

"Jerusalem," he repeats. "For Bev's sake. I just want this all sorted out."

"Once Uncle George is dead, I'll be gone." He's not used to this earnest attitude in anyone, it's all epic and final.

"I don't think Bev will want you to disappear. We'll stay here tonight and then tomorrow, we move again. I'll get help. I know people. You stay with me and it will all be okay. You'll be safe." He nods to the bed. "Sit yourself down."

He watches her take the mug and go over to the single mattress in the semi darkness of the converted garage. She is not much more than a child.

"Who was the first man that you killed?" she asks in the dim light. It's late. Our Dave lays on the couch and Jerusalem has the single bed. A lamp on the floor gives the one long room an eerie feel, and there's the rattling of the wind through the corrugated iron roof above.

"I don't remember the first person," he answers. He does. Jerusalem seems to know the darker side of Our Dave already.

"Why did you kill him?"

"I had to."

"Why?"

"If I didn't, one of mine would have been killed instead."

"How did you do it?"

"You ask Uncle George these questions, did you?"

"Yes."

"What did he say?"

"He laughed. He said he never killed anyone."

"He's smarter than me, then." Our Dave looks across from the couch at the young woman on the bed opposite. "You've got a lot of growing up to do, lass. Wait till your head starts to sort itself out, it's called the prefrontal cortex and once it sets by the time you're twenty-four or five, you'll start to figure out what's a good idea and what's not." Our Dave saw this on one of those short videos on social media. Really, he just wants to tell her to wait before she does anything stupid – like try to kill someone.

Our Dave lays back on the sofa and looks up to the ceiling planks that Big Steve fitted out so carefully a few summers ago. He can sense that the girl is looking up at them as well.

"Have you got a plan?" she asks.

"Of course," answers Our Dave.

"Are you afraid?"

"Not for me."

"Really?"

"I'm too old to be scared for myself anymore."

"What's your plan?" she asks.

"It won't work if I tell you."

"Is it because you don't trust me?"

"Not really," says Our Dave. "You did well with that gun today. I hoped you would. I won't tell you because I'm not sure myself how it will play out, and if I explain it to you, it'll seem stupid, then it'll seem stupid to me."

"You're not like other men," says Jerusalem. It's not really a compliment, more an observation.

"How so?"

"You treat everyone like they're your friend."

"They are."

"You sure?"

"I can't be sure, but everyone is my friend until they piss me off. We're all equal at the end of the day. We're all going to die and we all wipe our arses the same way." This is an old expression for Our Dave but a new one for Jerusalem. She's not used to the humour mixed into the serious nature of the conversation; it throws her somewhat.

"People in my country do not wipe their arses like

Europeans." Our Dave does not like to ask. "Those who are powerful speak down to their lessers."

"Then they're not powerful," answers Our Dave. Jerusalem likes this. It's something her father would say.

"When you killed that first man, how did it feel?"

Our Dave thinks back to the beach all those years ago, to the winter sky above and the wind whipping in off the North Sea. "The killing was the easy bit," he whispers. There's no point in lying to her. "It was all the things around it that were hard. It was the dreams afterwards, seeing shadows move out the corner of your eyes, hearing someone knocking at the door when there's nobody there. It doesn't leave you. You just get used to it. That's what I mean about Uncle George, lass. You leave him to me."

"Is that part of your plan?" she asks.

"Something like that."

"You're going to kill him, aren't you?"

"Well, I'd prefer to get someone else to pull the trigger, but not you."

The wind outside the little garage has picked up and the corrugated iron sheets pinned to the roof rattle against it. The big trees creak at the back of the church next door and far off in the distance, there's the booming thud of the dance music from the fair.

"You best get some sleep, lass," says Our Dave. "What I mean by that is, don't talk to me till tomorrow." It's best to be straight with her. Dilva taught him to be direct with those who don't speak English as their mother tongue.

"Goodnight," she says and he hears the bed creak as she rolls over.

Our Dave takes out his phone and the screen lights up his face. He feels for his glasses in his trouser pockets as he lays there on the couch and puts them on. He scrolls to contacts.

There is someone he needs to message if all this is going to go as it should tomorrow.

CHAPTER SEVENTEEN
A visit for Gaz

Downstairs in the living room, DI Wilson looks through the conservatory window at the River Humber. The sun peeps out from behind the clouds in the mid-morning, and the horizon is a blaze of golden light across the water. On late afternoons like this, with the heat through the windows at the back of his new build on Victoria Dock, it's as if you're in the south of France or the Caribbean. He's having a scotch in one of the cut glass whisky tumblers that he bought after the divorce went through – a sign that he could finally do what he liked without any of those comments from his little ex-wife. He takes a sip through thin lips. He shouldn't be drinking in the morning and however nice the setting, DI Wilson is in serious trouble. This has all gone too far. Harris is back at the station, PC Grace is on leave until next week with strict orders to keep her mouth shut, and Wilson is more nervous than he has ever been before.

After they crashed into the field yesterday afternoon, he called in an old favour from a retired officer he used to work with. It was expensive, but the man arranged for the vehicle to be towed and took Harris and he back to Tickton and to Uncle George. The Dutchman was already on top of the situation. He has connections with people in Leeds and they were on their way. Big Tony was not quite dead, but he'd made a right bastard mess of the off-white floor tiles.

DI Harris and a pale looking PC Grace got a lift back to the station with his old mate. Wilson was all for leaving Uncle George to sort the problems himself, but that wasn't what the Dutchman had in mind. George ordered him to sit tight until the men from Leeds turned up. They're called cleaners and are the opposite of the forensic teams Humberside Police use when investigating any crime these days. There were three of them in a battered Ford Transit van with rust on the wheel arches and hub caps – it didn't take too long for them to race down the M62. They were professional but dressed like mucky workmen in blue overalls and old hoodies with paint stains on their boots and dirty hands. There was no small talk as they got busy with the job they were paid for.

Tony had already lost too much blood and was too far gone to do anything with. There'd also be questions if they took him to a hospital. This could all be avoided if they let nature take its course. They bent his body double and put it in a big folding suitcase on wheels then took him out to the van. The three of them attended to the mess with all sorts of bottles and sprays and a fabric cleaner for the blood splats on the curtains. Uncle George talked on the phone in Dutch while they worked and it reminded Wilson of when he was first a uniformed copper, and how the older officers would treat him with disdain – like he wasn't there almost. It was as if he was a necessary annoyance.

It took an hour to get rid of all trace of Big Tony, and then Wilson was given the job of driving Uncle George himself in that big Land Rover they hired. The Dutchman wanted somewhere safe and quiet to go, a suburban setting perhaps, without the complications of hotel staff and the like. After the attack, Uncle George was back to his affable and level-headed self. On the drive back to Hull, he probed Wilson about policing and his personal life. He found out about the divorce and that Wilson kept the house in the settlement. It all sounded perfect and so, that's where Uncle George is now after he spent the night. He is upstairs in Wilson's house overlooking the River Humber taking a long shower, and no doubt using the posh towels that Wilson bought himself after his wife left.

Wilson sips his drink. It has definitely gone too far, but he cannot wriggle out without getting into trouble. He hears the stairs creaking and Uncle George enters the room wearing fresh clothes that look much the same as the ones he was wearing before. They are brown slacks and a black polo-shirt.

"That feels better," he says as he walks past Wilson at the window and sits down on the blue corduroy couch. George begins to put socks on his bare feet with Wilson looking at him over the rim of his whisky tumbler.

"This is far from ideal," says Wilson.

"Yes, I know but we'll get it sorted, you'll see. My friends over in Leeds are sending some of their people. We'll find this Dave character and it will be done and finished. I'll go home with the African girl and we'll have a little business plan in place."

"I mean me being involved like this. It wasn't part of the deal." Standing here in the house where he bullied his little wife gives Wilson more courage than he might otherwise have. Uncle George is not offended by this at all. He offers advice like he might do a brother or an old friend:

"It's become part of the deal now, friend. You should know better than to go too close to the fire, you might end up getting burned."

"Even so, I could lose my job."

"Yes, you really could. You could also get shot in the back of the head and left face down in the river here." There's a jovial quality to Uncle George somehow. You can't operate a business as large as he does without humour. "Could you make me a cup of black tea, Officer?" he asks. "I have to make a few calls, and as soon as my visitors from Leeds arrive, we'll get started."

Wilson does not quite know what to say. He walks through the living area towards the kitchen. At the doorway he stops and turns back. "I won't be coming with you to look for this Dave character," he calls over his shoulder, "I've done enough and more for the fee, so have my people."

"I didn't think about that." says Uncle George, "I mean you'd be the perfect person to come with us, you've worked in this city for years. Thanks for the offer. Oh, and don't leave the tea bag in for too long, I don't want it too strong and no milk. I'm not English."

Wilson better stop acting like he is some sort of big fish. He is the little man in this situation.

Uncle George spends half an hour at least on the phone sitting on the corduroy couch. He speaks loud Dutch and laughs a great deal. As he yaps, Wilson notices that the man has taken off his socks and is fiddling with his feet and toenails with his fingers. He leaves the bits he picks off on the clear glass table next to his teacup. Wilson feels some of the disgust his ex-wife may have felt for him.

When he's finished on the phone, Uncle George grills Wilson about the people in the van that he followed earlier. He wants as much detail as he can get, and because Wilson is a copper, and he notices things, he explains about the men who were in the vehicle. Apart from Jerusalem, there was Our Dave and Face who Uncle George is familiar with already. DI Wilson is keen not to say just how much he knows Our Dave, or the fact that he has met him and he goes out with his mother – there are so many ways that this situation could get even more sticky than it is. Wilson does not want his mother involved at all. When this is done, he will have to personally approve any of her boyfriends, indeed, he's angry that his policing experience did not allow him to assess Our Dave correctly at the first meeting.

The van driver is not familiar to Wilson, but he makes a phone call to the station and asks a few questions. It doesn't take him very long to get a name. Like all good coppers, he searches for 'Gaz Lockwood' on social media first – there isn't that much but he finds a picture of the same man who was driving the black van that afternoon. He has his arm around a pretty, blonde-haired girl outside a terraced house. Wilson narrows his eyes at the style of the little front garden, he knows this road, it's Belvoir Street. He can see the number on the front door. It reads 56.

The men from Leeds arrive within the hour. They are humourless professionals, probably ex-forces. There are three of them with wide shoulders and casual jackets, they have short, cropped hair and Adidas Samba type trainers so they could be any bloke in a northern pub. One of them has a parka-style jacket and bright Turkey teeth. George invites them into Wilson's kitchen where the copper makes coffees for them as the Dutchman explains his plans.

They are going to pay this man who calls himself Our Dave a visit and show him how they do things in Amsterdam. The three men from Leeds will exact his wishes now that Big Tony is no longer with them. It's businesslike, and it strikes Wilson that it's very much the same as the briefings they have before they do police operations. The irony is not lost on him.

Gaz taps on the door and stands back down the path to wait for an answer. This is East Hull, Lee Street, half a mile away from East Park and the houses are squeezed next to each other like the cars parked along both sides of the road. It's just after two in the afternoon. He had a sleepless night thinking about what Our Dave told him.

The door opens to a chubby older man with unkept black hair and a beard. His blue eyes twinkle but he is out of shape. Gaz found him on social media yesterday evening, and they talked about the man who Our Dave explained might be Gaz's father. The chubby bloke gives him a grin and motions his head for Gaz to step inside. His name is John Bird and he's a friendly sort.

Gaz follows him through the tidy front room and into the dining area where there's an open photo album on the table. There's the smell of bleach from the kitchen and children's toys are piled up in the corner neatly. The man smiles at Gaz and they stand in awkward silence looking at each other in the bright light from the bulb above.

"The wife and little ones are at the park," says John Bird.

"Maybe I shouldn't have come," says Gaz. "I don't want to cause any trouble."

"You look like he did, anyway," says the man. Gaz's stomach turns over. John is in his fifties now, but son to the man who Our Dave said was Gaz's father, a trawler skipper from Hessle Road way. Neither of these two knows what to say.

"I don't have any proof, and to be honest I don't know why I'm here," says Gaz. John nods. They spoke at length online and it was John who invited Gaz over to the house here on Lee Street.

"Just so as you know," says John, "there's no money. He died a long while back and he was skint by that time. If you're looking for gold, there's nothing here. Who was your mum?"

"A woman off Beverley Road, a working lass." This is a polite way of saying she was a prostitute. John Bird gives a half frown as if this is not an unusual thing for him to hear. "He put himself about a bit when he was older. I was in my twenties by then, and he'd split up with my mum. He drank a bit too. He had a way with girls, did my old man, he made them all feel like he was going to take them off somewhere. He was a good lad really, mixed up in the end though."

"No need to defend a man who I never knew," says Gaz. "He never defended me."

"He wouldn't have known," says John Bird.

Gaz's stomach tightens at this. The security of knowing your own father is a luxury most do not appreciate, for Gaz, this is cataclysmic somehow. He goes back to his old training to fight his feelings, but there's pressure on his chest. His face registers no change of emotion at all. "Who's to say he's my old man even, just Our Dave."

John Bird hears this. His father changed in his mid-fifties. Once he'd lost his skipper's ticket, he couldn't earn like he did. He left John's mother and set about pretending he was young again. John is not surprised this earnest young man has appeared. In the bright light of the dining room bulb, he is the image of Richard Bird, the dark-haired skipper that John knew and loved all those years ago.

"I got the photo album out," he says as he points to the dining room table. "I thought you might want to have a look, if you like." Gaz licks his lips in worry. He's got this far. He did not mention anything to Kate about what Our Dave said or the conversations he had with this man on social media. Like Gaz knows best, he keeps it all to himself. It's how he feels safe.

John Bird steps over to the photo album and opens it up. Gaz moves next to him. "He was a skipper in the seventies," says John. There's a black and white picture of a dark-haired man with a barge cap and sideburns. He's smiling and standing on the deck of a trawler next to a row of other sailors. "He sailed out of St Andrew's Dock. My mother said he promised to give it up when I was born, but it was all he knew." On the next page, the same man is leaning on a black car with a big grin on his face. In this picture he has a moustache and his dark hair is swept over in the style of the day. Gaz peers at the warm colours of his jacket. The black muscle car behind him is familiar somehow with its big front bonnet and low roof. Gaz's eyes move over the body work and to the number plate on the front, he reads the registration, B500 ELA. He draws in breath. It is his car. It's the Capri that he drove into the Humber some six months ago. It is Ela.

This man is his father.

Gaz's hand goes over his eyes to mask the shame of his tears. "I've made a mistake," he says to John Bird. "I've made a mistake coming here." He moves back into the living room and his eyes are watering through his fingers. Like lots of men from this city, Gaz sees emotion as weakness, he should be strong enough not to care. His stomach knots up, he has begun to sweat, he is not trained for this.

"Don't you want to have a proper look at the photos?" asks John Bird after him. Gaz shakes his head.

This man was his father. The one he has thought about since he was a little boy. A ghost made real in a faded picture in a photo album. The car that Gaz drove into the River Humber belonged to his father before it belonged to him. Now Gaz understands the magic of her – there was the engine that wouldn't start for anyone else, the way the steering wheel felt familiar in his hands and the low slung driver seat where he could see everything through the windscreen.

"I've made a mistake," says Gaz again. His first instinct is to leave.

"I can see it's a shock to you." John Bird follows Gaz as the younger man moves through the well-kept living room to the front door. "You can come back anytime, you know." Gaz manages to get himself to the hall and puts his hand on the front door to open it up. "He was a good man, you know, Gaz. If he'd known about you, and you were his, he wouldn't have just left you, you should know that." Gaz cannot turn round as he steps out the front door onto Lee Street and begins to stride away. He hears John Bird call to him as he hurries off: "You can come back anytime."

Gaz makes it back to the van that he has borrowed from Our Dave, the one that he is going to use as a taxi for airport pickups. He gets in and closes the door then puts his face into his hands, bends as close as he can to his legs so nobody will see, and weeps.

Your father is no big deal if you know him already – then he can be an arsehole, or a saint, or just a dull working man. This is not so for Gaz. He used to tell himself stories about who the man might be, an airline pilot or a professor, a rugby player, or a businessman. Deep down, Gaz knew his father was a sleazy nobody who went with whores. The tears come. He has held them back for so long that they will not stop. Until Kate, Gaz was a ghost himself, disconnected from history and place somehow. This knowledge shifts him. His father was a skipper, he was someone, Gaz has a half-brother too. He heard John Bird say that his father wouldn't have left Gaz if he had known about him.

There's a tap on the van window.

Gaz sits up to see a woman's face. She's middle-aged with a beanie hat and a red nose. He doesn't know her.

"You alright, love?" she asks through the window. This is East Hull – you can't sit and cry in a car without someone asking if you are okay. Gaz composes himself in the instant.

"I'm fine," he answers, "I just had some news."

She looks at him and her eyes are worried. Perhaps she had some news too, once upon a time. Her cockerpoo pulls on the lead in her hand, and her face is concerned. "Have you got somewhere to go?" she asks.

Gaz answers quickly. "I've got somewhere," he says, "I've got someone." The woman looks at him through the glass of the van and the words seem true to her.

"You'll be alright, love," she says. She hopes this is true. The cockerpoo pulls her away and she goes off down the street towards Holderness Road. Gaz takes a big breath in and composes himself. He may have been a lost soul once upon a time, but not so anymore – he has found someone and they are lost together. He dries his eyes on his palms and starts the engine. He needs to be at home. He needs her.

Gaz drives the van away from Holderness Road through backstreets past Garden Village and the steel pipework of the cocoa factory on the big roundabout. His guts gurgle under him. If he had known he had a father all those years ago, he wonders how different he would be now. Gaz waits at the lights on Beverley Road and the van engine ticks. He does not quite know what to think

In Belvoir Street, he takes the first parking space he sees. It'll be a minute walk to their house but this is the closest he will get on these terraced roads. His mind spins. As he drove back, he decided that he would tell Kate all about it, but now he thinks the words would spill from his mouth all jumbled and wrong. He will keep it to himself until it comes out. She will understand.

At the little path to their house, Gaz glances in through the front window and the curtains are open inside. He can see the shape of Kate sitting right on the edge of the armchair seat next to the fireplace. Her arms are folded and her legs are together. He can't quite make out her expression, but it is not at all normal. Gaz looks at his watch before he goes to the door, it is three o'clock. She has patients she should be speaking to upstairs online. He cocks his head. Kate does not miss appointments.

He steps closer to the window and angles his head so he can peer in through the glass just beyond the curtains. There's a figure with broad shoulders, dressed in a parka jacket, standing in the dining room. The autumn sunshine outlines the darkness of his shape. He has his hands crossed in front of him and is motionless. Gaz dips out the way unseen.

His blood freezes.

This is all to do with Our Dave. The old man did tell him not to go home yesterday.

Gaz grits his teeth in rage but the anger is silent. He grasps the door handle and pushes it down softly as he turns the key. He will play this as he is expected to do, only, Gaz has done this kind of thing before – more than a few times.

He unlocks the front door and goes down the little hall with his feet squeaking on the floorboards as he walks to the open archway into the front room. There's Kate sitting on the edge of the armchair seat next to the fireplace. Her arms are folded on her lap and her eyes are wide under her blonde hair. Gaz's face is without emotion. He knows who's round the corner.

"What's wrong?" he asks. His voice is flat.

"There's someone here," she says.

"Nothing to worry about," comes a voice from the dining room. "I've just come to make sure you're ok." The voice is Mockney, but cleaned up to make it sound more respectable. It's not at all the kind of accent you'd hear round here. Gaz steps through the door and sees the man. He's more than six foot tall and wearing a parka jacket, light blue jeans and Adidas trainers.

"Just sit yourself down," continues the man. "I'm waiting for a call from a friend of mine and then I'll be on my way." Gaz turns to face him. The man has perfect, false white teeth. He could be a model in a shopping catalogue with his chiselled jaw and fade haircut. This is Gaz's house. He feels level and smooth rage building within him.

The man's voice is calm. "There's nothing to worry about," he repeats. "Have a seat. Just don't go doing anything stupid. That way, nobody has to get hurt." It's this last line that is telling. Someone is more than likely going to get hurt.

"You work for the police, do you?" asks Gaz.

The man shakes his head. "I'm just here as security, if you like. Now, take a seat, please, and once I get the call from my colleague, I'll leave you in peace."

Gaz is sick of it. Not this man in himself. He's sick of not knowing what to expect. At least when he had nobody and worked nightclub doors, life was reassuringly monotonous. Ever since he got mixed up with Our Dave, surprises jump out the darkness at him, and he absolutely cannot let this continue. Gaz does not want to look after the whole of Chants Ave like Our Dave. He doesn't need the validation of women like Face. He is not lost like Bev is. He has something here that he will fight for, and when this is done, he and Kate will get out of this town and these streets that hide the skeletons of their past. There's not a moment to lose.

Gaz springs forward. The man with false Turkey teeth is quick to move back like a good fighter should, but he is not fully aware of the facts. He doesn't know who he is up against. He's been told to stand guard over the residents at this property, and if need be, in the next hour or so, Uncle George will call him and explain what to do to them. Like the soldier he once was, this six foot two man originally from Luton will follow orders, and he will not question them, or feel bad about them even. He's paid to be an instrument only.

He steps back as Gaz roars up at him with a wild right hook. Maybe he should have drawn the pistol he has in the pocket of his green jacket already – the woman seemed so nice he didn't want to. As he steps out of range of Gaz's fist, he realises that the man is running at him.

It's the speed that Gaz hopes will throw him off guard. He crashes into the man and they tumble through into the kitchen. Gaz lands on top of him. The surprise attack has worked and he brings his open palm to strike straight down on the man's chin so the back of his head cracks on the white tiles. Gaz goes at him with strikes to the face and nose, he feels the Turkey teeth break under the cheek, but he does not stop. However cruel this is, he cannot afford to get it wrong, not while Kate is in danger. Gaz's knuckles split and he feels himself yelling at the man on the floor below him as he works. Coming in a loud, strong voice from behind him, he hears Kate shouting:

"Don't kill him, Gaz, for God's sake don't kill him." She is right. Gaz stops but does not pause. He unzips the parka jacket as the man groans, finds a wallet in the inside pocket and a phone and tosses these behind him. The man is starting to come round.

Gaz has to get it over with as soon as possible. When he's done, he will see Our Dave and then finish this once and for all. Gaz has made up his mind as he turns the body face down tight against the tiles. He pulls the parka jacket off the man and hears the gun rattling in one of the pockets. He fishes this out and throws it into the kitchen corner. The white tiles are slippery with the man's blood. Gaz works quickly, he wraps one of the sleeves around his neck and yanks him up and towards the back door. The other sleeve goes around his right arm and Gaz ties them tight together.

The backdoor opens outwards into the little garden. There's a square lawn with a rusty swing before a long red bricked garage. Gaz pushes the man forward and he stumbles down the little path, falling onto his knees and face. Gaz glances up to see if any of the neighbours are at their windows, they'll most likely be at work at this time. He turns back to the man and boots up into his balls in the space between his legs – there's a groan. This man brought a gun into Gaz's house. Make no mistake, whatever this thug said would happen, he was here to do something unpleasant to Gaz and Kate, so all this, the way Gaz scuffs his face along the brick of the garage wall, the way he drives his head into a wheelie bin in the ten foot when they've got through the back gate – all this is part of the job he agreed to do. The man from Luton with his broken Turkey teeth is lucky that he has not been killed.

Gaz drags his body across the ten-foot alley and sits him on a sofa that the neighbours left outside for the council to collect months ago. It's swollen with rain and rotten with mould. The man's bloody face lolls backwards. Gaz leans in.

"I've got the gun, your phone and your wallet. Come and find me again when you get better, and I'll finish this job." This is intended to make sure the man does not return. He stands back and looks at the mess he's made. Gaz won't do this again, not to anyone.

He looks up and down the ten foot and it's quiet in the late autumn sunshine. The police or an ambulance will pick him up eventually, there are all sorts of battered and drunk folk down these streets – he could be from the homeless shelter down Princes Ave, he could be a spice head or a heroin addict from town.

Gaz closes the gate behind him and walks back down the garden towards the house. Kate is standing at the back door with her hand over her stomach. Her face is a mess of tears.

"We're not staying here," says Gaz as he approaches her.

"This is our home, Gaz."

He shakes his head. "Our home is with each other," he says. "It's Our Dave. I'm going to get out from under him once and for all, and then we're off."

"Where?"

"Somewhere new. I have money. Something like this is going to keep happening over and over. Do you see?"

She nods. It's not natural for Gaz to hug someone when he is upset, he feels like he should hold everything inside, but Kate has trained him and he leans into her. They embrace.

"Go to Viki down the street," he says into her blonde hair without letting her go. "Tell her you need a cup of tea and a chat. When I'm done, I'll pick you up, and we'll be gone."

"What about all our stuff?" she whispers.

"It's just stuff."

"You won't do anything stupid, will you, Gaz?"

"Not anymore."

She can hear his voice waver as he speaks. This is all too quick for her to process. The man at the door, the fight that Gaz had in the kitchen with him, the fact that he says they are leaving, but Kate trusts him. He puts his hand on her stomach where the baby will be growing.

"I'll go to Viki, and I'll be ready," she whispers.

HULL FAIR SIX

It's the last night of the fair.

The showmen are tired of these long days and endless punters. The cold gets into your bones when you stand outside all night, and fingerless gloves don't stop your hands freezing either. The owners of the rides have made a packet already, but they'll see the workers get their share as well, when it's all done.

The crowds still come on this last spin. It's the elderly man and wife from the North Hull Estate having a look round like they always do. It's the gang of young Kurdish lads –first generation here and more Hull than they are Middle Eastern. There's Diane who teaches yoga – she's here with her daughter to take pictures that help with the acrylic paintings she does. Red Faced Glen has been nagged all week, and he is with his mousey looking wife and twin girls. Carl Parker and his seventeen-year-old son Paul are here together because his wife wants them to bond – they walked through the graveyard on Spring Bank West and shared a spliff on the way. Carl says it makes the lights of the fair seem brighter. Paul agrees.

This time tomorrow, more than three quarters of it will be gone. The helter-skelter will be back in pieces on the side of a truck. All the soft toys on the hook-a-duck stall will be packed into boxes ready for the next fairground. They'll pour all the chip oil down the drain from the chip vans.

Walton Street Car Park will be swept clean and there'll be a cherry picker crane dismantling the big wheel. The chaos and the lights, the booming music and the hordes of people will all disappear. Mrs Turner who lives one street away on Anlaby Road will be able to let her cat out again. The nurses on the night shift at the Hull Royal Infirmary won't be able to look out of the eleventh-floor windows at the lights and wish they were there. Mr and Mrs Parkinson will move back from his sister's poky house in East Hull.

Until next year then.

Like a match bursting into life and fizzling out, this is Hull Fair, over and done within eight days.

CHAPTER EIGHTEEN
Mally Kemp

This is the Halfway House on Spring Bank West over the railway tracks and only two minutes' walk from the fair. It's a whitewashed building with a union jack flag behind the bar and cheap deals on lager. Ordinarily it does steady business but, like the Kingfisher chip shop a few doors down on the corner of Pulman Street, when the fair's in town, there's a small fortune to be made. This year, they've decided to let fair goers use the car park at the back for eight quid, and the landlord has set up a food stall just outside the front door selling sausage rolls, pies and chips that have been cooked in the kitchen. Punters come in for a pint before they go round the fair and inside it's busier than any Friday night of the whole year. They go through more beer in a week than they do in three months.

With their backs against the far wall and sitting next to each other are Jerusalem and Our Dave. This isn't a racist pub but people keep looking at her, and she just stares back as she chews her gum. Our Dave has bought her a water and he's having a half of bitter. They look out of place, especially since they aren't speaking to each other and Our Dave has his eyes fixed on the door.

"You keep staring at people like that," he says, "and you'll get us into trouble."

"They're staring at me," she whispers without taking her eyes off a man with a fat face and a bald head at the bar.

"Well, we're here on business, so I don't want you to start anything."

She holds the fat man's stare. "You're not my father," she whispers back. She's an angry one is Jerusalem. It's in her spirit.

"It's me who's going to get you out of this shite, lass." She turns to look at Our Dave. He has kind eyes. "You start any trouble in here and everything I've tried to sort out will fall through."

Jerusalem focuses on Our Dave and her brown eyes examine him with his well-kept teeth and close cropped silvery moustache and beard. "It would help if you told me what you've got planned. Who are we waiting for?"

Our Dave looks towards the door, and coming through the crowded pub is a small man with a bald head and red braces over a thick black jumper. This is the leader of the showman's guild here at Hull Fair, it is Mally Kemp, and he is on unfamiliar territory at the Halfway House even though it's just a couple of minutes' walk. He wouldn't have come if it wasn't important.

"He's already here," says Our Dave as he stands up. He holds out a hand and the smaller man shakes with a firm grip. They are friends. Mally sits down on one of the stools opposite and glances at the African woman sitting next to Our Dave.

"You've got married again, have you, Our Dave?" The tone is friendly but the man in braces does not smile. He is strangely out of place here in a Hull pub right next to the fairground that he is responsible for.

"This is Mally," says Our Dave to Jerusalem by way of introduction. "We've been friends a while," by this he means many years. Jerusalem does not respond as she takes in the man sitting in front of her on a stool. He has a sense of steel about him. Her stomach tells her something is wrong. "I won't be getting married again, Mally. Hazel died two years back. I've been on my own since. This is a friend of mine."

The man doesn't take his eyes off Jerusalem. "Sorry to hear that, Our Dave, son. You'll be as free as a bird these days then." There's a sense of musical humour to his voice but still no smile.

"I'm still tied to the business, Mally, just like you're still tied to the fair here." He turns to Our Dave and finally smiles. He has teeth that are yellowing with age, but not yet blackened.

"What have you brought me here for, Our Dave?" he asks. "I mean it's been a few years, and it's always good to see a fellow traveller and the like, but I'm a busy man."

"I heard you're looking for someone who attacked one of yours."

Mally's face drops when he hears this. "Tell me more."

"Someone robbed one of the rides and attacked some of your lads."

"The coppers got him, Our Dave."

"I heard the lad who works on the mega spin ride got paid a grand to take the rap. I also heard that whoever really did it is still out and about. Are you still looking for them?"

Mally rubs the stubble on his face. He wonders just how Our Dave gets to know information like this. He must have his ears very close to the ground. "As it happens, I am still looking, aye."

"Well, here she is." Mally looks to Jerusalem sitting next to Our Dave with her high cheekbones and her curly afro hair tight under a black Marx HU9 cap.

"What do you mean?" asks Mally.

"This is the person who attacked your showmen." Mally cocks his head. "I'm here to sort this out," says Our Dave, he keeps the same smooth tone of voice. Jerusalem on the other hand feels her heart jump in her chest. She glances at Our Dave in worry. She felt safe with him.

Mally's lips are a thin line across his wrinkled face against the busy pub behind him. There's the loud chatter of drinking men and the sound of the football on the screen next to the bar though nobody is watching. Mally would not be here if he did not know and trust Our Dave.

"I'm not joking, Mally. This is the lass who did it." Our Dave's voice is level. He nods to a figure making his way through a family group standing in the middle of the pub. "This is her boss and the man who put her up to it, and this is the fella that you want."

With a big, yellowing false smile that shows his gold tooth, Uncle George makes his way through the various groups that fill up the little pub. In his nineties style leather jacket, he stands smiling at Jerusalem without looking at Mally. Our Dave invited him here, it was easy, he found DI Harris on social media and sent him a DM. He asked for police protection and told him he would be at the Halfway House. The copper would have informed Uncle George straight away.

"Would you like to sit down?" asks Our Dave.

The smile does not fall from Uncle George's face, as if it's pinned up to his cheeks. They can see the anger in his eyes, and there's a red mark across his neck from where Our Dave tied his head in a plastic bag a few days before. "I think I'll stand. I don't expect to be here long." His accent is Dutch and he can't pronounce the s properly.

"You'll sit yourself down," says Mally.

"Who are you?" asks the Dutchman.

"Someone you should be a bit more respectful to."

Uncle George puts his soft hand on the table and leans down to address the little man with braces. He whispers through his yellowing teeth. "I've got business with these two only, and they'll be coming with me. If you know what's good for you little man, you'll stay the fuck out of other people's business." This is uncharacteristically rude for Uncle George. He doesn't like to insult people. It cheapens a man to do so. Mally stares back. Nobody who knows him would dare to speak like this.

Our Dave considers the two men in front of him. If you put two aggressive dogs in a cage, they're going to fight before they sniff each other's arses. One of the dogs will back down in the end – not like these two.

"This girl work for you, does she?" asks Mally as he motions to Jerusalem.

"Yes."

"Our Dave here says she cut one of my people up. He says

that you put her up to it. So, you better sit yourself down."

It's hard for Uncle George to be in a different city. Back in Amsterdam anyone with street sense knows who he is. He doesn't have to threaten or swap insults. What he wants done just happens and he can be the nice fellow that he pretends to be. He looks at Our Dave who is just putting down his half pint glass, and to Jerusalem whose nostrils are flared in fear. "You two are coming with me," he says, "you've caused me enough trouble already."

"You'll sit yourself down," repeats Mally, "and I don't want to have to say that again or there'll be bother. Bother the like of which you can't get yourself out of, fella." Mally has an Irish lilt to his voice when he issues orders even though he's originally from Bristol way.

Uncle George stands back up, unzips his nineties style leather jacket and pulls it open to show his lapel and the handle of the black pistol that is within.

"He told me to do it," says Jerusalem. She's as brave as they come. If Our Dave had explained that he was inviting Uncle George, she would have gone to pieces beforehand. She can see now that he has a lot more wisdom than he lets on. Jerusalem thought that she was here to learn how to be cold and unhuman, she did not realise that she was here to learn to be smart.

"He told me to do it," she repeats across the table to Mally Kemp. "He'll ask you to pay up next, so that it doesn't happen again. That's what he does. It's protection. It's extortion." Mally looks back at Jerusalem with her frightened eyes and he believes her. Uncle George cocks his head as he stands there. It's he who should be intimidating them.

"He's come from Amsterdam," says Our Dave as if the Dutchman is not there. "I thought it best that you know." Mally nods – this is very convenient for him. Mally has already offered up one of his own to the coppers for the robbery, but it's widely known by the fair workers that the kid did not do it. They are looking to Mally to find the real culprit, and, if what Our Dave says is true, this could be it. He's known Our Dave for a long time ever since he used to buy booze straight off the docks in the eighties and nineties.

"You don't want to do this, do you?" asks Uncle George. "I mean, really. in a crowded bar? It'll be on your head if people get hurt, and I can promise you that you'll feel terrible when the smoke clears. Maybe more than terrible."

Uncle George does not know who he is dealing with at all. He has no knowledge of this city. He is not aware of the scale of Hull Fair and that the little man with braces sitting in front of him runs the whole thing. The police are everywhere, but more than that, Mally has his own eyes everywhere as well. If there's a drunk man starting a fight at the back of the dodgems, it gets spotted by a girl selling hot dogs and before it can go anywhere, she's messaged Mally who's messaged one of the big lads who works for him, and he's there as quick as a flash. Everything that goes on here is Mally's concern. This is his fair and he looks up at the Dutchman with calm and serious eyes.

This is why, as Uncle George goes for the weapon in his leather jacket, a figure looms behind him with a metal club. Mally doesn't travel alone, even if it's just to the pub a few doors down. The man has a flat cap and a fat, pock marked face and he knows how to use a steel truncheon without making a fuss. The heavy end clobbers Uncle George across the back of his head and the man manages to catch and spin him so that he goes down and sits on the bench seat next to Jerusalem against the wall. Uncle George's head spins – he is out cold. Mally turns to the bar to see the landlord looking at him with frightened eyes.

"He's had a few too many," he calls over. "We'll look after him." The landlord gives him a weak, fearful grin.

CHAPTER NINETEEN
Our Dave comes clean

Two of the three men Uncle George hired from Leeds wait in their car. They're on double yellow lines and are not supposed to be here, not with the fair on. Buses honk as they pass. If they stay here too long, the police will come and move them along. DI Wilson is nervous in the backseat. He tells them he's going to see what's happening and gets out the car. They don't know him after all, and he sees this as his opportunity. He gets lost in a crowd moving towards the fair and keeps his head down as he goes. He doesn't want to be spotted by anyone he knows and he will not return to the car. DI Wilson hopes that Uncle George will let him go because it will be too much hassle to find him. He has to look after himself.

The men wait another five minutes before they drive round the corner where they wait another ten more. They call the number Uncle George gave them and it rings out. The driver calls the lad with bright white Turkey teeth they dropped off at a house earlier on, and there's no reply there either. They wait another half an hour and drive away. It's not like they haven't been paid already, and they couldn't really give a toss about Uncle George, or each other. This is a dangerous business to be in after all.

One of Mally's lads gives Uncle George some sort of stimulant up his nose to wake him but he's still groggy. Two big boys from the fair take him out the pub backway. They go down alleys and through the Walton Street Club building to get to the fair. The men hold Uncle George up and walk him through the crowds of the last night. They help him stagger past the food vans, behind the bright lights and take him to a caravan where he won't be seen. It's all very well managed.

Our Dave and Jerusalem have followed Mally back to his

caravan on the near side of the fair. That's where they are now, sitting opposite him at the little table with the glare from the strip light harsh above their heads. Mally gets up and locks the door then sits back down. In his hand is his chunky vape, and he takes a good long puff that makes the light on the end glow red like it really is a cigarette. The shelf under the window is filled with family pictures in front of the net curtains. There's a younger Mally with his arm around a woman next to a swimming pool somewhere hot, a family around a table, and an old couple standing next to a car in the seventies.

"You'll tell me the lot, Our Dave," says Mally. "Nothing left out and nothing made up."

Our Dave is a straight lad, and he's not the best liar there is. In the past he could convince Hazel that her curries were wonderful, he can make Bev feel better about herself, he can pretend that bad folk are okay and good folk are the best. That's how it's done.

"I'll tell you the truth," says Our Dave.

"We've been friends for a long time. I wouldn't like to think you'd fill me up with a load of shite, now."

"You'll have to hear me out before you react. Is that ok?" Mally gives a sigh in agreement. Our Dave begins: "One of my lady drivers picked up this lass just outside Bishop Burton a week or so back. She'd been battered and raped." Mally looks to Jerusalem's face and sees the fading bruise on her neck. Her calm stare holds his. "It was a group of your lads that did it, the ones from the waltzer ride. She's a hot head. You can see it on her. My lass took her in and it just so happened that the men who did this to her were over the road. I'm not saying it's right, Mally, but when she felt a bit better, she hopped over to the fair, found them, and fucked them up. She took the money too. You can't fault her for it, really."

Mally would disagree with this. "Who's the big bastard my man just knocked out?"

"He's Dutch organised crime. He runs immigrants into the

country as well as whores. He ran this girl next to me from Ethiopia to Amsterdam. He's a pimp with a smile, Mally. He wanted me to be part of his operation. I said no. We didn't have anywhere else to turn. I knew if you came face to face with him, something like this would happen."

Mally sits back on the bench in the little caravan as he thinks about what he's heard. This story appeals to him because he likes those that stand and fight for themselves. The backhanded compliment from Our Dave also helps.

"Is this true?" he asks the girl.

"Yes," she answers.

"Did you really rob that ride?"

Jerusalem flares her nose and nods. "They deserved it," she says.

Mally understands. Her story checks out from what the Waltzer owner, Rob, told him. That family won't work the fair again, and they did deserve it. "What's Our Dave to you?"

"He's looked after me."

"He looks after everyone, girl," says Mally, "that's what he does. Me on the other hand, I just look after the people at this fair. So now I'm mixed up in this as well, am I?"

"There won't be anyone coming to help Uncle George," says Jerusalem. "He's the top of the tree."

"Everyone's got friends," says Mally.

"They'll be glad he's gone."

The fair man with the red braces wrinkles his nose. He crosses his arms over his chest in thought. "I'll need that money back tonight."

"We'll get it for you now."

"I'll have my lads come with you."

"No need," says Jerusalem. "It's here." She reaches into the bag she's wearing at her chest that goes over her shoulder and unzips the top. She draws out a yellow, plastic supermarket bag that she sets on the table.

"Is it all there?" asks Mally.

"I spent fifty of it, maybe."

"You've caused me a lot of trouble, lass."

"I didn't start it," she answers.

"I understand that." He turns to Our Dave. "What am I gonna do with your mate?" He means Uncle George.

"The coppers will want him," says Our Dave, "what with him carrying a firearm and all that. I could have something happen to him."

Mally taps his weathered finger on the fake wood of the caravan table in thought. "Someone has to take the rap for the robbery, Our Dave, I'm fine if it's that man we got in the pub, but I don't want him, he's too hot for me to handle. I have to look after the people who work this fair. I'll say he put your lass here up to it and that organised crime was trying to shake us down, my people will buy that. It'll get me out of a spot of bother as well." Our Dave's throat is dry. The noise from the fair rages a few hundred yards away from them with shrieks of excitement and the dull thudding boom of dance music. Neon lights flash outside the net curtains.

"I'll kill Uncle George for you," says Jerusalem. Her stare is level and calm.

Mally shakes his head. "I think you've done enough, girl," He means this. "I'd apologize for what those waltzer lads did to you but you've had your revenge. Will you get rid of this Uncle George then, Our Dave?"

"I will."

Mally likes Hull. You know where you are with the folk round here. He takes another big toke on his chunky black vape and the light glows red, some of the smoke comes out of his nose like he's a dragon. "That's it all wrapped up then."

"I guess it is," says Our Dave,

"I'll leave you with this bit of advice, it's for the both of you in actual fact."

"Go on," says Our Dave.

"Never cross my path again, and never set foot on this fair, or any other fair that I'm a part of."

"Done," says Our Dave.

It's late, and the fair is about to close, for good this year. The food stalls are selling hamburgers for a quid, and five doughnuts for fifty pence. There are no more queues for the rides. The bins at the end of Walton Street are overfull with food wrappers and cans spilling out around them. The coppers on duty are yawning in the glow of the neon lights.

Jerusalem and Our Dave walk out of the fair and over the railway track to Chants Ave. It's not far to Avenue Cars from here, nearer than Bev's house and the pub. They are both tired. It has been a stressful couple of days. Our Dave is not sure he can handle any more of them; Jerusalem will use the experience to help her in the months and years ahead.

They stand at the back door to Avenue Cars and Our Dave takes his key out to unlock the door. Mally Kemp's lads are going to deliver Uncle George when the fair is all closed up and quiet. Our Dave will wait for them. Before he puts the key in the lock, he turns his head back to Jerusalem.

"I can take it from here, lass," he says over his shoulder. He feels her stare at him out of the darkness.

"I'll wait too."

He will have to speak plainly for her. "I'll do this alone. That's what I want to say."

"It will be by my hand, Our Dave," she whispers. "It's me who'll finish George."

He shakes his head and turns back to her. "I told you before that I'll deal with him, and I will. That's not open for debate, and it's not just because I'm a lovely old fella. Chances are, if I let you in on what I'm going to do with his body, you'll screw it up and we'll end up getting caught." His words are flat and serious. "I've been doing it for years, you wouldn't help."

"It's my right."

"It's not. You'll have to grow up. You've had your revenge,

lass. You're free and you're alive. That's what you've got." Our Dave puts his keys back in his pocket as he stands in front of her. He doesn't open the door.

"What do you want me to do, Our Dave?"

"Get yourself off."

"Where to?"

"That's your call. I'm not sure I'll be around here for much longer." She nods at him in the darkness. She will take Bev's advice; she will have to accept his help. She thought she could do it alone, turns out she's like everyone else. She needs other people. It was foolish to think otherwise. Time has educated her as Bev said it would. She steps forward and holds out her hand for him to shake.

"Thank you, Our Dave," she says. "I won't forget you."

"I want you to. I want you to forget everything about the last few days, understand?" He takes her hand and her grip is firm.

"I understand," she answers.

"Good luck, then."

"Good luck to you too."

It's Saturday night and the rides have closed up for the last time. Council road sweepers are out in their yellow waterproof trousers with white wellies and woolly hats. A rubbish truck turns the corner past the darkness of the big wheel and two men attach black wheelie bins to the mechanism on the back before they press the button. It gobbles up the trash. That fox waits behind the railings next to the train track – they never clean everything.

Mally's lad's gagged Uncle George at first and tied his hands behind his back, but when they found out that he was going to get put to sleep permanently, there didn't seem much point in making sure he could still breathe properly. As long as he didn't start bleeding. The fairground lads wrapped him in cardboard, taped him up and rolled him in some tarpaulin.

He fits on the backseats of a jeep with his legs up and the men have driven the short distance to Avenue Cars in the darkness. The streets are dead after being so busy all afternoon and night.

Our Dave waited in his Ford Galaxy in the little car park behind. He didn't want to go into Avenue Cars to get distracted with anything. When the lads from the fair arrive, he asks them to bring the body into the taxi office and they lay it on the floor. There it is wrapped in blue tarpaulin in the doorway between the back office and the kitchen. The lads step out into the oily darkness of the autumn night, and Our Dave hears them drive off. Our Dave doesn't know if the body will fit into his Ford Galaxy – he might have to walk down to Belvoir Street to get the van off Gaz.

In the dim light from the lamp in the kitchen he wonders if Uncle George is still alive in there. It doesn't make a difference if he is or not. Our Dave is still going to drive the body down to the incinerator on Cleveland Street. He'll make the same call as he always does to the foreman and say he's got something to burn. They'll give him a time slot, and he'll drive in, then unload the body straight into the furnace – the lads think he's getting rid of booze. It's not the first time he's done it. He hopes it's the last.

There's the squeak of a chair in the back office and Our Dave turns his head. He's suddenly conscious of a figure standing in the darkness behind him. He does not feel afraid.

"Is that a body?" comes the voice. It's Gaz. Our Dave turns round.

"It's that Uncle George. Mally from the fair fixed him up for me. How did you get in?" asks Our Dave.

"You keep a key under the mat outside." Gaz does not look like himself as he stands there. His face seems older in the shadows from the light in the kitchen.

"Did you put it back?"

"Aye."

They regard each other in the darkness.

"How long have you been here?" asks Our Dave.

"Ages."

"What can I do for you, Gaz?" he asks.

"A man was at my house before. He was meant to be some sort of insurance. One of Uncle George's lads, no doubt."

Our Dave licks his lips and gulps down the guilt. "I'm sorry about that. What happened to him?"

"I didn't kill him, if that's what you mean. I'm not like you are, Dave. I did sort him though."

"Well, that's good. It's late. I'm kind of busy, Gaz."

"I bet."

"What is it you want?"

"A man was in my house, Our Dave."

"You said."

"It's because of you he was there."

"Like I said, I'm sorry."

"So am I. I think you've come to the end of the road."

"What's that supposed to mean?"

"I want you to give up."

"Give up what?"

"Everything. Avenue Cars. The booze you bring in. The people you think you help out. I want it all to stop."

Our Dave steps away from the young man and into the office. He puts his hand to his forehead in worry. He never thought it would be someone so close to him who would ask him to do this. "It's not as simple as that, Gaz."

"It is. You stop. You disappear. You must have enough money. Face will close up shop properly." The young man's voice is earnest and clipped.

"This is my home too, Gaz. I grew up on these streets. I know people round here, and they know me."

"That's as may be, Our Dave, but you're not doing anyone any good. Everything you touch turns sour. People die. Like that poor lass shot against your fridge a few months back, like whoever this bastard is laid there on the floor."

"In my line of work, you deal with stuff like that, Gaz."

"In your line of work, not mine. Your shite has spilled over onto me too many times, Dave. I've had enough."

"You're free to walk away from me and this place and stay away too, kid."

"That's not it, though, is it? It always seems to follow me, even if I'm not involved, and whatever happens I'll get sucked in again because you're too old to deal with it."

"You won't be."

"I will. You know that as well." Gaz steps closer to the man. "She's pregnant. Kate's going to have a baby. We'll be a family." Our Dave doesn't look at the lad. "I can't have this. It has to stop."

"What do you want me to do?"

"Pack up. Disappear. Fuck off." The words are cold and hard. The anger of having Kate threatened is bringing out the worst in Gaz. It gives him the kind of venom that he usually reserves for himself. "You're not stupid, Dave. You can see it. Surely. Everything you touch ends up sticky with danger, you carry it around with you like dogshit on your shoes." Our Dave stares at the wall. Gaz is the one he wanted to protect.

"I never meant for anyone to get hurt. It's just how the dominoes fall. Life doesn't go as you plan. You'll see that. The only thing you can be certain of is that it won't work out as you thought." He turns to face Gaz and sees his brooding, dark face. "I'm sorry about what I said about your dad. It was my age talking, Gaz. I don't know if it was him. I shouldn't have said anything. I just wanted to help."

"That's what you need to stop doing, Dave. You need to stop trying to help people. If you really wanted to do something nice for this street, then you'd start by packing up."

"You don't know that, Gaz. You don't know the people round here either."

"I am the people round here, mate. I know I live in your

house and the rent isn't as expensive as it should be, I know that you've lent money to people who struggle, I know that it's you who bought the bloody tandoor oven in the Maya Spice Restaurant across the road. We're in debt to you. We want to stand on our own two feet without you sticking your nose in." Gaz does not like himself saying this but he's heard people slag off Our Dave behind his back and he is using this to fuel his anger. The older man looks hurt. His big eyes examine Gaz's face. He swallows.

"I know," he whispers. Our Dave pulls out a chair and sits down. He puts his head in his hands. It is not the response Gaz is used to – it disarms him. It makes him feel ashamed even, for Our Dave here has done so much for him over this last year or so.

"I'm sorry Our Dave, but I can't have Kate threatened. You do understand. I'm out of your games. I'll be out the house just as soon as I can get it arranged as well. You'll not hear from me again."

Our Dave hears him walk out the office, step over the body wrapped in a blue tarpaulin and go out the door. He hears it close gently. It leaves the whole of Avenue Cars in darkness. There's a light groan from the body on the floor.

"Never shut up, do you, Uncle George?"

The wind is strong outside. There's the bark of a dog fox and the whoosh of a car as it drives down Chants Ave. Gaz is not usually wrong. It's he who manages to see things as they are these days, and it's Gaz who has dragged Our Dave up by his collars more than a few times. He rescued him from a fire, he stopped him getting his head blown off, he showed him that a troubled soul can fall in love.

Our Dave believes in the kid.

The body groans again and the sound is muffled by whatever is wrapped around his face. Uncle George is a tough bastard that's for sure. Our Dave walks to the kitchen in the darkness and looks out at the car park and the shape of his Grey Ford Galaxy. He can't be arsed to shift the body. What's the point? He's kidding himself. It's been exhausting this week and he's an old man as it is.

Our Dave's wife is dead. He pretends that he has a new life. This is a show. It's all designed to give him value. His new girlfriend is just a way of covering up the truth that his time is over. Self-pity is taking hold.

Folk round here would be better off without him too. Imagine all the debts that wouldn't get collected. Like Gaz says, he pokes his nose into other people's business. There's the will that Face helped him write. People might get more out of him dead than they do while he's alive.

Our Dave opens the drawer under the kettle and there's a box of matches there from where Bev used to smoke and not vape. He takes them out and walks into the office. The body of Uncle George groans again and rocks from side to side in the doorway. The Dutchman is coming round, and Our Dave doesn't know if he has the energy to finish him off properly. The body begins to give out low, muffled groans. Our Dave opens the box and takes out one of the matches.

What about the business? Face has it in hand. He has all the documents online as well. Nothing upstairs matters at all. The drivers will still have their council contracts, they just won't have an office. It will be business as usual.

How will Bev be? Happier. She'll find a new direction. She won't be mixed up in these gangland stories that Our Dave finds himself in. Like Jerusalem, she'll be free.

And Gaz? He'll make his own way, as he should have already. Our Dave was not wrong about his father, now he thinks about it. Once upon a time, Skipper Richard Bird set him straight. That was his name. He had bright blue eyes and jet black hair. All those years ago, on a Scarborough beach, he put Our Dave on the path he is still on. Perhaps his lad is here to set Our Dave on another.

What will Wendy think? She'll be on the dating apps faster than she could open a bottle of Pinot Grigio. That's not true.

Face? He's as hard as they come. He'll have the insurance sorted as quick as a flash. Our Dave blinks a minute – this has to be done properly, if he pauses now, he'll never make the step. His eyes moisten as he strikes the match and watches a yellow flame burst from the end.

He hopes he'll see Hazel again, maybe his mother as well. Maybe he'll see that man from Scarborough in 1983. There's a simple green sofa in the corner of the back office, and he tosses the flame onto the seat and watches it take light. The fire eats greedily at the foam and black smoke begins up the wall. You wouldn't believe how quickly fires start with sofas that don't have a safety tag – that's why this one was so cheap.

It was time to sell Avenue Cars anyway. It's easier this way.

There's no one to say goodbye to, nobody to explain anything to either – they wouldn't be bothered anyway. There'll be no drama at all. Once the fire has eaten up Avenue Cars, the building will be as cold as this city can be.

Our Dave won't have to take that body to Cleveland Street incinerator. In fact, he'll never have to drive down Cleveland Street or any other street ever again.

Jerusalem has just left Our Dave. There's someone she has to see. She waits outside Bev's house in Lynton Avenue and looks up at the front bedroom window. The lamp light is still on. Bev will be awake. Jerusalem looks up and down the deserted street. This is not going to be easy. She could leave without saying goodbye, this would be easiest, but Jerusalem is made of better stuff than that. She'll face Bev because it's the right thing to do.

The front door is locked and she taps on the glass. It takes a few seconds for the curtain to twitch in the front bedroom and then there are footsteps coming down to the frosted glass.

"Who's there?" she calls through the door.

"It's Jerusalem."

They stand in the kitchen looking at each other. Bev is in her loose grey pyjamas and her hair is scraped up into a top knot. Without the mascara under her eyes, she looks washed out and ghostly, and with no lipstick her face is anaemic. Jerusalem has explained. Uncle George is gone by Dave's hand. Bev takes the news with her serious face.

"I'll make us a drink," she says.

Jerusalem shakes her head. "I came to say goodbye."

"At this time? You can at least stay until the morning. Then I can give you a lift somewhere."

"It has to be now," says Jerusalem.

"Why bother coming back then?"

"I wanted to say goodbye."

Bev looks out of the kitchen window at the darkness outside. She had it all laid out. Jerusalem was going to live here with her. She was going to get a job and claim asylum in the UK with Bev's help. Maybe she'd go back to college; she'd be happy and settled, she'd become someone. Bev has spent the evening looking at the Home Office website reading up on the details. She looks back at the girl. Bev always goes too hard into anything; she thought she would have learned by now. "Where will you go?" she asks.

"Back to Holland to start with."

"It must be half eleven, you can't just walk away."

"It has to be now," says Jerusalem. "You're the bravest woman I ever met." She steps forward and as the two women embrace, she feels Bev silently shivering as she cries.

"It's the menopause," says Bev in explanation as she steps back and wipes her eyes.

"You don't have to make a joke about everything."

"Yes, you do."

Bev stands at the front door as she watches the tall woman walk down her front drive. Jerusalem stops just after the big white BMW. She turns. "I love you, Bev," she says.

CHAPTER TWENTY
Aftermath

Bev gets a phone call at half six in the morning. It's Linda who runs the café a few doors down from Avenue Cars. Bev doesn't really register what the woman is saying as she sits up in bed in the darkness. According to Linda, Avenue Cars has burned down.

"Call Our Dave," says Bev.

"He's not picking up."

"Call Face."

"I haven't got his number. Anyway, the fire brigade has put it out now. It's a bloody mess though, all the upstairs has been gutted and the office too." Even though she is not quite awake yet, Bev can hear the sense of glee on Linda's voice as she explains.

"I'll be there in ten minutes," says Bev.

Bev goes out of her house and walks down Lynton Ave towards Chants. As she turns, she can see the fire engine parked up on the corner outside Avenue Cars. A policeman in a yellow jacket is directing the traffic.

As she gets closer, and in the light of the early autumn morning, Bev can see that Linda from the cafe was not lying. It looks like a bomb has hit the building. The windows have all been put through, and the bricks are charred where the fire must have burnt out of them. There are police cars, a police van, and the whole corner is cordoned off from the public. Bev approaches and her eyebrows are raised. There's not a great deal that can shock her these days. She gives a huffing sigh. Our Dave will be well pissed off.

Face stands with his arms folded as he looks up at the building from the other side of the street, he's dressed in smart jeans and a flat cap. He gives Bev a worried look as he wanders over to her.

"Does Our Dave know?" she asks.

"I can't find him," answers Face. He looks across at a fireman peering in through the front door. "Apparently, they put the fire out about an hour ago, but it's still too hot to go inside."

"What else do you know?"

"They say it's an investigation." Face turns to look at Bev properly, her blue eyes look more honest somehow without the heavy black mascara. "I think they've found a body inside." Bev wrinkles her nose in disgust.

Jerusalem thought she would be more at peace now she knows that Uncle George is dead. After she spoke to Bev that night, she walked into the city centre and carried on going. In the early morning, she ate a full English at a café on Holderness Road and left a twenty quid note. There's no need for her to go robbing anyone anymore. She's learning.

Of course, she did not pass all the money back to Mally from the fair, she kept some of it, only a thousand or so. She caught the bus out to Withernsea, and watched the landscape change from the top deck, so that the rows of houses were replaced with fields and the high-rise flats swapped for the blue and open East Riding sky. Jerusalem fired up her old email address too so she could access her online bank. There's money there.

At Withernsea, she walked due south according to the map on her phone. It's a few miles to the airfield that Uncle George had told her about. She met the man with the plane for sale and followed up the story Uncle George started with, that he was an air enthusiast from outside Amsterdam. Jerusalem knows too much about her former boss's business and too much about planes to be anything less than an expert. She inspected the P28–200 Arrow II. If he were still alive, Uncle George would have bought it.

She agreed seven thousand and paid the lot up front with

a full tank – she waits until the money has transferred to the man's account. It is all the Euros she has saved, but it doesn't matter, not now Uncle George is gone.

The plane handles well. It's old, but there's quality in the machinery. Jerusalem looks at the flat horizon of the North Sea as she flies over the choppy water. There's a lot for her to do back in Amsterdam and she has big shoes to fill now Uncle George is gone. She won't begin from where he left off. When she's back on Dutch soil she'll go to the police. They'll have an enormous network to untangle once she tells them about Uncle George's operation.

She wonders if she will see Bev again. She has her details so she will wire money, but as to whether they will meet; probably not. Their paths crossed for a moment only, and Jerusalem loves her, but in the moment is where it will stay.

Bev is a mess.

She does all her taxi runs still. Her comments are more barbed than ever. She cleans the house and washes the bedding in Chloe's room where Jerusalem stayed. She batch cooks curry and chili to put in the freezer. She cleans the oven and to take her mind off the funeral that's happening at St Ninians on Friday, she logs into those dating apps again and sets a slutty picture as her profile. It's a distraction.

As he explained to Our Dave, Face has uploaded all the business to the cloud. He still has insurance policies and all the paperwork for the taxi company, so he runs everything from the office upstairs in his big house on Westbourne Ave. He has Our Dave's will as well – he wrote it. It's Face who organises the funeral at St Ninian's, it's he who talks to the vicar and orders the cards that will be given out to mourners. He chooses a picture from social media with Our Dave on Pearson Park, it's a sunny day and his sleeves are rolled up to his elbows, he's smiling and his eyes twinkle too. There's something unreal in the fact that the tall man is no longer across the road and Face cannot call him up or text. He knows how it is to lose people. Face is not looking forward to the funeral.

Chants Ave is a working road as always. Dundee Street Fisheries carries on as normal, although Alan sometimes looks across to the burnt-out building and feels sorrow wash over him. He won't say. He keeps with the jokes as he's frying fish. The Estate Agent on the corner won't have to pay their loan back. Steve from the cycle shop won't get his weekly visit from Our Dave. Linda won't see him at the café. He won't be back to see if his boiler repair worked for the couple on Park Ave. Lilly won't chat to him over the polished bar of the Avenues pub. There'll be no more visits to the car lot on the riverbank on Sundays after a pint in the German beer house on Princes Ave.

Gaz hides his darkness. He papers over his feelings when he is in front of anyone, especially Kate. She says how much she will miss the old man and he hugs her while she cries, but Gaz does not grieve. He goes back to that lost man who keeps everything tight inside his chest. It was his fault after all – he was the last person to see Our Dave and told him to get rid of himself too.

Wendy finds out from her son, Brian Wilson, that Our Dave is dead. The DI is pleased that it all worked out and pleased too that his mother has dodged a bullet in his opinion. He tells her over the phone in lurid detail of how they found a body burned to a charred crisp in the taxi office. He goes on to explain how they had to use dental records to identify the body – that's how they're sure it was him. When she puts the phone down, she sinks to her knees on the floor next to her bed and weeps like she is a teenager.

Mally stays behind to make sure the fair is packed up right. The rides get dismantled into pieces and loaded onto wagons and lorries; the cherry pickers roll in to start on the big wheel. They dig up all the electrical wires that have been tarmacked to the cement floor. Caravans unhook from the electricity sockets and there's a line of show kids and wives emptying their portable toilets into the main drain in the centre of Walton Street car park. It's done for another year. Mally gives Fat Rob back most of the money he lost, the man won't know how much it was anyway and explains that him and his group will never work fairs again. Mally has put the word out about what they did to the girl they picked up, they won't be welcome anywhere now. They'll have to sell the waltzer ride because there won't be a site in the UK or Europe where they can put it up. It's the power of a community.

Mally watches the last of the big wagons roll out down Walton Street on huge tyres. They will be off down the M62 to Leeds, or Nottingham or somewhere. It's not been the easiest fair for Mally, but he's got to the end of it, and all the loose ends have been tied up tight and neat as well. He wonders how many more fairs he has in him, at his age.

Wendy doesn't go to the knit and natter that she runs for the old folk at Willerby Library on Tuesday afternoon. She gives the gym a miss this week. She just says she feels tired when the girls ask her for a coffee one afternoon. She doesn't respond to any of the emails or messages from the book club. People notice, but they don't mind. They don't know about Our Dave or what happened to him, and anyway, that Wendy with her big smile and blonde hair, she looks like she's forty-five, she'll be fine. She doesn't have problems like the rest of them do, her husband is dead and she can do as she pleases.

Wendy lays in bed till two in the darkness. She doesn't open the curtains downstairs for days at a time. Her little sporty Fiat is quiet in the driveway of the big house in Willerby.

On the Sunday night, late on, at half ten, she puts on her trainers and her tracksuit, throws her wax jacket over her shoulders, and leaves the front door unlocked with her keys still in the keyhole. She's not drunk, not at all. She walks over

St Georges field and past the private hospital to Hessle and then up the long, gentle hill towards the Humber Bridge. It doesn't take that long, she's a fit lass, and the journey is perhaps two miles only. The wind and the rain start up as she walks past the big roundabout and towards the great bridge twinkling in the autumn night sky.

Wendy has thought about Our Dave a lot. She did what she ought not to have done – she placed all her eggs in one basket, and it was lost. She should have known better. Now, here she is, not dressed at all for a night walk across the Humber Bridge in the darkness. Cars zip by leaving lines of red from their backlights in the blue black of the night and she makes her way onto the big footpath that goes alongside the bridge. She'll go halfway along. Then, things will start to change, she hopes. The jacket isn't suitable for the wind. She didn't put any socks on.

She hopes she's doing the right thing.

CHAPTER TWENTY ONE
Wrap up

Face has poured himself a glass of wine and is in his kitchen on Westbourne Ave. He doesn't plan to drink it, but he is just looking at it. Within the glass are all the answers he needs, and more. There's comfort and familiarity and rest.

He could just have one drink. He has just lost the best friend he ever had. That doesn't happen every day. There are people who have a drink on their birthday or Christmas or just because it's Friday night. Why should it be different for alcoholic Face here?

There's a knock at the door. It's Sunday night. Alex is off at band practice over in Blenheim Street and will walk home when he's done, so Face is alone. He doesn't have many friends. This is odd.

He opens the door and it's his ex-wife. She's wearing a long coat against the cold and a woolly black hat. She gives him one of those smiles that says she is sorry for what happened. She will have heard about Our Dave.

"Can I come in?" she asks. Face shrugs.

In the kitchen she takes off her gloves but not her coat and looks at the full glass of red wine on the table.

"Are you drinking again?" she asks.

"I was about to," says Face. These last months he has learned that it is okay for him to be himself, and so he tells the truth. That's why he has given up being called Tom. "How can I help?"

"I heard about Our Dave? I just wanted to say I'm sorry. I know he was your friend."

"He was that to everyone," says Face.

"You know, I still want to be your friend too, even after everything that's happened. We were married a long time. I still think about you." This is the warmest Inma has been to him for many years. Face is not sure if he trusts her, but the smooth brown eyes and her dark hair peeping out from under her woolly hat bring him to his senses. He walks over to the wine glass, picks it up and goes to the sink where he pours it away. He has to be honest with himself. It's what Our Dave taught him. The booze won't help with that. He turns back to her.

"I heard you left the chiropractor," he says.

"Yes. He wasn't a very nice man."

Face nods. It's unlike her to admit this. He will have to nip this in the bud right away, she will be here to hurt him, like always.

"Inma, I've changed since we were together. I'm not the same man you married or even who you were married to. I'm in a better place. Thanks for coming round, and thanks for what you said, but I'm busy."

Inma sighs. "I saw you on one of those dating sites," she says.

Face shrugs his shoulders as if he's done nothing wrong. "Everyone's on them these days."

"You know I've changed as well," she says. "It's helped me understand a lot of things too, Tom." Face shakes his head.

"You know that's not my name anymore."

This is hard for Inma. She's a proud woman. Her mother is from Galicia in the north of Spain and she does not really know how to say sorry or accept defeat. She is learning the best way that she can. "I didn't like Tom, in the end," she says.

"He was a knobhead," says Face. "Everyone walked all over him, and he liked that. It was what he wanted."

"Do you think we could get to know each other?" Tom would say yes. Face is much wiser.

"It would have to be slow for me. Tom didn't like you either, in the end." She smiles and her teeth are white. Inma puts her gloves on and turns to the kitchen door to leave. She looks back at him over her shoulder.

"Shall I come with you to the funeral?" she asks.

"Yes," says Face. "You'll come with me and Alex."

When she is gone, Face leans his head on the closed front door. He will use everything he has learned about people over the last few months to get her back. It will take all of his guile and his skill. He allows himself a smile.

Gaz doesn't say much at the best of times, but now he is largely silent. Kate feels like she has lost him. He runs all the way to the boxing gym up on the Orchard Park Estate, trains for an hour and a half and then runs back. He is returning to his old ways of keeping it all locked up in his chest. Kate cooks spaghetti hoops on toast, she gives him space. He apologises for his behaviour and tells her, earnest and sullen, that he will be able to talk about his feelings soon, just as soon as he has processed them. She can see that he is nervous around her – he is protecting himself from revealing how he feels.

Gaz helps Face with the funeral preparations. They meet up in the big house on Westbourne Ave in the upstairs office and when he comes home, Gaz smells faintly of Face's aftershave. He explains scant details about Our Dave's business only that it is now a trust, and the taxi business will have to close, but it's not the same Gaz she knew. He doesn't have the same twinkle for her.

In the darkness, on the Sunday evening, Gaz returns from the same big run and a training session at the boxing gym. He showers and gets dressed into loose fitting jeans and his dark jumper. At the bottom of the stairs, he sits down to put on his trainers that Kate knows have steel toe caps. She stands leaning on the door to the front room with her arms folded.

"Where are you going?" she asks.

"I've got a job."

"What job?"

"I've got to deliver something."

Kate stands above him. She looks down as he ties his shoelaces and she can smell the moisturizer he's used on his face. She has observed Gaz all these months, and this is how he works; when he's scared, he gets ready to fight. The loose pants and jumper will allow him to move if he needs to.

"You didn't tell me you had a job."

"You didn't ask." Gaz isn't like this. He is afraid of something.

"We need to talk, Gaz."

He looks up at her and his blue eyes are honest. "I know. I just need to get this out the way."

"You can't do this to me, not again. You can't just shut me out. Tell me what job."

"I have to deliver something. The less you know about it, the better."

"What?"

"Something for Barry at the garage."

"At half nine on a Sunday night?"

"It's big."

"I don't want you to do it, Gaz."

"It's not dangerous," he answers as he stands.

"I'm coming." She steps near him and looks up to his smooth face. Kate did not come all this way, and through all the shite she's had to deal with to lose Gaz now. "I'm coming or else this is all over. I mean it. Since that man died you haven't said a word to me. I'm coming with you now and you're going to drive and talk." She can see that tears are just behind his eyes. "What are you delivering?" she asks.

"A plane."

Barry thinks that Sunday night is a good time to deliver it because the roads will be empty. He's looked at the weather forecast and the winds aren't bad. Gaz is taking the Cessna over the Humber Bridge into Lincolnshire because Barry has sold the plane to a businessman overseas. Face arranged it. Gaz is going to deliver it over the Humber Bridge and to the little port at New Holland where they'll load it onto a ship.

Barry has a flatbed truck that he and his mechanic lads have strapped the body of the plane down to. The wings are still not attached and they've been fitted tight under the plane as well.

Everything is set up for Gaz. Barry has the gates to Richmond Street Garage open, and the truck is facing the ten foot alley ready to drive away. Gaz and Kate have walked from Belvoir Street but they didn't talk. Gaz does not want to.

"She's all ready to go, Gaz," says Barry. He has that happy look on his fat face. "I've sent you the postcode, you'll just have to follow your phone directions. It's the dock at New Holland, just north of Barrow. It's not far."

"You seem pleased with yourself," says Gaz.

"I got three grand for it," he answers.

"Face set that up for you, did he?"

"Yeah, some fella up in Denmark bought it. He paid for the shipping too."

"Oh Aye," says Gaz. "Face arrange that as well, did he?"

"He did. I got the money through yesterday." Gaz gives a knowing nod as Barry hands him the keys. "There'll be someone there waiting to help you unload it onto the ship."

"At this time?"

"I'm just doing as I've been asked, Gaz. What the customer wants, they get." Just as long as he's got his money and the plane is out of his garage, Barry will be happy.

They drive slowly down Westbourne Avenue and go careful over the speed bumps. As he passes Face's house on the left-hand side, Gaz cocks his head to look up to the bedroom. There he is, with his ugly burned face looking out of the window at the flatbed truck.

"He's in on this too, then," says Kate. Gaz nods.

Chants Ave is deserted. They drive past the burned-out shell that was Avenue Cars and then wait at the lights on Spring Bank West. The radio in the truck doesn't work, so there's the awkward silence between these two. The sound of the indicator is loud and Gaz turns the corner and goes super slow over the bumps of the railway tracks. Kate is not going to make him talk. Maybe she is trying too hard. He seems nervous.

At the Humber Bridge they stop to pay the toll at the little booth and they drive up towards the lights of the bridge towers stretching up into the night. The plane rattles on the back.

"You'll be cool, won't you, Kate," he says.

"I wish you'd level with me."

"I don't know how, not about all this."

The bridge is empty and Gaz keeps the flatbed steady at forty till they get nearer the middle. He begins to slow down and switches on his hazard lights while he looks in the rear-view mirror to the deserted road behind.

There's another reason they are here on Sunday night.

The truck comes to a stop, and he checks through the windscreen and out the passenger window.

"What is it?" ask Kate.

"You'll have to move up," he says.

The flatbed truck door opens and a figure climbs up inside. She's dressed in her long wax jacket and a grey tracksuit. Without the make-up and smile, she seems old. She has blonde hair and her face is pale and cold.

It's Wendy.

They are moving again. Kate sits in the middle of the cab while Gaz drives and Wendy sits next to her. The wheels hum on the tarmac as they accelerate away from the bridge.

"You're supposed to be alone," says Wendy.

"You can trust her. Did you throw the shoes in?"

"My best pair," says Wendy. Kate looks down to see that the older woman is not wearing any shoes and her bare feet are wet with mud and dirt.

Something is going on.

It's just after eleven when they get to New Holland. It's a timber dock, and nothing like the huge port east of Hull. Gaz drives the flatbed truck through the open, raised gate to the car park. There are great stacks of wooden planks wrapped in plastic ready to be shifted, and he drives slowly through a sliding gate onto the dock proper. Floodlights illuminate the two cranes that jut out at an angle over the water, and there's a long boat waiting on the high waters of the Humber. Two men in fluorescent jackets clamber off the vessel when they see the headlights of the truck.

Gaz parks up next to the ship and turns off the engine.

Kate wishes she had not come. He gets out the truck and closes the door as he goes to talk to the men standing in the headlights, it leaves Wendy and Kate sitting together. They've never really chatted properly, and they don't look at each other in the darkness of Barry's flatbed truck.

"You can't say anything about this," whispers Wendy. "I mean when it all comes out. It'll hurt you more if you do."

"I'm frightened," says Kate.

"Don't be that. Just make sure when you get home that you don't remember anything about this."

"I don't know what this is."

"He's not dead. Neither am I. He's been in that plane for a week. I can't imagine how he smells." Kate looks to her and sees that Wendy's face is smooth and calm. "The boat is Danish; we'll board the ship with the plane and it'll take us across the sea to Esbjerg. I don't know where we'll go from there. I don't know how it'll be either, but it's the first time in my life I'm doing what I want." They watch as Gaz chats to the men in hi-vis coats in front.

There's a tap on the passenger side window next to Wendy and she turns to see him. It's the same old face and kind blue eyes with a close cropped white beard. He opens the door and smiles.

"I've brought you some trainers," he says as he hands her

a plastic shopping bag. "Size five, if I remember right." She fishes out the white shoes from inside then begins to put them on. In the space where she's leaning down, Kate gets a good look at Our Dave's face. She is seeing a ghost.

"I didn't expect you to be here," he says.

"Nor me you," she answers back. She looks pale.

"Your Gaz sorted me out again," he says. Her eyes have begun to water. She will have to learn to trust Gaz from here on in.

Kate watches as Wendy gets out the passenger side and they close the door. The men in fluorescent jackets are behind them now, undoing the straps and hooking up the crane to the aeroplane on the back of the truck. She can hear their low voices and the whirr of the winch cable. There's a clunk as they lift the weight from the back and the truck rocks as the plane is removed. Kate looks through the rear view mirror to see Gaz and Our Dave carrying the two wings. It doesn't take long for them to set it onto the ship and then, in another two minutes, Gaz opens the driver's side door and gets in. He sits down and looks across at Kate in the lights from the dock.

Outside it's begun to drizzle. Our Dave steps forward and gives two bangs on the bonnet of the truck. Wendy stands next to him and he holds his hand up in a wave to say goodbye. Gaz starts the engine and they reverse with the two figures getting smaller in the bright headlights.

This really is it.

It's the last time Gaz and Kate will ever see him.

It's the last time anyone will.

They drive across the dark fields away from New Holland and the world around them is silent in the late night drizzle. There's the hum of the engine and Gaz's face is just visible in the lights from the dashboard.

"All those people will cry for him," says Kate. Gaz turns on the wipers and they clear the fine rain from the windscreen in front.

"Not for him. More for themselves."

"This is why you didn't talk to me about it."

"Secrets are hard to keep, the less you know, the better."

"Did Barry from the garage know?"

"Just Face and me. We took him food every day."

"Not Bev?"

"No. The less she knows the better, for her."

"I thought they found his body."

"It was someone else. Face got in touch with a copper. DI Wilson. They switched the DNA records as long as Our Dave promised to disappear. It wasn't Our Dave at all."

"Who burnt Avenue Cars down then?"

"Our Dave did. I had that row with him. I went back half an hour later to say sorry and there he was, standing in the car park watching the place burn. I made him run before the fire engines and the coppers turned up. He was in a state, saying all sorts of stuff about killing himself, so I arranged it with Face. We sorted it. That's just what happened."

"It's the kind of thing Our Dave would do," she says.

They can see the Humber Bridge in the distance and the lights stretch across the river back to Hull.

"What about Wendy?"

"The coppers will find her trainers; they'll assume she jumped in."

They drive through the little town of Barton and up the hill. At the big, deserted roundabout, Gaz pulls into the petrol station in front of the closed supermarket. He parks at the pump and turns off the engine but doesn't get out. It's been a rough couple of days. He needs a minute to gather his thoughts.

Kate puts her hand on his lap and he turns to face her. The lights from the twenty-four hour service station are bright after the darkness of the road. Her clever blue eyes have been worrying about the situation.

"Someone will have seen you pick Wendy up on the

bridge," she says. "Our Dave and her will need passports to get into Denmark too."

Gaz shakes his head. "Face planned it all. There are no cameras in the middle of that bridge. They'll record her walking on but not walking off. More reason to think she jumped. They have passports already. Face sorted it. He's a clever bastard. No more questions after this. It's done. There's so much that I don't even know." Gaz takes her hand and she threads her fingers through his.

"I don't want to leave Hull, Gaz."

"Me neither. Now he's gone, I don't think we'll have to. We'll be able to play it by the rules from now on. It'll be easier that way."

"So, it will be back to normal then," she whispers into the cold air of the truck. This is her old Gaz.

"Aye, it will be back to normal without Our Dave." They embrace on the front seats in the lights from the petrol station. Gaz is going to have to tell Kate about his half-brother and the trawler skipper who was his father. He feels her soft, blonde hair on his face as his hand goes up to hold the back of her head. He is going to have to be a father as well.

"It will be ok, Gaz," she whispers. "You and me and everything, it's all going to be ok. We'll be a family." Kate believes in herself as she says this. Gaz believes in her too.

Bev has poured herself a neat glass of gin without ice. She likes the horrible taste of it. It numbs her. She stands in the darkness of the kitchen and drinks it down in one go, then pours another one. She knows that tomorrow won't be any easier with this drinking, but at least she doesn't have anywhere to drive. Even though it has only been a week since the taxi office burned down, the council has cancelled all their contracts with Avenue Cars. The lease for her white BMW expired and so did the insurance – it's not like she can drive anywhere.

She has lost, again.

Jerusalem has gone. The taxi office is finished. Chloe is away at university, and now the only man she ever trusted, Our Dave, is gone as well. The story is still the same. Everyone she loves leaves in the end.

Her phone buzzes. She has been back on the dating apps again. She'll meet the first man she likes and let him take her out and do whatever, like she's done before. The attention will be nice. This is a message from a lad in his late twenties who has a twinkle in his blue eyes but can't spell. She is about to reply when a call comes through with a name, it's Chloe, her daughter. She puts the phone to her ear.

"What's wrong?" she says.

"I need help. I need to come home, mum." Chloe's voice is clipped and worried.

"What's happened?"

"I might as well just come out and say it. I've ruined my life, mam. It's me and Robin. I've got pregnant. I'm pregnant and I don't want to give it up." Bev wipes her eyes and sets the glass down on the counter in the darkness. She feels her eyes focus and her chest swell as she takes a breath. Bev is designed to look after people, she can be cruel and petty, aggressive and rude, but take away her family and she will self-destruct.

"You come home, Chloe," she says without a thought, "you just come home and we'll work it out together." She hears her daughter sniff back tears on the other end.

"I'm gonna come in the morning, mam. Robin's gonna drive me back."

"I'll be here," she says. When her daughter hangs up, Bev pours her glass of gin down the sink.

The universe has thrown her a lifeline.

#

Sign up for the Chris Speck newsletter here:
https://www.chrisspeck.co.uk/
Follow on insta here:
https://www.instagram.com/chris.speck.writer
For more of Chris Speck's books visit the Amazon page here: https://amzn.to/3Nq27eQ

The Witch at the End of the Lane is set in 1794 in Beverley. It'll be out in July 2025.

More West Hull drama to follow: **Queen of The Queens** will be out Oct 2025. It's Halloween in the Queens. There's a murder.

A Grand Christmas will be out in Nov 2025. It's a novella. It features Our Dave in 1983.

Printed in Great Britain
by Amazon

57444352R00128